BROKEN ANGEL

Brian Knight

82339334

First Paperback Edition: December 2007

Published by:
Delirium Books
P.O. Box 338
North Webster, IN 46555
sales@deliriumbooks.com
www.deliriumbooks.com

ISBN 978-1-929653-89-8

Copy Editor: Troy Knutson

This book is dedicated to the Broken Gods; word-masters, creators and destroyers of worlds. They are mortals, but they are also much more. Life has broken them, but cannot destroy them. They and their words live on.

Charles Grant, Ed Gorman, Ray Bradbury, and Stephen King.

Extra special thanks to Dr. Ron Wallen, for being a good sport, and to his lovely wife, Lisa Wallen; my accomplice.

Special thanks to Donald Koish, Tracy West, David Solow, Jen Orosel, and my step-father, Roger Burnham, for helping me make this novel better than it would have otherwise been.

Writing is a solitary job, but no one publishes alone. There isn't enough room on one page to list everyone who has helped me along the way, but I will do my solid best to remember as many as I can.

Douglas Clegg (the nicest big-shot in the biz), Matt Schwartz (horror's #1 pimp), Monica J. O'Rourke (who discovered me, but only after I discovered her), Tim Arsenault (Timm-aay!), James Newman (who's always there a step ahead of me), Brian Keene, Shane Ryan Staley, Russell Davis, Ed Gorman, David Sparks, Nanci Kalanta, Ron Dickie, Joseph Kroeger, Tara Noble, Michael Myers, Adam Troy Edwards, Sean Wallace, Jack Fisher, Caniglia, Alan M. Clark, Mort Castle, Simon Wood, Weston Ochse, Tom Piccirilli, Dennis Latham, Andonis Dragassias, and Matt Maquire.

And you, dear reader. Thank you too.

Last, but certainly not least, my family: my wonderful wife, Shawna, my brilliant boy, Christopher, my beautiful girls, Judi and Ellie, my mother, Ellen Burnham (it's your fault I turned out like this, you know), my step-father, Roger Burnham, my father, Eddie Knight (I still miss you), my step-mother, Winnie Knight, Grandpa Bill, Grandma Betty, Uncle Kelly, Aunt Kay, my cousin Michael, and his better half, Carrie.

There are more, but I'm running out of room, and I have to get on with the story.

"Mysteries are not necessarily miracles."
—Johann Wolfgang von Goethe

"The final mystery is oneself."
—Oscar Wilde

"Now comes the mystery."
—Henry Ward Beecher (dying words)

Part 1
CLEARWATER

Chapter 1

She was a mystery from the start.

*   *   *

But was she a miracle?

*   *   *

The yellow Oldsmobile idled in the gravel and dirt parking lot, in front of a *No Place* Idaho greasy spoon called Canyon Jack's.

I'm a coward, he thought. *I should just cut her throat and drop her in the river.*

He couldn't make himself do it, though. He was afraid.

He was already cursed.

He didn't want to be damned.

"What are we going to do with her?"

*   *   *

His girlfriend sat beside him, hands clenched in her lap. Waiting for him to do something.

Anything.

The girl sat in back, slumped against the passenger side door. Eyes open, but not awake. Breathing, blinking only when the autopilot in her brain told her to do so.

Just a piece of living meat.   The ghost inside the machine was subdued.

For now.

"What are we going to do with her?" his girlfriend asked.

"We're going to leave her here," he said at last.

She glanced back at the girl behind them, gave her a look both frightened and sympathetic. "We can't leave her. She's your sister."

"No," he said. "She's not my sister."

"Then what is she?"

*   *   *

He focused on the rearview mirror, watching the monster in the back seat. She'd moved, or at least he'd imagined she had. Then her unfocused eyes turned toward the mirror, found his, made the short hairs on his neck prickle.

"What is she?" his girlfriend asked again, raw desperation cracking her voice.

"I don't know."

Chapter 2

The fight hadn't even started and Eugene Grim was already exhausted. The long way to the salvage yard was a half-hour walk from town, down the highway and over a neglected logging road through the woods. He'd have taken the Yamaha, but it was broken down in his front yard, awaiting repair. He didn't trust himself to fix it alone, and Danny was just too busy at work lately to help him.

If his plan worked, the long walk would be worth it.

Old Ron Wallen's salvage yard was the ideal place for the year's first game, he thought, since they had lost it to Alex Cain and his friends the last game before winter. Alex and his buddies had handed them their collective ass.

The added excitement with Wallen's place was the possibility of getting busted. It all depended on how drunk the old man was, the drunker the better, and if one or both of the Sheriff's Jeep Wagoneers happened to be in the shop.

Of course, it was always easier if you held that ground. The salvage yard was easier to defend than it was to take.

After ten minutes of pounding dust, Grim turned off the dirt road, into the trees. He could smell the salvage yard's odor on the wind—old oil, burnt rubber, rust; the perfume of dead machines. And beneath that, the heady scent of pine sap.

He stopped, took a deep breath to steady himself.

Pucker time, he thought.

He shrugged out of his backpack and leaned it against

the trunk of a tall spruce tree, unzipped it and took inventory. He'd loaded the pack with more than he could carry up a tree, and he didn't feel like climbing with the extra weight strapped to his back. He needed the binoculars and his paint gun. The spud launcher, on the other hand, might be tricky to fire from up there.

What the hell, he thought, and pulled a potato from the bottom of the pack. He shoved it into the spud launcher's tube, packed it down with a stick, and hung the launcher from his shoulder by the twine strap. He shoved a can of aerosol hair spray into the front of his pants, checked the load of paint balls in his gun, and holstered it. The holster was homemade; leather and twine, road-kill ugly, but it would keep his hands free for climbing. He hung the binoculars from his neck and zipped the pack up again.

He jumped and caught a low limb, was about to hoist himself up when he changed his mind.

Clay wanted him to stay far enough away that Alex and his friends wouldn't be able to hear him, or see him if they happened to glance up the right tree.

If you get a shot, take it, Clay had said. *But stay back. If they catch you alone and take you out before we get there, we're screwed.*

Clay, his best friend in Clearwater, Keith, and Kelly were counting on him for recon, first and foremost.

Grim wanted to get in closer though. He'd be a lot more useful closer to the fight.

Besides, the thought of sitting high up and plugging away at Alex Cain and his friends, Raif, Bo, and Kelly's older brother and arch enemy, Clint, filled Grim with a giddy anticipation. He wanted to show those fuckers up in the worst way.

He dropped back to the needle-covered ground, picked his pack up by the straps, and crept onward..

He went closer to the salvage yard, almost daring himself forward, and didn't stop until he heard their voices, amplified, but tinny in the steel jungle that was the salvage yard. They were probably hiding in the old boilers, or lying low in the stack of rusted culverts.

Waiting. Smug bastards.

Got a surprise for you guys.

Grim set his backpack down, found a sturdy looking tree, and climbed.

He scanned with the binoculars but didn't see them. He waited and listened, then heard their voices again a few minutes later, coming from inside the old cement mixer. The cement mixer was a long time fixture of the salvage yard. It had settled into the ground over the years and was pocked with large rust-holes. Grim knew it was a great place for an ambush. He had used it before.

He unclipped the walkie-talkie from his belt. This was the part he didn't like. Alex and his friends carried talkies too; there was always a chance they'd get lucky and guess which channel he was using.

He turned the talkie on, pressed the send button, and said, "Hey, you guys awake down there?"

*   *   *

"This is bullshit," Keith said. He lit a cigarette, shook his match out and tossed it into the grass at the edge of the road. "This is the last time we trust *Eugene* to plan a raid."

Clay shook his head, bent and plucked the burnt match from the grass, tossed it onto the pavement. "Better not let Grim hear you calling him that," he said. Grim didn't like his first name, had talked about changing it for as long as Clay had known him, but his foster mother, the only one in Clearwater who got away with using it in front of him, wouldn't let him. So, to anyone who didn't want to start a fight, he was just Grim.

Keith made a disgusted noise and dismissed Clay with a wave. Keith had caught Grim screwing his older sister the year before and had never quite forgiven him. As much as he liked to badmouth Grim behind his back though, he didn't have the stones to take Grim on..

"What's up your ass?" Clay asked.

"Just remembering last time," Keith said.

"You can't blame Grim for that."

"Nope, but I'm gonna tear him a new one if he makes us late."

It was nearing sundown, the magic hour, when Wallen would be at his drunkest and the sheriff's office would be more interested in coffee at Canyon Jack's and completing the day's paperwork than patrolling. If they waited too long, the dark would catch them, and they might as well go home. No way in hell they'd take the salvage yard in the dark.

"Hold on to your dick," Clay said. "We'll make it."

"Call him," Keith suggested, and slapped the walkie-talkie clipped to Clay's hip. "Ask him what the fuck he's up to."

Clay laughed. "You're feeling brave tonight. How about you ask him?"

Kelly swiped the smoke from Keith's hand and took a drag. "Shut it. We're almost there."

They were coming up on the packed dirt road to Wallen's place. The salvage yard was not visible yet. The road twisted an S through the trees to Wallen's shack, then past it to the yard.

They turned down the dirt road. When Wallen's shack came into view, they broke into the woods. They passed it, keeping quiet, putting enough of the forest between them and the road to mask their passage.

When the salvage yard came into view they crouched down in the trees, unloaded their backpacks, and prepared for war.

Minutes passed, and they didn't hear from Grim. The sun dipped to the edge of the western evergreens. Silence from the salvage yard.

"Quit jerking off, Grim," Keith whispered, and drew snickers from the others.

Then it came, a low crackle of static on the talkie, and Grim's voice. Clay cranked the volume down and pressed the speaker to his ear.

"Where are you?"

"Looking down at them," was Grim's reply.

*   *   *

Grim prepared himself for a little dose of the old Clay attitude and said, "Looking down at them."

"Shit, how close are you?" Clay asked.

"Close enough to be useful."

A moment of radio silence, probably Clay cussing him out on the other end, then, "Where are *they*?"

"In the cement mixer." He lifted the binoculars to his eyes and scanned the salvage yard again. "Don't know if they're all there. They could be spread out." He paused, looked back toward the declining sun. Not much of it left. "I'd like to wait for a while and make sure but I don't know if we have the time."

"We're cutting it pretty close," Clay said.

"It's your call."

A few seconds pause, then Clay said, "Let's do it now. Keith's gonna piss himself if he has to wait any longer."

"Gotcha," Grim said. "Hit it with the spud guns, aim for the holes if you can. If we can scare them out we'll have a better chance."

"Gotcha. See you on the other side," Clay said, then was gone.

Grim clipped the talkie to his belt and unstrapped his spud launcher. He straddled the branch he sat on, back pressed against the rough skin of the spruce, pulled the hair spray can from the front of his pants, and fumbled in his pockets for a lighter. He almost panicked when he didn't find it.

"Shit," he said under his breath. *Lost it!*

Then he found it and relaxed. Almost relaxed.

He sat with the spud launcher drawn across his lap, the hair spray can in one hand, and the lighter in the other, and waited for it to begin.

It started with the bang of rusted metal as the first

potato struck the concrete mixer. The metal rang like a gong, startling birds from the trees around him. A second bang followed the first, and he steadied himself on his limb before uncapping the can and spraying the flammable aerosol into the small hole on the back end of the tube.

He heard shouting, cursing from below—if the noise was this loud from as far back as he was, it must have been ear rupturing inside. Alex and Raif scrambled toward the mouth of the mixer.

Grim couldn't help himself; he had to take the shot. He gave the tube another shot from the spray can, aimed a few feet over the top of the mixer to adjust for drop, and used the lighter.

The spud left the tube with a hollow sound and pounded through a rust pock in the hull of their hideout.

Grim didn't have time to appreciate the excellent shot. The recoil had thrown his balance off. He slid sideways, the spud launcher falling as he grabbed for a handhold. He caught the branch with a hand as he went over.

"Oh shit!" He swung one-handed from the branch, straining for a hold with his other arm, but not finding it.

He heard the *ping-ping-ping* of paint pellets on metal, and spun to see the action. Raif was on the ground beneath the lip of the mixer, crouched and firing. Alex leaned from the mouth of the mixer, gun pointed down the salvage yard's main path. He fired.

"Fuck! I'm out," Kelly said, and came into view, arms in the air and a splatter of red paint on his chest. Then he dropped to his knees and Clay rose up behind him.

Pop-pop-pop.

Alex ducked back inside and the pellets splattered the wall behind where he had been.

Clay took cover behind a row of rusted culverts stacked like logs along the path.

Raif rose and chased after him.

Where was Keith?

Still swinging from his limb, Grim wrestled his paint-gun from the holster and squeezed off a half dozen shots.

One of them was lucky, taking Raif in the small of the back. He stopped and kicked at the dust. "I'm out!"

Grim took no time to gloat. His arm ached, and his shoulder felt stretched out. He fumbled the gun back into its rough holster and strained for the limb. The hand keeping him from falling some fifty feet to the ground was slipping. The fingers of his free hand found wood, and lost it.

Then the first paint-ball exploded against the trunk, just above him, splattering him with red paint. Another followed, just missing him as he twisted around for another grab at the limb.

"*Hey*," he shouted, then realized how stupid it was to expect Alex to cut him any slack. He wouldn't have given Alex any if their positions were switched.

Grim made another grab, and breathed easier when his hand caught wood and held. He shimmied toward the trunk, another paint-ball flying over his head, then he hugged the trunk and lowered himself down to the next limb a few feet below.

It bent beneath him, then let go with a dry snap.

The fall was over before he had a chance to scream. He hit the ground with his feet, his knees buckled and he landed hard on his ass. There was a moment of darkness, the muted sound of footfalls coming toward him. Someone said *Oh shit*, but he couldn't tell who it was.

Then the darkness morphed into pain, a pounding inside his skull, a line of pain up his spine. He was able to sit up without stirring more pain. He flexed his legs. They worked.

"You okay, man?" Clay ran toward him, gun hanging forgotten in his hand.

Alex followed close behind. He actually looked worried.

Grim took a moment to appreciate Alex's concern, then unholstered his gun, and aimed.

Clay's eyes went wide and he jumped aside. "What the fuck, Grim?"

Alex stopped, turned to run, but too late. Grim fired

and the paint-ball exploded against Alex's shoulder. He looked down at his red-splattered shirt, then back to Grim. "Dirty fucker," he yelled, then raised his hands to the graying twilight sky. "I'm fuckin' out!"

Grim smiled, and rose to his feet. It was a cheap shot, he knew it and felt a little guilty, but the satisfaction outweighed the guilt.

A second later Clay was at his side. "That was dirty, man," he said, then laughed.

"Thank you," Grim said. "How we doing?"

"Good so far," he said. "Bo and Clint were hiding behind the gate. They got Keith on the way in. I nailed Clint."

"Two to one?"

"Yep."

"I like those odds," Grim said.

Clay opened his mouth to reply, then stopped. He reached around with one hand and rubbed his back. His hand came back smeared with red.

"I'm out." He raised his hands, paint-gun aimed at the clouds, and winked at Grim.

Grim nodded and pointed his gun at Clay's chest.

Clay stepped aside.

That trick would not work again; there was no one behind him.

Grim ducked behind the trunk of his tree, and waited.

The others were on their way to the waiting point outside the gates of the salvage yard. He heard Clay say something, then laugh, and heard Alex's surly reply.

Cheap shot motherfucker!

Yep, he was pissed.

It was just him and Bo now. If they lost this time it *would* be his fault.

He peeked around the trunk of the tree and saw no one. This did not comfort him. There were a lot of places to hide in the salvage yard.

He stepped into the open, bracing himself for the sting of a paint-ball, and sprinted out of the trees. Inside the yard now, he ducked behind the iron bulk of a World War II era boiler, the first in a long row of its fellows, and listened.

There was nothing at first, then the approaching thunder of footfalls coming down the main isle.

He steadied himself, paint-gun raised, and stepped out to meet Bo.

"Watch it," Alex said, and pushed past him. The others followed, Clay at the rear.

"Haul ass," Clay said. "Big brother's here."

Shit! So damn close!

"Hey, Grim."

Grim turned and saw Bo standing only a few feet away, gun pointed, a grin splitting his face. It wasn't his paint-gun; it was his spud launcher.

Phut!

The flying potato caught Grim in the stomach, doubling him over, knocking the wind out of him. He dropped his paint-ball gun and fell to his knees, trying futilely to suck air. A paint-ball exploded against his shoulder, close range, and added to the pain.

"Say it," Bo said.

Grim struggled to catch his breath, then finally sucked in a lungful. The salvage yard's decay-scented air had never tasted so sweet.

"Say it, Grim."

Grim raised his hands resentfully and said, "I'm out."

Bo nodded. "Bet your ass," he said, then followed the others into the woods.

Grim knelt in the dirt, panting, listening as their passage through the woods faded. Time to go.

He picked up his paint-ball gun and started to rise when the voice came from above.

"Drop the gun, punk. You're coming with me."

Chapter 3

Michele was fifteen years old, looking forward to the last week of school, when the workload would lessen and softball season would begin. Softball wouldn't last long; the Clearwater team never made it to the post season. There wasn't a big enough talent pool to build a *good* team. Still, it was fun, and a great excuse to hang around the diamond after their games to watch the boys from visiting teams.

She knew almost every girl her age in Clearwater, but she didn't know the girl sitting alone in the corner booth — the girl who was sleeping with her eyes open. Except for the slow, rhythmic movement of her chest, she could have been dead.

"Don't stare, Michele. It's not nice."

Michele turned to face her mom, but her eyes flicked back to the girl. "There's something wrong with her, Mom. Look at her."

"Michele!" Her mom's lips pulled into humorless lines, her eyes widened and scanned the tables around them, almost hoping, Michele thought, that she wasn't the only one incensed by her daughter's rudeness. "You can be such a little monster sometimes."

Michele rolled her eyes and dipped one of Canyon Jack's limp fries in catsup. "She's been sitting there since we walked in, and I haven't seen her parents once. Don't *you* think that's weird?"

"They're around somewhere," her mom said, but she sounded unsure. She looked around the dining room, as

Michele had earlier, but saw no strangers she could match with the girl; just Jack working the kitchen, the waitress, Darla, and a few townies. She looked through the dining room window, scanned the half dozen cars, and frowned.

The strange girl just sat there, staring at nothing in particular.

Then her head turned and she looked at Michele.

Michele felt a sudden, electric shock of fear—those dark, bottomless eyes seemed ready to swallow her, and giving way to the fear, a loathing she didn't understand for the strange girl. Her stomach gave a sudden, slippery roll. Her throat burned, and she had just enough time to duck beneath the table before her dinner came back up.

"Michele," her mom shouted, and tried to pull her back up. "God, are you okay?"

"Yeah," she said, then wiped her mouth. "Let go, I'm fine." She opened her eyes and saw the pile she'd left between her feet. Not much there, she hadn't eaten much, but what was there was tinged with red. Michele almost screamed, then realized it wasn't blood, but bile-thinned catsup.

"You okay, Michele?" It was Darla, standing at the table with a half-pot of coffee in one hand and a bar rag in the other. She frowned at Michele, then the mess under the table.

"Do you know who that girl is?" her mother interrupted.

Darla followed her mother's pointing finger and flinched when she saw the girl. "Oh m'god! I didn't know she was still here!"

"You know her?" Michele ventured. She chanced another look at the girl, bracing herself for another wave of sickness. There was none, just her natural curiosity and a creeping pity—she wanted to go and hug the girl, to tell her everything would be fine.

"No," Darla said. "She was here when I came on shift. Sitting with her friends." She looked thoughtful for a second, an almost alien expression on her face. "They left about the same time you came in."

While Darla and her mother spoke, Michele looked around at the other patrons. Not many, especially not for a Friday night. They'd arrived about the same time as usual, just ahead of the normal Friday rush, but tonight that rush hadn't come.

There were a few kids, stopped over on their way to some Friday night party or other, a few mill workers from down-river.

Old Man Wallen sat at the bar, nursing what was probably his twentieth beer of the afternoon. He'd come in earlier, already half-toasted, bitching about the *Damn Punk kids foolin' around his salvage yard again.*

He was the only one, besides her, her mother, and Darla now, who seemed to notice the strange girl. He watched her, blood-shot eyes unblinking, muttering.

"Maybe you should check the restroom," her mother said to Darla. "I'll look around outside. They have to be here somewhere."

"Yeah," Darla said, then set the coffee pot on the edge of the table and wandered toward the restrooms.

"Stay put. I'll be back in a minute."

"Yeah," Michele said. "Sure."

Her mother pulled out her pack of Saratoga's, the vice she usually kept well-hidden in view of other people, and lit one on her way through the door. When the door swung shut behind her, Michele got up and walked over to the lone girl's booth.

"Hey," Michele said, and stopped in front of her. "You okay?"

She didn't respond, not even a blink of the eyes or a turning of the head in the direction of Michele's voice.

"Where are your friends? Did they leave you?"

Nothing from the girl.

Michele heard footsteps from behind and turned to find Old Man Wallen approaching, his cane leading the way like an arthritic third leg.

"You best get now," he said to Michele, but his eyes

remained fixed on the unresponsive girl. "Get on back to your table and let me deal with her. You don't want to get mixed up with her lot."

Michele was suddenly scared of him. He'd always been just the cranky old junk man, but she felt something coming off of him, a stink that was more than beer or whiskey. There was something very wrong with him.

Michele backed a little closer to the booth, standing in front of the girl. "She didn't do anything wrong, Mr. Wallen. She's just lost, I think."

Now his eyes did find hers, locked onto them, held them in an electric grip. What she saw in them was worse than his irrational drunk talk, worse than the stink that seemed to ooze out of his pores. What she saw in his eyes was a simple, brutal rage.

He dropped the cane. It hit the tile floor with a wooden clatter, then he limped forward a step. His right hand flew at her, and before she could duck it slammed into her face.

She heard the shocked gasps that came as one from the other diners, then felt the dull, metallic pain as her head hit the floor. She tasted blood, and spit it onto the tile in front of her.

She tried to scream for her mother, but her traumatized lips wouldn't cooperate. They were fat, rubbery.

"I'm going to do this," Wallen said. "Oh, you little bastards I'm going to do what I should have done a long time ago!"

Michele pushed herself up from the floor; there was a lot of blood on it.

That all came from me, she thought, amazed. *That asshole really hit me!*

"Asshole," she said, but it came out slurred through her swollen lips. More blood spattered the floor.

She began to cry.

From the other side of the dining room, Darla screamed.

Wallen was laughing.

Michele turned her head, looked up.

He was choking the girl.

Michele couldn't see the girl, only Old Man Wallen, bent over her, arms thrust out, tendons standing under the skin like strands of bailing wire.

"Help her," she said, but no one did. They just stood around, watching, faces ashen, eyes big.

Michele stood, slipped in her own blood, fell to her knees. She saw Wallen's cane lying on the floor and picked it up. Before she even knew she meant to do it, she was standing behind him, cane upraised like a club.

"Michele, no," she heard her mother scream from somewhere behind her, but she was already in motion.

The cane came down on the top of the old man's head with an almost comical *bonk* sound.

Wallen grunted, lurched forward, but didn't release the girl. Her face had gone a sickly shade of lavender.

Michele raised the cane again, held it with both hands, and brought it down as hard as she could.

The *bonk* sound was less comical this time. It was accompanied by a brittle cracking sound, like an eggshell breaking on the edge of a mixing bowl. He fell to his knees without a sound, leaned forward onto the booth's seat — he looked like a man searching for a lost contact lens — then rolled off, onto the floor under the table. This time the blood staining the tile floor was his, and there was a lot more of it.

His eyes were open still, but he didn't see Michele. They were not accusing as she might have expected, like a dead person's eyes sometimes were in the books she read. They were like the eyes of a mounted deer head.

Michele dropped the cane, turned away from him. She found the strange girl lying on the seat of the booth. There was an ugly red ring around her neck; a raw red peppered with grime from Wallen's ever dirty hands.

She was breathing though, drawing air in ragged gasps. Her eyes were red, leaking silent tears.

Michele began to bawl. She dropped next to the strange girl on the seat, lifted her up and wrapped her arms around her, fists locked behind her back, and cried for both of them.

*   *   *

Deputy Danny Grey allowed Grim to sit in the front passenger seat of the old Jeep that served as Deputy Sheriff's patrol rig for Clearwater, instead of the back seat. Being a lawman's brother rated that much at least.

Not a real brother, Grim supposed, but close enough. They'd both been raised under the same roof, by the same woman—Clara Grey, Clearwater Post-mistress, President (ten years running) of the local chapter of The Sisters of Mercy, and foster mother.   Clara Grey—Clearwater's answer to Mother Teresa.

Grim's arsenal was zipped up snug in his backpack again and stashed behind the Jeep's back seat, where it would likely remain until Danny decided he'd been punished enough. He'd replaced his paint splattered shirt with a spare he'd packed for afterward.

"It had to be the salvage yard, didn't it?" Danny said, trying to sound stern but not quite accomplishing it. The salvage yard had been a favorite playground to the kids of Clearwater since time out of mind, and he'd heard stories about Danny's exploits in his younger years. Not a serial rapist by any means, but he'd got up to his own mischief.

"You knew we were going," Grim said. "If you're so concerned about Wallen's property rights why didn't you stop us?"

"Hell, I don't care what you do in that old crap-yard, so long as you keep it low key." He winked at Grim, gave a little chuckle. "It was those damn spud-guns. Sounded like you were beating war drums. Wallen was damn near frothing when he called."

They rolled slowly along the dirt path from the salvage yard to Wallen's shack. Grim's heart played a little tango in his chest when it came into view.

"You're going to make me apologize to him, aren't you?"

"That would be a sight," Danny said, then laughed. "No, I told him to be gone before I got there. Said I didn't want to have to worry about restraining him and a gang of juvies at the same time."

They passed Wallen's cabin and found smoother ground. Grim noted with some relief that the old man's green International was gone.

"Didn't know you could do that."

"Can't, but I did anyway. He was too drunk to question it." Danny pointed at Grim as they turned the next narrow corner, almost running them into a tree. "Tell your friends the next time I get a call from Wallen I won't give them a running start. You're lucky as hell it was me instead of Everett."

Everett Johnson was Clearwater's daytime deputy, the main reason they'd planned their game for the evening, rather than the middle of the day. "He'd just love to bust you."

"I know," Grim said. "He's had a hard-on for me from day one. Thinks I'm a bad apple."

"You are a bad apple," Danny said, but not without another hint of a smile. "Incidentally, you want to duck down when we get to Jack's. Wallen's waiting there for a full report."

"What're you going to tell him?"

Danny screwed his face up into a sour mime of Wallen's and croaked, "I'll tell him the shit-lickin' bastard punks were gone when I got there."

"Thanks," Grim said. It wasn't the first time Danny had covered for him—most likely wouldn't be the last.

"Don't mention it. Especially not to Mom. She'd kick my ass."

They rounded the last corner through the trees and the road to town came into view. As they turned onto it, Danny's radio blared static, then a voice. "Danny, you been to Wallen's place yet?" It was Lydia, the volunteer dispatcher. When the office was empty, all calls routed to her.

"Just leaving now," Danny said, then held a finger up to pursed lips; a little *be quiet or we're both in for it* gesture.

"Good, you need to get over to Jack's, ASAP."

"Copy," he said, rolling his eyes. "Tell Wallen to keep his pants on."

"Wasn't Wallen that called, it was Darla."

"Come again," Danny said.

"Darla called. I couldn't understand most of what she said, but she's pretty upset. Sounded like she said Michele Kirkwood just killed someone right there in Jack's dining room."

Grim gawked at the radio, then at Danny. He knew Michele Kirkwood, not well, but well enough to doubt what he heard. He just couldn't make his mental image of Michele gel with the word *Killed*.

Danny looked doubtful too, indicated it with a little shake of the head.

"You have got to be mistaken," Danny said. "Michele wouldn't kick a dog if it was chewing her leg off."

"I know," the radio squawked back at them. "Dear God, I hope I am mistaken."

*   *   *

Danny had seen dead bodies before, mostly on the highway; truckers run off the road by exhaustion, and a few town folks that had been t-boned pulling onto the highway by Jack's without looking first. This was his first murder.

Well, not exactly a murder. Wallen had attacked Michele first, then the strange, silent girl sitting alone in the corner booth. Not exactly a murder then, but the thing was, he didn't know how else to think of it.

A fifteen-year-old girl that he knew from town—a nice girl, a good girl—had busted Wallen's old head wide open with his own cane, and had saved the other girl's life.

So really, she was a hero, not a murderer.

He had trouble convincing himself though, probably it was the sight of the old man, lying cold in a pool of his own blood. He didn't think Michele would buy it either. He'd had to pry her off of the strange girl.

Grim sat with her now, holding her, trying to comfort

her while Danny took a statement from her mother, Evelyn Kirkwood.

Jack had closed the place down and left for home after giving his statement — which was nothing really, since he was in the back cooking when it had happened. The other patrons were gone too, having given their individual statements and perspectives.

The consensus was that Michele had been brave and acted before any of the others had a chance to.

This didn't feel right though. Wallen had backhanded Michele out of the way — and a damn wonder she wasn't out cold after the hurting he'd put on her — and then attacked the girl in the booth. The girl's throat had swollen, and there were ugly purple imprints where his fingers had closed around it. That had taken more than just a second to inflict.

And Michele had hit him twice before his skull caved in. Twice. There should have been plenty of time for someone else to step in and help.

What it looked like, though Danny didn't quite dare say it, was that the others had just stood around and watched.

That didn't make any God damn sense either. He knew these people, thought he did anyway.

"Thanks, Evelyn." He closed his notepad; he wasn't going to get anything new. "You better get Michele home now. Poor girl's had the worst night of her life." There was a lump on her head where she'd hit the floor, and her split lip still dribbled blood, but she would be fine. No concussion, nothing broken. The emotional shock seemed to be the worst of it.

Evelyn glared at him. "Well, no shit? Where ever did you get your spectacular grasp of the obvious?" She turned away from him, purse clutched to her chest and nose in the air.

Let it slide, he thought, face burning with equal parts embarrassment and anger. *She's having a shitty night, too.*

Shitty night or not, that kind of antagonism was par for the course when dealing with Evelyn Kirkwood. She was a bitch on her best days.

He watched her approach Grim and Michele and willed her to keep a civil tongue with Grim at least.

"Lets go, baby," she said, holding out a hand to Michele. To Grim she said, "Thanks." At least her mouth said *thanks*. Her tone said *stay away from my girl*.

"Take care, Michele," Grim said, and didn't even acknowledge Evelyn, just stood and walked past her like she wasn't there.

Just let it slide, as Grim liked to say.

Little brother: kind of; troublemaker: definitely, but sometimes that kid impressed the hell out of Danny.

Grim waited until the door swung shut behind Evelyn and Michele, then said, "How did such a nice girl ever come out of that bitch?"

"Shut up," Danny said, even though he'd been thinking close to the same thing.

Darla was sitting alone in the employee's break room in back, probably helping herself to Jack's beer (and could Danny really blame her?). So it was just them and the girl in the room.

That weird fucking girl.

Danny had an idea why no one else had helped. It was his job, and he didn't want to. The thought of touching this strange girl made him cold.

The girl had settled back into the far corner of the booth, hugging her knees to her chest. Not comatose, not a vegetable. It was almost like she was sleeping with her eyes open.

"Shouldn't the ambulance be here by now?" Grim asked.

"Naw," Danny said, a little disgusted. "They're all tied up right now. There was a pileup on the highway."

"We taking her then?" The nearest hospital was fifteen miles east, in Orofino. The girl seemed to be breathing fine, so there was really no huge rush, lucky for her.

"I am," Danny said. "You can go back home if you want, but I won't stop you if you want to come along." He gave the girl a sideways glance, barely a flick of the eyes, and shivered. "Tell you the truth, I could use the company."

"No sweat," Grim said.

For a moment neither moved, neither spoke.

"What the hell do you make of her?" Danny asked. He supposed it was silly, him asking a garden variety juvie what he thought of anything, but he'd spent his whole life here, and Grim had lived in Seattle most of his life, a street kid until he'd found his way to Clara. He had seen things, experienced things that Danny never had.

After a brief pause, Grim said, "E-Z-Lay."

"What?"

"Roofies," Grim said. "I've seen what they can do." He looked away from her; must have seen the disgust that Danny felt and looked at the floor. "She's probably so drugged up she can't remember her own name."

Danny was still trying to take it in. "Roofies? The date rape drug?"

"Yeah," Grim said.

She was just a kid, looked about the same age as Michele, maybe younger.

Grim sat down next to her, "Hey there, can you hear me?"

No response, no acknowledgment.

"My brother and I are going to take you to the hospital." He reached out and gave her shoulder a light shake. "Don't be scared. We're going to take care of you."

A small response that time; she raised her head from her chest, just a little, rolled her eyes toward him. Then she shifted toward him and rested her head against his shoulder before blanking out again.

Grim put an arm around her narrow shoulders and held her.

"We better let Clara know where I am. She's probably passing a stone by now."

"Yeah," Danny said, and walked to the phone to make the call.

*   *   *

The ride to Orofino was quick and quiet. Neither Grim nor Danny spoke more than one word at a time. The girl spoke not at all. She sat buckled in next to Grim, slouching against her restraints.

The only time she showed any life was when they passed the pileup he had mentioned. Danny turned the flashers on as they approached it, and the State cops waved them by.

Only one ambulance remained on scene, waiting for the extraction crew to peel open the last of the vehicles involved. An old car, mustard yellow, looked like it might have been a Buick, California plates.

The girl turned her head and watched the crew working to open it up. When they were past it she twisted around in her seat, still watching. She didn't settle back into her seat until the next bend in the road put it out of sight.

*   *   *

A sound in the blustery, star dappled night. A sound that made dogs whimper and hide under porches. A sound that roused men and women stumbling zombie-like from beds to lock doors and latch windows. A sound that made children pull blankets over their heads and bunch pillows over their ears.

The gusting wind picked up the pace and dark clouds snuffed out the starlight.

Then the sound came again, louder.

Outside, somewhere in the deserted streets of Clearwater a voice called out. A loud schizoid wailing that sounded like laughter—or maybe laughter disguised as wailing. Crying.

Then a scream.

"Oh no!" A woman's voice.

Her silhouette moved against the Old West Style false

front of the post office, dragging something behind.

She stopped, dropped what she dragged behind her. A bag.

"Oh my god, oh-my-god, ohmygod!" She held her hands up and looked at them. Then down at the bag.

Then she ran away into the darkness, leaving the bag where it lay.

The sound that followed her, like the heartbeat of the night, the squelching sound of footsteps in blood.

*   *   *

The night crawled on, the darkness endured. Total darkness. The sky was dead.

Canyon Creek grumbled past at full flow. A deep gash carved into the earth by a thread of water over the long years.

Splashing feet disturbed the water, and the ragged breath of runners cut the wind.

He caught her in the underbrush on the other side, the wild side of the creek, and threw her down.

There was a struggle, but it was brief.

Ripping cloth, the wet smack of flesh on flesh.

Slobbering, grunting, yowling, painful pleasure. Animal. Organic but unnatural, like a monkey fucking a cat.

Only one returned.

*   *   *

The night grew old, bleached out like something dead. The stars returned, but they were pale, weak.

The darkness was not finished yet, the darkness endured.

Chapter 4

Grim hated hospitals. He hated the way they looked; straight and bland and fluorescent-bright. He hated the way they smelled; pine and bleach on top, piss, shit, and human rot beneath. If dread had a scent, it would be Orofino Municipal.

Grim felt sorry for the girl, but he wished like hell he hadn't come.

The people were the worst, not the doctors and staff, the visitors. So much anger and pain. The patients he ignored as best he could. It was easier if he could think of them as non-people; fixtures, inventory, diseased merchandise. If he could ignore their discomfort he wouldn't empathize as much. Empathy was a path to misery.

Danny had been gone a long time. He was with the doctor.

The ER was busy with injured from the car wreck, but the waiting room was nearly deserted. An old woman at the other end of the room pretended to watch the early morning news, but kept a suspicious eye on him.

He'd picked through the stack of magazines on the table next to him; *People*, *Time*, and *Better Homes & Gardens*. There was a *Readers Digest* and a few *Field & Stream*. He'd read these already, all the interesting parts anyway.

He was bored and tired, but couldn't sleep, not with the old lady watching him. He didn't like being stared at. A woman from the kitchen had come through earlier and started a fresh pot of coffee. He decided a cup of coffee was as close to happiness as he was likely to come this morning.

He stood and groaned as he stretched away the weariness. He rolled his head, popped his neck, then walked across the room to the coffee pot. He walked closer to the old woman than was necessary, and smirked when she moved a heavily-veined hand over her purse.

The waiting room door opened as he filled a Styrofoam cup, and he heard Danny's voice.

"I understand you have to wait for the test results, but if you had to guess, would you say she is drugged or retarded?" He sounded as tired as Grim felt. Irritable. The doctor would do well to just humor him.

"First," the Doctor said, "we don't use the word *retarded* anymore. Second, I'm not in the business of guessing, Deputy." He emphasized the word Deputy as if it were vulgar. "Sheriff Davis is free to contact me at any time to check on her condition, but I won't have anything definitive for a while."

The doctor's eyes strayed to Grim and narrowed, his face puckering into a grimace. "This isn't a flophouse, young man. If you don't have family here I'm afraid I'll have to have the Deputy escort you out."

"He's with me," Danny said. "He's a witness, and he's had a very long night. He can have the whole damn pot for all I care."

The doctor looked not the slightest bit abashed. He gave a curt little nod and turned back toward the door.

"Sheriff Davis is out of town on business. You're stuck with me for the time being."

It was a formal inquiry actually, something to do with the misappropriation of County funds from what Grim understood. He thought there was a pretty good chance Sheriff Davis wasn't coming back. Probably the doctor already knew that, just thought he was being clever.

"When will you have the test results? Could you be a little more specific?"

"No, I can't." The doctor turned around again but didn't face Danny. He consulted something on the chart he held, made scribbled notes. "The specimen will go to St.

Joseph's in Lewiston. I'm afraid the budget won't allow for a proper lab here."

"Or doctor, it seems," Danny said, then walked away, leaving the white-coated man to glower over his chart.

"Let's get you home now," he said to Grim. "Mom is going to kill me for keeping you out this late."

* * *

"What are they going to do with her?"

A strange question coming from Grim. It was not like him to care, at least not past the moment. He was a good kid, Danny thought. A little troubled, but who wasn't? He could be counted on to help when a need came up, but when the hour of need was past he tended to just fade into the background. Not one to get too attached.

Except for Clara, but Clara was another thing. She had been there in his time of need, and had not faded out on him. He'd once been suspended from school for beating up an older kid who'd made fun of her.

Nothing seemed to touch Grim, except for Clara, and now, it seemed, this girl.

"State Hospital North," Danny said. "For now anyway." State Hospital North was a little ray of sunshine tucked in the pines behind the state prison. In the '70s it was called State Asylum North. It had been little better than a prison itself back then, but progress had seen to that. The locals simply referred to it as *Up River*.

He noted Grim's look of dismay and added, "Really no alternative at the moment. If she's not too," —he searched for the right word, but didn't find it—"messed up they'll probably send her along to one of the children's homes in Lewiston."

"Just how *messed up* is she?" Grim ventured.

"They don't think she was raped, if that's what you mean."

Grim grunted his response.

He said nothing else for the rest of the trip home.

*   *   *

The old house had been impressive and elegant in its time, but that time was long gone. Now it was little more than a curiosity to passing history buffs, a functioning relic. When Clara's mother bought it, she'd taken down the sign on the old western building's edifice that identified it as THE CLEARWATER SCHOOLHOUSE, and hung a brass plaque that said THE OLD CLEARWATER HOTEL—A STOP ON THE TRAIL OF THE INFAMOUS JAMES BROTHERS. The school had been moved to a more modern building years before a young Clara called it home.

She'd lived in it a year before contractors had introduced the miracle of electricity and modern plumbing to its ancient frame, and how she had hated it then.

But she'd grown to love it. Even after her mother died in a fall down its old, creaking staircase, Clara—then only seventeen—had fought to keep it. She'd fought off the bank with her mother's life insurance policy, her own part time jobs, and a series of small personal loans, but just barely.

She owned it now, free and clear, except for the yearly curse of property taxes, and as much work as she had to put into the aging beast, she still loved it. There were times, more and more as she grew older, when Clearwater and the people who called the little gash in these mountains home, exasperated her to the point of unchristian thoughts, that she would swear that old house was the only reason she bothered to stay.

But that was not exactly true. She stayed for the kids, her kids by love if not by blood. There had been three of them, all orphans.

One had run away and been arrested a few years later for a murder in Lewiston—a bad seed that one had been, sometimes nothing could change that in a person.

Danny, her second, was still around, living in Clearwater, a Sheriff's Deputy. He could be the Sheriff, she knew. She'd tried to convince him to run, but he'd resisted thus far. Maybe when the problems with the current elected crook came to a head that would change.

The third. Her third broken angel was something in between. Not the wasted second chance her first (she could not bring herself to say, or even think his name to this day) had been, but no saint either.

Her Grim—the reason she'd not slept at all the night before, the reason she still paced the foyer of her old crumbling beast of a house at six in the morning.

He was with Danny, she had that much to be hopeful for, but she'd heard there had been trouble at Wallen's salvage yard the night before, and then the old bastard had attacked a girl in Jack's, near killed her from the gossip.

And poor Michele, such a sweet girl. Clara just didn't know whether to believe the stories going around about poor Michele Kirkwood bashing his head in with his own cane.

Such craziness, far too much craziness for a place like Clearwater, and she couldn't dismiss the sinking feeling that her Grim was at the center of the trouble, not just a bystander.

"How much trouble are you in this time, young man," she said to the empty hallway.

"Not too much, Ma."

Clara jumped a little, then spun toward the open front door, her right hand fluttering theatrically over her heart. "Merciful Jesus, Danny, don't do that to me." But then she laughed a little, a nervous laugh, but also a grateful one. Danny was back, and when Danny came back everything was made right again. It had always been that way.

"I'll walk louder next time, Mom," he said, and gave a brief smile.

She had known him most of his life, and could read him well. Something in the pained smile, and the downcast of his gaze, told her his bad night wasn't over yet. Suddenly she wasn't sure she wanted to know what had happened.

"Where's Grim," she asked.

"Waiting in the car. He's afraid to come in until I've talked to you."

"Why? What's he done?"

"Aside from fooling around the old Salvage Yard, not a thing. In fact he was a big help to me at Jack's, and on the way to Orofino. He just wanted you to know that before he showed his face was all."

Clara relaxed. She closed her eyes and leaned against the old plank wall. "Thank you," she whispered to no one in particular.

Danny motioned out the door, and a second later Clara heard a car door slam and footfalls crunching the gravel of her driveway.

"What happened last night?"

"What have you heard?"

"A lot," she said. "Just don't know how much of it I believe."

"You can probably believe most of it," Danny said. "Don't think there's much room for embellishment. It was Goddamn crazy."

"Watch the language," she scolded, but without real force. It was just a reflex to Danny's slip of the tongue. There was no feeling behind it.

Grim entered behind Danny, looking tired and embarrassed. He hated being the center of attention. A throwback to his time on the streets, she imagined, something he'd not been able to outgrow yet. He'd only been with her for three years. He'd been on the streets much longer than that.

"Oh, come here, you," she walked toward him, arms outstretched, and forced him to accept her hug. Another form of attention he wasn't comfortable with, but he'd just have to suffer through it. The hug wasn't for him, it was for her. She just needed to touch him, to know he was really okay.

He returned the gesture, then pulled away quickly.

Danny gave his back a light pat. "Why don't you head upstairs, bro? Get some sleep before you tip over."

"Yes," Clara said, suddenly in charge of her emotions. "Up you go." She clapped her hands together — *Clarese* for *Now, Now!*

"All right, all right," Grim said, falling comfortably into the roll of indignant teenager. "I have to get rid of some coffee, then I'm there."

"You let him have coffee?" Clara huffed, as if she'd just discovered the two of them had been out fornicating at the Stateline brothels.

"You got a big mouth, bro," Danny said, then cringed as Clara let out an incensed *harrumph*.

Grim had enough energy left to laugh as he mounted the stairs.

For a second everything felt normal, then Grim was gone — it was just Clara, Danny, and a silence that was a little too heavy.

Danny cleared his throat. "You could use a few hours sleep before work, Mom. You look as bad as I feel."

Clara shook her head. "No, no. Too late in the morning for that. I have to make breakfast. I'll get my second wind soon. I can sleep this afternoon if I need to."

Danny nodded. "I have to get to the office. I'll stop by after my shift is over and tell you everything."

He turned and stepped out into the still-cool morning, then paused.

"Mom, can I ask you a question?"

"What is it, dear?"

"Have you ever wanted to have a girl?"

"Yes. Yes," she said, her voice low so it wouldn't carry up the stairs. "God saw fit to bless me with two wonderful boys, so I can't complain." No mention of the first boy, the bad seed, the one who'd broken her heart.

Danny nodded. "Get some sleep if you can. I'll bring something from Jack's when I'm off shift. We need to talk."

Chapter 5

Someone had killed Mr. Spritzer that morning; Danny found him on the sidewalk in front of the post office on his way to the office. Beaten to death by the looks of it. There had been a lot of blood, more than he would have expected considering Mr. Spritzer's size.

Also unexpected, was his feelings of sympathy, even loss — all things considered Clearwater would be a happier place without him, and Danny knew it. He was a biter.

Mr. Spritzer, ten pounds of furry, ankle-biting, yard-shitting evil, was Darla Spencer's dog. She let it run loose in town, and he took complaints at least once a week from people whose ankles he'd bitten or yards he'd shit in.

"Finally took a dump in the wrong yard." He shook his head.

God damn, what a mess.

Danny didn't know if there was a humane way to put a beast like Mr. Spritzer down, but he knew this wasn't it — dropped inside a bag and beat to death against the light pole in front of the General Store.

The most troubling part of it, the part that honestly frightened him, was the bag itself. Old burlap, drawstring on the top, the letters USPS stenciled in black.

Laying at the post office's front door like a macabre special delivery.

But to whom?

It was a question he didn't care to explore just then, so

he walked two doors down to the Sheriff's Office, let himself in with a key from the miniature handcuff key ring Grim had given him for Christmas the winter before, and went to the broom closet for a garbage bag.

He'd used the disposable camera from his glove box at Canyon Jack's the night before, so he borrowed the one from Everett's Jeep.

When the crime scene was photographed and Mr. Spritzer, burlap sack and all, were sealed in his makeshift body-bag, Danny poured kitty litter on the bloodied parts of the sidewalk, hoping it worked as well with dog blood as it did with oil leaks.

He wanted to have the worst of it swept up by the time Clara came to work.

Technically, his shift had ended, but he couldn't go home yet. There was still too much to do.

Everett arrived as Danny was sweeping the last of the bloodied kitty litter into another plastic bag, unusually late for his shift.

"Road kill?" He said, walking up behind Danny in that endlessly creepy way he had; silent, nowhere one moment, right behind you the next.

"Not exactly," Danny said, setting the broom and dustpan aside to tie the drawstrings on the bag. "Someone finally got tired of Mr. Spritzer shitting in their roses."

Everett nodded, arms crossed, face serious. "Any leads?"

"Nope," Danny said, and dropped the bag next to the red-tinged straws of the broom.

"Shame," Everett said. "I'd like to buy whoever it was a drink."

"That is just plain wrong," Danny said. "You know damn well Darla's going to cry her eyes out."

Everett shrugged. He could afford to shrug it off—he hadn't seen the little dog's broken body, or the blood that soaked through the burlap of the mailbag.

"You should have called me up last night," Everett said. "No need to handle everything yourself."

"Wasn't much to be done by the time I got there," Danny said. "You can meet the Coroner if you want. Should be arriving soon."

"Where's Wallen's body?"

"In the Dumpster cage behind Jack's place."

Everett gave Danny a disapproving look. "Now *that* is wrong."

"Hell, no disrespect meant. Not much else to do with it. Jack sure as hell wouldn't let us put it in his cooler."

"How is Michele?"

"She's fine. Physically anyway."

"What about the girl?"

Danny shook his head. "Up river."

Around them, Clearwater was beginning to wake. People were headed to their jobs at the mill in Lewiston, local shops would open soon. Danny bent down, picked up the bag, the broom, and the dustpan. He nodded toward their office, a pathetic thing; small front room, no private offices, a small bathroom in the back and a single cell in the reinforced concrete basement.

Everett followed him inside.

Danny replaced the broom and dustpan in the closet then walked the bag with the litter to the back door and dropped it in the trashcan.

"No one knows about the girl." He walked to the front of the office and dropped into a chair by the front counter. "She's not from around here. There was a wreck outside of Orofino last night; happened about the same time Wallen attacked Michele Kirkwood and the girl. There was a yellow Buick with California plates, so I suppose she could have been with them."

"Kidnapped?"

Danny shrugged, then nodded. "It's likely," he said. "Couple of joy-riders maybe, picked her up somewhere between here and Cali. Dropped her off when they were tired of her."

Everett's face reddened, his lips thinned. "Was she raped?"

"The doctor that examined her doesn't think so, but there was more wrong with her than being lost and out of place." He braced himself and said, "Grim thinks she was drugged."

"And what would Grim know about that?" Everett barked. He began to pace the carpet between the front desk and front door, keeping an eye out for pedestrians and potential eavesdroppers.

"Grim's seen some things in his time," was all Danny had to say. He didn't feel the need to elaborate. Everett knew Grim had a past, but he didn't need to know the details. Danny himself knew very few of them, only that Grim had been on his own most of his life.

Danny knew about the homeless man in Seattle who had kidnapped him and taken him to a bum-infested park called Green City. He knew Grim called his kidnapper The Rag Man, and that he was only able to escape when Seattle's police stormed Green City in force to drive the outlaw homeless out.

Everett nodded, a curt movement of the chin. "You catch him out at the salvage yard last night?"

Damn it, Danny thought. *Doesn't miss a thing.*

"No," he lied. "He was on his way there and I picked him up before I got the call."

Everett watched him intently for a few moments, then nodded.

"Okay. Tell me what I need to know to wrap this up then head on home. You look like you're ready to drop."

Indignity swelled Danny's chest at the tone of command coming from someone who was not his superior, threatened to spill from his mouth, but he bit it back. It was too early in the day, and he was too damn tired. He knew there was no disrespect meant. It was an awkward situation, Davis having to leave them on their own. The pecking order had to work its way out somehow, and Everett, who had five years on Danny, had naturally assumed the role of Alpha dog.

Davis would resign, or be removed, soon enough, and

the constituents would decide who they wanted in charge.

Until then, just let it slide.

"Sounds like a good plan to me," Danny said.

* * *

Grim turned on the radio, stripped down to his shorts, then fell into bed. He couldn't remember ever being so tired.

He was drained.

But he couldn't sleep.

He kept thinking about the strange girl, couldn't get her out of his head.

At some point sleep did come. It was thin and dreamless.

He awoke with the sun shining through the parted black curtains of his upstairs window, warming his face, burning his eyes. He rolled over and looked at his alarm clock. It was ten in the morning.

Still in his shorts, he gathered his discarded clothing and deposited them in the hamper next to his dresser, then picked out his clothes for the day, reaching into drawers almost blindly. Fashion was another thing Grim didn't give a shit about.

He carried the fresh clothes — black cut-off shorts and a T-shirt — under the crook of his arm, bound for a long shower, then some coffee to wake his sorry ass up, when a rain of pebbles hit his window from the outside, startling him.

"Fucking inbreds," he grumbled. He slipped the shorts on and went to the window, expecting Clay, or Kelly, or both. Keith wasn't likely to come by this morning, or any time. They weren't exactly the best of friends, only hung together because they happened to have fallen into the same crowd.

Of course, it could be Alex or one of his friends. It wouldn't be the first time they've come to his house looking for a fight.

He walked to the side of the window, head low, and peeked through the edge of the half-drawn curtain.

It was Michele.

*   *   *

Michele didn't expect to find Grim awake, and she didn't want to wake him if he wasn't already up, so she stood and waited instead of shouting, or throwing more pebbles. A few minutes passed and she didn't see him. She'd decided to leave when the front door opened.

"Hey," Grim said, gave a kind of half-wave. He looked tired, annoyed.

"Hi," she said, and felt stupid when the words she wanted to say wouldn't come. She'd wanted to thank him for helping her last night, when everyone else only stood back and stared. Even her mom hadn't wanted to touch her after...

"What do you want?" he asked, a little impatient but not rude. Looked like he hadn't slept at all.

She hadn't either.

His house was at the fringe of Main Street, as far away from town as you could get without actually leaving town. Still, it was close enough to Clearwater's downtown that she could hear the occasional car and the crack of baseball bats, early morning softball practice at the school playground.

That was where she was supposed to be, practicing with her team. She had argued with her mom just to let her out for practice.

Anybody who happened to drive by or look her way might see her, and if it got back to her mom that she was seen with Eugene Grim, she'd be grounded for life.

"Can I come in for a minute," she asked, then blushed when she realized that he wore a shabby pair of cut-off shorts, and nothing more.

"Yeah," Grim said, and left the door open for her as he passed back into the cool interior of Clara Grey's old house.

It wouldn't be cool for long, she thought. It was a hot spring; record-breaking days every week since April, and she doubted the old house had air-conditioning.

She followed him inside and shut the door behind them.

She stood in the foyer for a few moments, trying to figure out where he'd disappeared to. She hoped it wasn't upstairs to his bedroom; she'd be too embarrassed to follow him up there. Then she heard banging from the kitchen to her left.

She'd never been inside the old house before, and was surprised at how nice it was. Old, sure it was, the oldest standing building in town, but Clara had not let it fall apart. The hardwood floors were waxed and clean, the wall planks straight, the fixtures rustic. A small wagon-wheel chandelier hung from the high ceiling, almost too high to provide more than a hint of light down where she stood.

The kitchen was only a little more modern. The appliances were old, she recognized their style from the seventies sitcom reruns her mom watched.

Grim stood in front of the gas stove with an old percolating coffee maker, the kind she thought people only used while camping. He fumbled in an open cabinet and brought out an old tin mug.

"Drink coffee?" he asked.

"Uh, no. Thanks though."

"How are you doing?"

"Fine. I guess. Never killed anyone before." She tried to laugh, but it came out a sob. She realized she was tearing up and willed herself to stop.

Grim, facing the other way, hadn't noticed.

Michele wiped the moisture from her eyes. "Thanks for sitting with me last night," she said.

Grim turned toward her. "Sure," he said. "Not much else I could do to help."

"Well it helped me a lot," she said. "No one else would come near me."

The coffee began to perc. Grim turned toward it, head

low. "Sorry," he said. "I'm not trying to be harsh. I'm just tired is all."

The phone rang, breaking the tense silence. They jumped up in tandem.

"I should go now," Michele said. "Mom will kill me if she knows I'm here." She realized her poor choice of words and blushed again.

Before Grim could say anything she ran from the kitchen, through the foyer, and pushed out the front door.

*   *   *

Grim stood a moment in Michele's proverbial dust, still half-asleep, stunned by the suddenness of her departure.

The phone, an old wall-mounted thing hanging next to the foyer entrance, as outdated as everything else in the house, rang again.

It was Clay.

"You're getting slow, Grim. We saw big bro escorting you into Jack's last night on our way back into town." He chuckled, a sound both perverse and contagious. "Were you there when Killer Kirkwood beaned Old Man Wallen?"

"Suck shit and die," Grim said, and hung up.

He walked back to the stove to check the coffee. It was done. He turned the burner off and poured a cup.

The phone rang again.

"Yeah?"

"I should be the one pissed at you, you know." He did sound a little upset too. They'd come damn close that time. "Bo was laughing it up all the way back to town, telling us how you stood there like a retard and let him shoot you."

"That's not exactly how I remember it," Grim said, and entertained himself with visions of where he might stick Bo's spud-gun next time they came face to face.

"Tell me what happened at Jack's," Clay said, shifting to the topic that really interested him at the moment. "Did Michele really club the old fucker?"

"Why don't you talk to Keith? His sister was there

when it happened."

"Tried man, Keith's gone AWOL, and Gina hates me."

"Yeah she does," Grim agreed. At the beginning of the last school year Grim had dated her. Hadn't lasted long, just long enough for him to get into her pants. After the split-up, Clay had tried, and she'd shut him down. She'd even handed him the nickname Clay-Midia, and to Clay's lasting embarrassment the unfortunate handle had stuck for a while.

Clay was silent for a few moments, deep inside one of his perverted thoughts, Grim supposed.

"I've decided," Clay said at last, "To make it my personal mission to get down Gina's pants."

"How noble," Grim said, beginning to get irritated with the conversation.

"Fitting," Clay said. "Show that bitch *Clay-Midia*."

"I gotta go, man."

"I'll be at the park watching the girls practice," Clay said. "Come on by if you feel like hangin'."

"Later," Grim said, now thoroughly tired of the conversation.

Clay laughed on the other end of the line. "Maybe I'll see Killer Kirkwood there. You know, if she can handle a bat as well as Old Man Wallen's cane, they might have a chance this year."

Grim hung up and tried to drown himself in coffee.

*   *   *

Grim decided to go out despite the encroaching lethargy, and the headache that began squeezing at his brain just after he'd got off the phone with Clay. He drank coffee, took a shower, drank more coffee, craved a smoke. He'd promised Clara he would quit, and he'd done pretty good keeping that promise.

It was eleven o'clock when he finally made it out the door. At first he just stood outside the door staring at the path beyond the front patio, which spanned the length of the big house. A porch swing, so old no one dared sit in it, sat at one end. A propane grill, end table, and lawn chairs at the other. His Yamaha sat on a spread-out tarp, still in pieces, in the yard. He wondered where he was going.

Clay's house was his usual destination, but Clay was not home, he'd still be at the schoolyard ogling the girls playing softball. Softball practice didn't let out until after noon on the weekends. Grim was simply not ready for his daily dose of Clay at the moment. He decided to cut through The Jungle, Clara's name for their overgrown back yard — as in, *Grim, how about you get the mower out and give The Jungle a shave today?* — and walk the back way to the post office.

He'd heard Danny ask Clara if she'd ever wanted a girl, and say they needed to talk after he was finished with work. Grim thought he should be there to hear what Danny had to say, even though he already had a good idea.

Despite his sympathy for the girl, something warned him that it was a very bad idea.

Grim understood this was probably just a natural fear of change, especially when the last three years had been so calm, a paradise compared to the previous fourteen, but the fact was he had just as big of stake in this decision as anyone. He at least wanted to be there when/if Clara made it.

Just as Danny had been there the day Clara had met him.

*   *   *

It was a wet and miserable fall afternoon, the day Grim found his way to Clearwater. He had run away from a foster home in Seattle, Washington, and was following a blind course inland. He didn't care where, just away from Washington State. After a week on the road, hitchhiking most of the way, he found himself on a little highway winding through the Idaho mountains, following the Clearwater River toward Montana.

He'd decided at some point that Missoula was where he

wanted to be. He'd searched maps of all the western states, and after deciding that California was too far away to hitch, ditto Oregon, the only decent city in his range was Missoula.

Traffic on this stretch of road was sparse, and no one was feeling particularly generous. At first there was no sign that he was anywhere near a town of any kind—just the green-covered mountains, and the river cutting through them. Then he saw Canyon Jack's. Then the pitted black-top breaking from the highway and a sign that read:

CLEARWATER

POPULATION 800

1 MILE

The road was visible for maybe a quarter of a mile, then disappeared around an evergreen-lined bend, cradled by the mountains, just a narrow rest stop in the wild.

He would have passed it without a thought, but he was hungry. It had been a few days since his last meal, a bag of rest-stop tacos provided by the trucker who had driven him from northern Idaho's mountain plains to the valley where the Snake and Clearwater rivers came together and had grown the small city of Lewiston.

In Seattle and Spokane, he had dined and dashed. It was easy to do in the packed restaurants, escaping onto streets boiling with activity. The gravel parking lot of this grease-spot was near empty, and this was not the city. For all he knew these country people could be crazy, and a man on his own (he may have only been fourteen, but he was on his own, and qualified himself as a man) could disappear very easy in a place like this. Who would even know to look for him?

So he walked on past, glancing through the front picture window to see if he was noticed. He was, of course. These country people must have *Stranger Radar*. A dozen eyes watched him pass, forks forgotten midway to gaping mouths hungry for their next shovel-full of grits, or whatever it was they ate. He waited until the little restaurant was out of sight, then went into the trees.

It took much longer than he thought it would to walk through the dense underbrush and dead tangles that seemed to thrive beneath the shade of the larger evergreens, but the restaurant finally came back into view through the boughs. He came out of the trees into a small field that seemed to be sprouting junk—metal barrels, parts of old tractors, the squatting hulk of an old shed, rotting slowly back into the earth, a few long dead cars. The junk field, not Wallen's Salvage Yard, but a lesser place of the same stripe, lay between a lone doublewide trailer and the restaurant.

Behind the restaurant, as he'd hoped, was a Dumpster. It sat inside a three-walled shed, the open wall closed off by a tall, bared gate. This, he later learned, was to keep the wild animals out, coyotes, wild cats and feral dogs, and the rare mountain lion that came this far down the valley. The gate was latched, but not locked, so he opened it.

It was the squeaking of long-ignored hinges that gave him away.

Jack had seen him and alerted an off-duty deputy who sat in his dining room eating a late breakfast. A strange kid walking alone, wearing clothes that were little more than dirt caked stitches by then, warranted some attention out here.

"Kid, I don't know what you hope to find in there, but I'm sure we can do better than that."

That was the day he met Danny.

*   *   *

That was where Old Man Wallen was now, unless the Coroner had already come from Orofino to pick his carcass up.

Grim felt regret for having given Wallen so much trouble in the past few years, but would not let himself feel the guilt that tried to surface when he thought of the old man's body stiffening on the floor of Canyon Jack's.

It wasn't his fault the old fucker had finally come unglued. Not at all. And it wasn't his fault, Wallen had hit

Michele. Not one bit. Hell, it was Danny who'd sent him there.

But that was where his logic failed, so he forced his thoughts in another direction.

He heard the crack of a bat and cheering—the girls practicing in the field beside the school—and thought of them instead. Running bases, swinging at practice pitches, chests pushed out at the end of their swings. Short shorts, bare legs, sweaty T-shirts. Grim loved softball season.

He wondered if Michele had gone to practice after seeing him, or gone home to hide from the sidelong looks and hands cupped over whispering mouths. Michele had friends, quite a few from what he could tell, but few very tight ones. She hadn't fallen in with any of the cliques, and that made her an easy target.

Killing old men was an effective way, Grim thought, to kill a social life.

High brush and stunted trees flanked the path he followed, mostly blocking the school from view. He thought about leaving the trail, getting a closer look at the girls in the playground to see if Michele was there, but Clay might see him, and he didn't want to get held up by Clay until after Danny and Clara's *talk*.

Canyon Creek burbled past at his right, narrow, but deceptively deep at many points. Spring runoff from the mountains fed it to the point of overflowing, turning the land around into a kind of seasonal swamp.

Ahead the trail curved toward town, would meet up with an empty lot at the bottom of Angel Ridge Grade. He'd be at the post office soon.

Grim saw the shoe out of the corner of his eye, barely registered it. It was the shoe's bright color that caught his attention, sparked recognition, and made his chest tighten with a new dread. It was a red canvas high top, like the ones Keith had worn to their game the night before.

It jutted at a crooked angle from the muddy water of Canyon Creek, the current rocking it to and fro.

It was not empty.

Chapter 6

Jack's was closed that morning, so Danny made Clara a breakfast of scrambled eggs, bacon, and toast, then packed them in Tupperware for the drive to the post office. He stopped by her house first, knocked, and when no one answered, went inside to find Grim. He thought Grim had a right to be there when he told Clara about the girl, but his little brother was not home, so he moved on. He saw Clay on the way, and had to fight the urge to give him hell about last night's trouble in the Salvage Yard.

Clara must have been watching for him. She met him at the door with a smile and kissed his stubbly cheek.

"Bless you," she said, taking the offered food. "My poor stomach thinks my throat is cut."

"Welcome, Mom," Danny said, smiling at her gratitude. A simple smile from Clara had the power to brighten the gloomiest of days, always had, always would. "Get some sleep?"

"A few hours," she said. "Enough to get my bounce back." She pulled at his sleeve with his free hand. "Come on, come on. We're going to melt out here." She led him in. The air conditioning was like a parcel of Heaven.

She seemed not to notice the hint of red Danny had been unable to wash from the sidewalk, and Danny felt no need to mention it. She would have enough to consider today without pining over the violent death of Mr. Spritzer, the ankle biter and yard shitter.

He let her eat first, which she did with the slow deliberation of royalty. She finished her breakfast in ten minutes without spilling a crumb.

"So," Clara said, fitting the lids over empty bowls, "tell me about the girl."

Danny smiled, nodded. "I thought you might have heard about her by now."

"Vicky told me about her, said someone abandoned her at Jack's." She looked into Danny's eyes then, locked onto them, her expression almost childlike in its innocence. "Did Mr. Wallen really attack her?" A question that begged disavowal, like a child asking a parent to prove that the bogeyman does not exist.

Danny nodded. "Near killed her too. Probably would have if Michele Kirkwood hadn't brained him."

Clara nodded, resigned to an unkind truth she'd already half-believed. She sat silent for several moments, blinked away silent tears. "When are you going to town next?" Town was a generic phrase for any place bigger than Clearwater, usually meant Orofino or Lewiston.

"I'll be going to Lewiston tonight before my shift starts," he said. "Have to see someone at St. Joseph's hospital. I might need to light a fire under someone's ass for some test results."

"The girl?" Clara asked.

"Yeah. She wasn't all there last night. Grim thinks she was drugged."

"She at St. Joseph's now?"

He shook his head. "Up river."

Clara signed. "Well, if she wasn't ruined on drugs before, she will be when they're done with her." She slapped the counter with the flat of one hand, her usual sign of a shift of subject.

"I'd like to go with you to town, if I could. Pick up a gift for Michele."

"That is a sweet thought, and yes, I'd love for you to tag along." He knew a gift wouldn't take away Michele's trauma, but the sentiment would help. No matter how he saw it, he didn't think Clearwater as a whole was likely to see her as the hero. Michele could use any friendly gesture they might give.

"Does this strange girl have a name?"

"Not yet," Danny said.

She nodded again. "I think I'd like to meet this mystery girl, if you can arrange it for me."

"I can," Danny said. "Mom," he said, then faltered, afraid to commit to words what he was thinking. "Mom, you know what I'm asking, don't you?"

"Why, yes," she said, and the hint of a smile touched her lips. "I knew before you came.

"If no one else is willing to take this child in and love her, then I will."

*   *   *

Michele didn't think she could handle practice today, so she'd gone straight home after seeing Grim. She didn't want to be around people right now. Accusation seemed to burn in every eye that found hers, and she knew what they thought, but were afraid to say.

She'd already got that speech from her mother, the shrill rant emphasized by an angry, prodding finger and punctuated by crushing hugs.

Damn it, Michele, I told you to sit still — point, point — *and I know how you are but you're not responsible for every stray cat and ragamuffin who wanders into town* — point, point — *and what the hell were you thinking anyway? You should have stayed out of his way and let us handle him* — point, point — *my God he could have killed you* — hug.

Beyond the words, a sense that there was something wrong with a girl who was capable of doing what she had done, killing a man. It was as if they thought, at least on some level, that she had enjoyed it.

And she knew what the other kids were calling her now, she'd heard Amy Johnson, Deputy Everett Johnson's daughter, whisper it to her friend as they passed her on their bikes.

Killer Kirkwood. Had quite a ring, she thought.

"Honey, I'm going to work now," her mother called from the kitchen. "Are you sure you'll be alright alone?"

Michele had gone straight to her room when she got home, dressed down to her nightshirt and laid down on her bed, trying for a few more hours of sleep. She was still tired, the hour or two of sleep she'd stole early that morning seemed like a cruel teaser for a main event that would never come. She'd been in bed for over an hour now, eyes closed and a pillow over her face to block the sunlight streaming through her blinds.

"Fine, Mom," she called. "Sell a house, buy me something big."

Her mother didn't laugh. "Stay inside. There's pizza for lunch. I'll see you tonight."

Michele doubted that. Most nights she didn't make it home until Michele was in bed, and sometimes not at all. Her mother had taken to spending nights in Lewiston when she worked too late.

Then the door slammed shut; she heard the deadbolt turn with a snap, and her mother was off to Lewiston to maintain their standard of living. When the sound of her car faded down the street, Michele rolled over onto her stomach and cried into her pillow.

* * *

Heads turned toward Grim as he stumbled down the short main street toward the Sheriff's Office. He recognized faces, but could not remember their names. Mud covered his arms and legs, his clothes, his face. He couldn't feel the ground beneath him. His feet carried him on, outside of his control. His legs were numb. Hanging loosely from one hand, a bizarre pendulum, was part of a leg in a muddy red shoe.

"Jesus Christ." A shout from the open bay of Gavin's

Service Station.

Grim, turned his head toward the sound and recognized Gavin Fox, Keith's father, standing inside next to an old red Ford. Without meaning to do it, Grim found himself walking toward the open bay door, holding out the leg like an offering.

"I found it in the creek," he said. His voice was conversational. "I looked but I couldn't find the rest of him."

Gavin stood there, gaping. "What happened to my boy?" he said at last, as Grim stopped in front of him.

"I found it in the creek," Grim repeated, and thrust the leg at him. "Might want to go back and find him before he washes into the river." He tried to pass the leg to Gavin, but the stunned man wouldn't take it, and it dropped to the oil-spotted bay floor.

He looked down at it. The breeze stirred a small forest of curly black hairs on it. The calf muscle seemed to twitch.

"What is happening?" Gavin asked.

Grim didn't hear him. He reached down for Keith's leg again. A cloud must have passed overhead, the dirty concrete faded to a deeper gray. Grim's legs failed, dropping him toward the disembodied leg. The concrete beneath him had faded to black before he reached it.

* * *

He awoke to a graying afternoon full of frantic voices and flashing lights. There was crying, too; Gavin, sitting in the service station's office.

Someone had folded a seat cover and put it beneath his head in a hurried attempt to make him more comfortable. Grim sat up, his head throbbing. He lifted a hand to the back of his head and winced as the fingers brushed a small goose egg.

"Easy now," Clara said, then her face appeared in front of him. She was wearing her Post Mistress uniform, her face was pale. She wrung her hands nervously. "You were exhausted," she said. "In shock, too, I suppose."

"Hey, Grim, you okay?" Clay shouted from the parking lot.

"He's fine, you just stay back," he heard Everett Johnson say.

Clay grumbled, but stayed back, and Everett went back to his conversation with a thin-bearded man standing in front of a *Clearwater County Search and Rescue* van. There was an ambulance parked parallel with the service station's front door. The EMT saw he was awake and approached.

"Did they find Keith?" Grim asked.

Clara shook her head, them made room for the EMT as he bent down before them.

"You took a nice knock on the head," he said. The man grabbed Grim's arm and led him toward the ambulance.

"I'm fine, really," Grim said, trying to free himself from the man's grip.

"Humor me," the EMT said, pulling him along.

Clara nodded. "Go on now, I want to make sure." She leaned in toward him and kissed his cheek, then hurried to the office, where Danny stood, trying to talk to Keith's grieving father.

The EMT shone a light in his eyes and prodded at his pounding head, asked a few questions, then let him go. Everett was waiting, arms crossed, stern eyes narrowed. "You seem to be the center of all kinds of shit just lately. Care to tell me what happened?"

*   *   *

There was nothing Gavin Fox could tell him right now. He was too caught up in the grief of loss. Danny didn't push him, only patted his shoulder and left him with a few commiserating words. Clara stayed with him. If anyone could ease this kind of pain it would be her.

He saw that Grim was awake now, standing at the rear of the ambulance talking to Everett, and started walking toward them. A hand clamped on his shoulder from behind and stopped him.

"Deputy Grey? Hey, Danny." It was a man he knew by face but not name. "The phone was ringing in your office so I answered it." He looked a bit apprehensive, as if he expected to be chewed out. "Someone from St. Joe's in Lewiston asking for Everett." The man's eyes turned toward Everett and Grim, then back to Danny again. "He looks busy, so I thought you might take it."

"Thanks," Danny said, then ran down the street toward his office. It was only a block away, but the short run left him drained, a combination of heat and creeping exhaustion. It felt like days since he had slept.

The phone's handset lay on the desk. The man who had answered it had not put it on hold, only set it down and left. He picked it up, hoping for some good news for a change, but prepared for more of the same.

"Deputy Johnson is disposed at the moment," he said. "Deputy Grey speaking, how can I help you?"

"Afternoon, Deputy Grey," a young woman's voice, sounding a little relieved to be talking to him instead of Everett. Everett sometimes had that effect on people. "I'm returning Deputy Johnson's call. We have the test results on your Jane Doe."

Somehow Danny was not surprised. Everett could be a real bastard to work with sometimes, but he got results.

"And," Danny urged.

"Tell him he gets a gold star. There is a high concentration of Rohypnol and Ketamine in her system."

Gold star for Grim, Danny thought. "Date rape drugs?"

"Yes," she said. "Club drugs. Mostly a problem in bigger cities." A pause, he could hear paper being shuffled. "Her file says she wasn't raped though."

"That's right," Danny said.

"Odd," she said. "The amount evident in her blood suggests prolonged use. These kinds of drugs have been known to turn people into vegetables. Usually in cases like these the victims are sex prisoners."

"I'd be grateful if you could send me a copy of the

results." He said, wanting to end the conversation.

"You have a fax?"

"That would be fine. Same number."

"Okay, I'll send it right over."

"Thank you. Have a good day."

"I'll do my best."

Danny hung up and waited. A few minutes passed, and the fax machine began to hum. He waited as a dozen sheets piled into the tray, then he copied and stapled them. He folded the copies and slipped them into an envelope, then slid it into his desk drawer and walked back to the scene at Gavin's Service Station.

Chapter 7

Everett finished with Grim quickly then set off to see Gavin. There was nothing else he could do, so Grim started walking for home. He saw Clay waiting for him down at the corner, smoking a cigarette and watching the girls as they pretended to keep up their practice, lobbing the ball at each other and missing more often than not, running listlessly round the rough diamond. Some didn't even pretend to be interested in practice, just stared down the street past him, with naked curiosity.

Clay saw him approaching and rushed to meet him.

"What happened, man?" The manic Clay of this morning was gone. His eyes were big, a little frightened. Smoke hung around his head like a low fog, blurring worry lines, making him look older. "Is it Keith?"

"Yeah," Grim said, not feeling the need to elaborate. He figured Clay had seen the Search and Rescue guys arrive and scatter toward the creek. There was nothing to explain.

A couple of younger girls in softball uniforms had walked along the school yard fence-line to eavesdrop, and one of them gasped as they turned and walked away.

"Fuck," Clay said, and said no more. A distant peal of thunder signaled an approaching storm.

He followed Clay home through the graying day.

*   *   *

A distant crack of thunder woke Michele from her thin sleep, and the first thing she noticed was that it was much darker than when she lay down. How long had she slept?

There were no dreams to remind her of the thing she'd done the night before, but the guilt returned upon waking. She didn't understand why she felt so bad about it; Wallen had hit her first and was choking the girl in the booth. If she hadn't hit him, he might have killed her.

No one else had helped. No one.

And the strangest thing, she did not remember picking up the cane, that part of her memory seemed to have abandoned her. She hadn't realized she was doing it until a second before the first swing connected with the top of his balding head. That first crack had brought it all into focus though.

She rose, feeling somewhat refreshed, and walked to her window. What she had mistaken for an approaching sunset was the premature dark of gathering clouds — a welcome early summer storm. It was still early afternoon; her mom wouldn't be home for a while.

Stay inside, her mom had said.

The first spot of rain streaked her window, and others joined it in a sudden cloudburst. She decided outside was the place to be, walking in the cool rain. She could call Rachel Wisher over, meet her halfway, then come back for pizza and a movie.

The thought of pizza brought an image of French-fries in blood, and she felt her gorge rise. If she'd had anything in her stomach to lose, she probably would have lost it.

Maybe just a movie then.

She pulled on a pair of shorts and tucked the long shirt into them, slipped on her sandals, and hunted down the cordless phone, which always seemed to be hiding from her in some out of the way nook.

She found it at last, in the bathroom next to her mom's unplugged curling iron, and dialed Rachel.

No answer.

She sighed, put the phone back on its charger before the

battery could run dead, struggled the front door's stiff old dead-bolt open, stepped out into the rain. It had already let up some, probably would only last for as long as it took for the clouds to blow past, but it felt good. She stood on the front step and let it soak into her.

The rain did not magically wash away her guilt, but it cooled her, and that was something.

She debated; go back inside or take a walk to Rachel's and see if she was home. Michele had a suspicion that Rachel's mother had seen her name on the caller ID and let it ring. It was the kind of thing she expected to start happening now, worried parents wanting to protect their kids from the influence of Clearwater's new #1 most wanted, Killer Kirkwood.

She started walking the two blocks to Rachel's house, dreading the reception she was likely to find there, but determined to make them face her before they judged her.

She passed lighted windows, families hiding from the turning weather; barbecues moved hastily indoors, girls from her softball team as they rushed home through the downpour. A few saw her and waved, but did not smile. A few stared at her unashamedly, whispering to one another. Most seemed not to notice her.

A girl from her team walked alone, turning onto her driveway half a block away. She was crying.

Michele passed Rachel's house without stopping, the lights were off and the car gone. They were probably at the shop where her dad worked, visiting, or off to town shopping.

She regretted her suspicious thoughts—not ignoring her call after all, just not home—but did not quite let them go.

The County Coroner rolled past her as she turned on to Main Street, and she was shocked with the sure knowledge that Old Man Wallen's corpse was laying in the back, zipped in a cold black bag. Because of her. Probably it was headed toward the Sheriff's Office before going back to the Coroner's Office in Orofino.

It passed the Sheriff's Office, and Michele followed its slow progress with her eyes. It pulled up next to an ambulance at the service station where Rachel's dad worked. The gravel parking lot of the station was busy with people despite the rain, Deputies Johnson and Grey among them.

What the hell?

The honk of an approaching car startled her, made her jump, and she saw Rachel staring from the window of her mom's car as it pulled next to her.

The front passenger window rolled down a few inches.

"Come on, get in," Rachel's mother called. "You're getting soaked." Her face was tight with worry, but Michele had a feeling it was nothing to do with her. Rachel, sitting in the back seat, pushed the door open and scooted over to make room.

Michele felt the first spark of happiness since the horrible night before; she knew there were people who would see her different now, people who would think she was something less than human after what she'd done to Mr. Wallen, but Rachel and her mom weren't among them.

She hurried into the back seat beside Rachel, who gave her a brief smile, and shut the door.

"Your mom is going to be so mad if you give yourself a cold," Mrs. Wisher said, then started driving.

"Yeah, I know," Michele said, and turned to get a last look at the scene behind them before Mrs. Wisher turned the corner toward her home. "What happened back there?"

Several uneasy seconds passed before she got an answer.

"Keith Fox is dead," Rachel said, and found a spot on the floorboard between her feet to look at.

*   *   *

"Looks like we're not going to town after all," Clara said. She stood with Danny and watched the Coroner depart with Old Ron Wallen, and what Grim had found of his friend.

The Search and Rescue had explored the creek from where Grim found Keith's leg downstream to the mouth of the river and not found him. He had not come home last night. His dad had said that was not unusual, that he liked to take impromptu overnighters down on the beach when it got warm. Danny thought if he had gone into the creek last night he was likely in the river by now anyway.

"That's okay," Danny said. "Everett got hold of St. Joe's this morning and got a rush put on the tests. They faxed them to me."

"And?" Clara prompted.

"Grim was right, she was drugged." Danny watched the Search and Rescue guys reorganize at their truck, one of them checking the scuba tank levels as they prepared to move closer to the river and dive. "If he's in the river they're not going to find him, and they know it. He'll probably wash up on the rocks down in Lewiston next fall."

"Why bother?"

"It's their job," he said. "They have to try at least."

The Rescue captain waved as they pulled away. Danny recognized him, Roger Burnham, and old friend from Orofino, and waved back. The crowd thinned with the departure of the Search and Rescue truck, even Gavin Fox had gone home, driven by Chuck Wisher, his only employee at the shop. Everett was searching the area around the creek, from the overgrown flat to the edge of the trees. Danny had offered his help, but Everett had told him not to worry, to wait until things calmed down at the shop, then to get home and catch as much sleep as he could before the next shift.

Probably won't find anything but poison ivy anyway.

It was about as calm now as it had been in the last twenty-four hours.

"Walk you home?"

"I'd love it." The Post Office closed early on Saturdays, not that she had spent much time there since noon. She hooked an elbow out at him, and he took it in his arm and led her away.

"What about our girl?"

Our girl already? He thought.

"Don't know much yet, just that someone put enough drugs in her to turn her into a vegetable. They say there's a good chance she'll come out of it, though, just take some time."

"What kind of drugs do that to a person?"

"Hold up a second," Danny left her on the sidewalk and went to his office to retrieve his copy of the test results fax, then met her back on the sidewalk, shuffling through papers until he found what he was looking for.

"Rohypnol and Ketamine," he said. "It's all right here," he shook the fold of papers in his fist, then slipped them back into the envelope and tucked it in his back pocket.

"Pervert drugs, right?" Clara asked, a little more venom in her voice than he was used to hearing from her.

"Something like that," he said.

His Jeep sat at the curb past his office. He opened the passenger door and let her in, then walked around to the driver's side. The rain had turned to a light drizzle. He was soaked through, but it felt good.

"Do you have plans for tomorrow?" Danny asked as he pulled out and made a U-turn on the deserted street.

"What do you have in mind?"

"Thought maybe we could go up river and see about getting our Jane Doe out of that nut house."

"I don't like that name," Clara said, and rubbed the wet chill out of her arms. "It's so anonymous."

"Well then, what do you think we should call her?"

She was gazing out the window, staring into the green as they passed the winding road into the mountains, and a battered sign at the bottom that said ANGEL RIDGE GRADE.

Clara smiled.

"I think I'll call her Angel."

* * *

Danny decided to make one more call before he turned in, knowing that Everett was too busy with the search for Keith's body to do it.

He sat on the edge of his bed, a singlewide in the small bedroom of what could only be properly described as a shack. There was a small bathroom, a living room and kitchen occupying opposite ends of the main room, and his bedroom. His home was a half-mile up Angel Ridge Grade, down a narrow dirt path in a clearing overlooking Clearwater. It had been a rarely-used hunting cabin before he'd bought the land and moved in. Danny's favorite thing about it was that it was paid for.

He kept a two-way radio on the nightstand between the alarm clock and the phone. The lines running up there had a bad habit of going down, especially in winter, and couldn't be counted on.

He'd changed into boxers and a light T-shirt, tossing his rain-drenched clothes into the hamper on the other side of the bed. He found his Rolodex in the top drawer of the nightstand, where he also kept his personal revolver and ammunition, and searched for the number he needed.

Orofino Police Department. Something else Grim had mentioned to him, something about the way their Jane Doe — Angel, he corrected himself — had almost come alive when they passed the wreck the night before.

The Orofino PD dispatcher, Doris, greeted him by name, no magic trick since they had a caller ID, but it still unnerved him.

"Hi, Doris. How're things?"

"Quiet," she said. "Bored out of my mind to tell you the truth."

"Be grateful you don't have our kind of excitement right now." He untangled the phone's ever-winding chord and lay back in bed, propping his head on a mound of pillows. As soon as his head sunk in it became a struggle to keep his eyes open. He hoped he could keep the call short. He would likely fall asleep, leaving her confused on the other end if it took too long.

"Yeah," she chuckled. "So I hear. I think every town is due for something like this at least once a decade. Not to worry," she said. "You'll probably have nothing but drunk drivers and speeders for the next ten years."

Danny heard the ringing of a door buzzer through his speaker, a muffled greeting, and when Doris spoke again her voice was a little more formal.

"So, what can I help you with, Deputy Grey?"

"Tricky Dickey?" he asked, indicating Richard Bell, their Chief of Police, by his much hated nickname.

"Uh-huh."

"I'll be quick then, don't want to keep you from him. I suppose you have the cars from last night's pileup impounded?"

"Yes," she said. "Back lot. What a mess."

"What have you got on the yellow Buick with the California plates?"

"Give me a second," she said. "I just filed that report." She put him on hold, instead of the typical muzak he listened to weather reports—hot and humid expected tomorrow, overcast with a chance of continuing thunderstorms. Distant thunder sounded from the west as if in agreement.

Danny felt himself begin to drift, and shook himself awake.

There was a click, a pause, then Doris's voice came back to him.

"Driver was a young male, female passenger, both approximately eighteen to twenty-two years old. No ID for either of them. We're running a check on the plates."

"Dead?"

"Very," she confirmed. "The lady they hit said they'd followed her for a few miles, then just up and rammed her. No alcohol evident, but we're waiting for blood tests to confirm." She paused, he heard pages turning, then she said, "sounds to me like a case of road rage."

An awful lot of rage going around just lately, Danny thought.

"What about their possessions? Anything to suggest

there may have been a third person with them earlier?"

"Nothing that stands out," Doris said. "Why, you know something we don't?"

"There was a girl, thirteen I'd say, abandoned by the highway at Canyon Jacks last night before the accident," he said, but did not elaborate.

"I see," she said. "Well, there was some luggage in the trunk. I suppose we can go through it and take a closer look."

"That'd be helpful," Danny said. He was about to bid her a good day and surrender to sleep when he remembered the test results in the envelope.

"One more thing. There may be drugs. Rohypnol and Ketamine."

"Never heard of them. What kind of drugs are those?"

"The lab tech at St. Joseph's called them Club Drugs." Danny took a breath, steeled himself against a fresh rush of anger, and continued. "They're date rape drugs. The girl was damn near comatose when I found her."

Doris was quiet for several seconds, maybe searching the report for any missed bit of information, but he didn't think so. It felt like tense silence, a shocked silence.

"I'll tell Richard," she said. "We'll get on it right away."

"Great, thanks, Doris." He sighed. He hadn't expected any great revelations or immediate proof that the girl might have been with them, but he was still disappointed. With all the bad shit that had happened since last night there was nothing he could do for any of them except fill out reports and count bodies. He hated being useless.

He was damn well going to do right by that girl.

"Give me a shout the second you find out anything." He reconsidered, then rephrased. "Give me a shout in about four hours if you find anything out."

"Will do, Danny, goodbye."

Danny said his goodbye then stretched his arm toward the nightstand and dropped the receiver back into its cradle.

Seconds later he was asleep.

Chapter 8

Some time later the phone rang. Danny rose far enough from sleep to hear it, but not to care. It rang incessantly, on and on, weaving its metallic warble into his dreams.

Then it stopped, and a static-filled voice shouted him awake.

Danny's eyes slammed open, stared at the ceiling, his heart hammered, he was sweating.

He groped for the two-way on his nightstand and lifted it from the charger, pressing the talk button.

"God damn it, what now?" he shouted, and immediately regretted it.

"Sorry," Everett barked through the two-way, "but we've got another situation here. Gina Fox, Gavin's daughter, is missing."

"Shit," Danny said, then yawned. "I'll be right down."

"No," Everett said. "No need for that. I just need to know if you've seen her around."

Danny lay back down. "Last time I saw her was Jack's. Last night. She was there when Wallen lost it. I took her statement and let her go." A thought occurred to him, and he cursed Everett for not having thought of it before waking him up. "She was with her boyfriend, from Lewiston I think. I have his phone number on my report. Why don't you call him, she's probably with him."

"Already tried that," Everett said, irritation in his voice. "He said they had an argument after they left Jack's. He dropped her at home and hasn't seen her since."

"I'm coming down," Danny said. "My shift starts in a few hours anyway."

"No you're not. I'm handling it right now," Everett countered. "You just go back to bed and I'll call when I need you. I think you've earned a few hours off tonight."

"Thanks," Danny said. "I appreciate it."

Silence from the two-way.

He replaced it in the charger and closed his eyes.

This time sleep did not come as easily. He was still wrecked, but his stomach churned with anticipation of the fresh trouble that awaited him — two killings, a mutilated dog, and now a missing person.

But even with all of that on his mind, the image that followed him down when at last sleep did find him, was the blank face of the girl.

Angel.

*   *   *

At last, night fell. It seemed to Grim, who sat reclined on Clara's overstuffed and comfy sofa trying to be interested in a rerun of *The Simpsons*, that the impossible day had finally drawn away, leaving a bruised, but welcomed peace in its wake. Clay had left when Clara came home that afternoon, and hadn't called since. Neither had Michele, but that was fine. Grim had never wanted company less in his life.

There had been no word on Keith yet, or Gina.

The search and rescue had packed up and left under the pale orange glow of twilight. Everett was, presumably, still searching. Grim expected he would be by some time soon to question him again, and more thoroughly than before. In a town like Clearwater the pool of suspects would be small, and Grim knew where he rated as far as Everett Johnson was concerned.

Clara sat in her rocker reading, not the Bible, but one of the dozens of inspirational companion books she owned.

Every now and then she'd *tisk-tisk* and shake her head as something she didn't approve of played itself out on the television, but other than that she was unusually silent.

At least she didn't ask him how his day had been.

Once in a while Grim heard the hum of an approaching car and would peek through a gap in the drawn curtains to watch the passerby. Everett Johnson had gone by three times, moving at a crawl, illuminating the wild beyond the road with a searchlight.

Grim drifted again, and awoke what felt like a short time later to see Clara walking across the living room to turn off the television.

He yawned, stretched, and decided he was finished for the night. Clara stopped him before he made it to the stairs.

"Grim, are you up for a talk?"

"Sure," he said, and walked back to the sofa.

Clara sat beside him, the book clutched to her chest behind her left arm, and placed her right hand on his knee. "I just want you to know that I've never regretted taking you in, not once." She smiled at him, "I know we've had our moments, and I know you've thought about leaving more than once."

Grim opened his mouth to protest that, then closed it again. What was the point, she knew better. Instead, he nodded.

"I love you as much as if you were my flesh and blood, and I like to think you feel the same."

She chuckled, a soft sound, a sleepy sound.

"You're a good boy." Her hand moved to his shoulder, squeezed briefly, then returned to her lap. "I know you're going to leave me some day," she said. "I've accepted it. I'd like nothing more than for you to stay close, but I don't think you will." She looked into his eyes, holding them with her steady gaze. "I hope you will be as good of a man some day."

"Thanks," Grim said, and though it sounded grossly insubstantial, he could think of nothing else to say.

Clara didn't let him go though; she watched him for

several seconds, searching his eyes, his face, for what he did not know.

Then she said, "I'm thinking of taking someone else in. Someone who may need a home as badly as you did."

Again he responded with only a nod. He'd expected this, and though the news, finally articulated, brought some anxiety, he was not disappointed. This was Clara, it was who she was, what she was, and he did love her for it. It would be a big change, but he would not fight it. He knew Clara's need to be needed.

And he knew that he was not the only one who deserved a second chance.

"It's the girl from Jack's, right?"

She nodded, smiled. "Yes. I'm going to try to see her tomorrow. I suppose it'll be clearer when I see her. For all I know she may have a family looking for her somewhere, but if not..."

Grim interrupted, "You're going to be a great mom to her." Then he surprised her, and himself, by leaning toward her and taking her in his arms.

They held each other, the would-be mother and son, for a long time.

*   *   *

Danny never did get the expected call from Everett. He awoke late in the night to the distant, muted sound that may have been a straggling peal of thunder from the storm now moving east. Or a gunshot.

He sat up in bed and drew the curtains back from his small window, checking the heavens for clouds. There were none. The storm had come through and dropped its payload of light and sound and rain, then moved along. Outside the stars were very bright.

He heard the sound again, and knew it for what it was.

Danny turned on his bedside lamp and picked up the two-way.

"Everett, were those gunshots I just heard down there?

Copy?"

But Everett did not copy. The only reply was static.

He pulled on a pair of work pants and a fresh white T-shirt, his boots, strapped his gun-belt on and checked the loads in his revolver, then was out the door.

He was at the bottom of the winding road in less than a minute and turned toward town.

He saw Everett's Jeep in the ditch, its steaming grill tangled with the front bumper of an old blue Dodge. Everett lay halfway out of the driver-side door. His feet rested on the floor of the Jeep's cab, the rest of him lay on the shoulder of the road. Blood soaked through his work shirt and stained the ground around him.

Gavin Fox sat in the dirt beside him, his face cupped in one hand, a gun clutched in the other.

Then Gavin saw Danny and turned on him.

He fired once, wildly, missing Danny's car entirely.

"He's dead! You let it happen. He's gone and I'll never see him again!"

Danny stomped the brakes and slid to a broadside halt only yards away, then dove for cover beneath the dashboard.

Gavin fired again, taking out the window, showering Danny with glass.

"What are you doing?" the crazed man shouted. "You're not even trying."

"Drop your gun, now," Danny yelled, still taking cover, groping for the revolver that now seemed glued into its holster.

Gavin fired again. The bullet ripped vinyl off the sprung seat, and sunk into Danny's flesh. He felt fiery pain travel through his shoulder.

Danny fell to his back on the faded upholstery of his old Jeep, a rig that would have been replaced by now if Sheriff Davis hadn't pissed away the town funds. He tugged at the butt of his revolver again, and it finally came free. He thumbed back the hammer and lifted it.

"Where is she?" Gavin screamed, and then his face

came into view, framed by jagged teeth of glass that still hung in the door.

The gun was pointed at Danny's head, the hand that held it shaking. "You don't even care!"

Danny fired.

Once.

The wild man's face vanished in a jet of blood, then was gone.

Danny lay there, panting. Gavin stayed dead, so he dropped his revolver and gripped the torn flesh of his shoulder.

He thought he heard voices, but it might have been the ringing in his ears — the gun had been incredibly loud, the cab of his Jeep a great tin-can amplifier. The scent of spent powder burned his eyes.

Smelling that tombstone scent, half-deaf from the incredible noise of gunplay, Danny began to fade. He thought he heard Grim's voice just before the worst day of his life finally slammed closed on him.

Part 2
SYNCHRONICITY

Chapter 9

In the two weeks after the craziness that started with Michele clubbing Old Man Wallen to death in Canyon Jack's, and ended with Danny blowing Gavin Fox's head off on the out of town stretch of Main Street, Clearwater seemed to become the center of the universe. A horde of reporters came from back east, people from *Hard Copy* and a host of knockoff news shows, people from the networks, and writers from every newspaper from Seattle to New York.

In a wider world filled with violence of every stripe, this was a small tragedy, but the vultures had fallen in love with it, and soon, too, had the American public.

The reporters called it *Blood Storm*, which was catchy, if somewhat exaggerated.

The locals called the time that followed it The Press Storm, shaking their heads over burgers and beers at Canyon Jack's, which was doing a boom business. Jack, at least, did not mind the army of strangers one bit.

The reporters had found their own form of Heaven in Clearwater. Killer Kirkwood was the flavor of choice, but when there was no more blood to squeeze out of that particular story they were happy enough to pick at the other scraps. Mr. Spritzer was famous for a day, Keith Fox's leg, ripped off at the knee joint, not severed, was a great, grisly tid-bit, but Gina Fox became the greatest source of speculation. Rumors surfaced that Everett Johnson had backtracked a trail of blood from the creek and found Keith's clothes wadded up in the bushes at the edge of the woods. And, in the end, it was Gavin Fox that came out the villain. The popular story was a tangled knot of incest, jealousy, and murder. After lord knows how many years of sexual abuse by their father, Keith and Gina tried to run away, only to be caught and murdered by their abuser, who would later kill one of the town's deputies when he came under suspicion.

That the press had not one bit of evidence to prove this story was inconsequential.

Everett Johnson was barely mentioned at all, and when they were finished with Danny, he came out looking like every city slicker's image of small town incompetence, a modern day Barney Fife.

Everyone knew that The Press Storm was winding down when the news people set their sights on the strangely absent Sheriff Davis, and stories of petty corruption replaced the horror stories.

Through it all, Grim did what he did best; he kept a low profile and faded into the background whenever he saw a TV camera.

Then a sanitation worker in Las Vegas went on a rampage one day, running down pedestrians and smashing cars over several city blocks before the cops finally put him down. Nothing extraordinary at first, just another case of middle age rage, until they found the bodies of his family and in-laws crushed in the back of his truck with the morning's garbage.

What had started as a slow exodus of reporters from Clearwater, Idaho became a full-scale desertion.

Life in Clearwater returned, more or less, to normal.

*   *   *

Then Angel returned.

*   *   *

Pariah—Michele turned the word over in her head, examined it from different perspectives. It sounded fierce, like Piranha. It sounded powerful, like Pharaoh. Dangerous, like Pyromaniac. It was what she was, so she supposed she'd have to get used to it. She wanted to paint it in big red letters across the walls of her room, have it printed on her summer shirts, maybe get it tattooed in big block letters on her forehead. Maybe then her mom would figure it out too, and get them the hell out of Clearwater.

Michele had always suspected that teenagers were horrible people, needing only the right circumstances to bring out their worst potential, but the ugly truth went far beyond her suspicions. Alone they usually ignored her, but in packs they were vicious. She'd never been in a fight in her life before the night she'd killed Old Man Wallen. She'd been in two in the two weeks since.

The first was outside the general store, filling a dinner list for her mom. Amber Ipstien, an older girl who was always in some sort of trouble with her parents and the teachers at school, was with a small group of her friends, loitering in the back alley behind Main Street and smoking cigarettes, when she saw Michele walking home, a plastic bag hanging from the crook of her arm.

"Hey, there goes Killer Kirkwood," she'd called out with a recognizable *here comes trouble* edge in her voice. It was usually the first sign of trouble with her, prompting any adult in earshot to keep an extra close watch on her and scattering the smaller kids like a tornado scatters trailer trash. "Wonder whose head she has in the bag?" This drew laughs from her friends the way shit drew flies.

Michele knew better than to respond, she'd seen what happened when other kids took the bait. But Amber's words—*wonder whose head she has in the bag?*—conjured up an image of Keith's severed leg, red shoe and all, floating in the high water of the creek.

"Shut up, Horse," she called back over her shoulder, proving yet again that any teenager in a bad situation will almost always do, or say, the wrong thing, also proving that she was not above the fault of cruelty.

Not even a big, rough girl like Amber was immune to the razor tongue of adolescence. Words like horse, cow, and pig were the words that cut her deepest.

Amber moved very fast for a big girl. By the time her friends had caught up she already had Michele down, punching her in the face, the chest, the stomach, kneeing her ribs. It had taken Danny Grey, the new interim sheriff, one arm and shoulder still trussed up in a sling, and his volunteer deputy of the day to pull Amber off.

The second fight, happening on her way home from the last softball practice, turned out different. Even with as much savage satisfaction it gave Michele as each fist and foot landed, she had felt horrible when it was finished and the rush was gone.

Some of the girls were still friendly as they had ever been to her face. They saved their venom until they thought she wasn't listening. Paranoia was a terrific sensory enhancer if nothing else. Somehow these quiet attacks were even worse.

She'd quit the softball team.

And still her mom went on like nothing had changed, like killing an old man at the local eatery during dinner and becoming a social outcast—a pariah—was just a normal bump in the road of life.

Rachel had not turned on her; Rachel had no interest in maintaining social status, she had no clique. Rachel was a good friend.

But Rachel had gone.

Gavin's Shop was a husk now, what the creditors had not taken, the local vultures had. Rachel's dad had worked in Gavin's shop, but now that job was gone, and there were none in Clearwater to replace it. A big truck had come early that morning and towed Rachel's singlewide mobile home away.

Rachel was gone, and Michele had to stay.

Now I know what it feels like to be Grim.

This thought shocked her into a smile. Bitter as it was, it felt good on her lips.

Yeah, Grim knew *alone*. Michele had watched him from a distance made up more of age than space, since he'd come to town. Less than two years between them, but when you're young two years is a big chunk of time. She'd watched him the way one watches a favorite character on television — distant but close.

She knew him. Grim had a little group of friends, but he was alone just the same. Only with him it seemed, alone was the choice.

Suddenly, like an itch that must be scratched, Michele needed to see Grim. She had avoided him since the uncomfortable thank you that day when all hell broke loose in Clearwater.

She'd been holed up in her little house for so long that the walk to his house seemed a formidable journey, but she made up here mind to make it.

"I'm off," her mom said, hurrying down the hallway, slipping her cell phone into the side pocket of her purse and pushing a pair of sporty sunglasses up her nose as she passed Michele's room. "No trouble today, okay?"

"Sure," she said, and waited.

The front door banged shut, and a minute later Michele heard her mom's car pull away, headed for her office in Lewiston.

Michele got out of bed, ran a brush through her hair, slipped on a pair of worn sandals, and walked out into a too-bright day to find Grim.

*   *   *

Kelly was talking about getting another war game on, but that subject seemed to border on sacrilege with Clay. At this point in the day Grim no longer cared. It was too god damn hot to care, let them hash it out by themselves and he'd go along with whatever they decided.

Grim didn't think it would happen. They were three

now, and he seriously doubted that Alex, Raif, Bo, or Clint would bow out to even up the teams, even if they were the only ones who would game with them. Better for them to not play and remain the champions.

Grim would rather ride his bike or take a swim. The river looked inviting, cool. Low, slow, and comfortable. Plenty of beach to lounge out on afterward.

Instead of doing either, Grim sat on a boulder at the edge of the sand and watched the highway. Clara would be back from Orofino soon.

Clay had brought his radio today. Kelly had set up a line of tin cans along the rocks on the other side of the beach and plugged away at them with his pellet gun, missing more than he hit. The sounds of nihilistic heavy metal blended with a shout of surprise and laughter as Kelly turned and put a pellet into the Budweiser tallboy sitting in the sand next to Clay. The can ruptured with a spray of foam and beer, drenching Clay.

"You dirty son-of-a-bitch," Clay shouted, sitting up and surveying his soaked shirt. "That's alcohol abuse!"

Kelly had dropped his pellet gun and was doubled over, hands braced against his knees, shaking with laughter.

Clay, several inches taller and fifty pounds of muscle heavier, charged Kelly and pushed him to the sand. Kelly held up a warding hand but was still laughing too hard to defend himself. Clay looked down at him, smiled, winked at Grim, then grabbed Kelly by the front of his shirt and the waistband of his shorts and lifted him from the sand.

"Oh, fuck," Kelly shouted as Clay bore him toward the water.

Clay charged into the water, not stopping until the cold water hit his crotch, then, laughing himself now, heaved Kelly into the river.

Kelly resurfaced a second later, arms thrashing, churning water in twin whitecaps, eyes wide in shock. "Think you're getting away with that?" He took a few slow steps through the water at Clay, then dove below the surface, clutching at Clay's feet.

Morons, Grim thought, watching them wrestle in the water, a little jealous that he was missing the fun.

"Hey, Joe Cool," Clay said, pushing Kelly under the water with both hands and holding him there. "You can sit in a corner and brood in your house." He released Kelly's head with a yelp as a hand reached from the water, grabbing a nipple through his shirt and giving a twist.

Kelly surfaced again and put some distance between him and the scowling Clay. "You gonna come and help me with this big stupid fucker or what?"

Grim shook his head. "Nope." He watched the highway again and thought he saw Clara's car in the far distance, approaching. "I have to be home when Clara gets back."

Kelly made a disgusted sound and waved him off.

"See you around then, mama's boy," Clay said with a mock salute, then turned his attention back to Kelly.

Grim gave them the finger as he walked to his bike, parked at the edge of a worn dirt path that led to the tunnel under the highway. The tunnel was the mouth of Canyon Creek, thirty feet of graffiti-covered concrete (graffiti in small town Idaho was something Grim would never understand — who the hell was out here to appreciate it?) tall enough to stand upright in and wide enough for the three of them to walk side by side. There were no more than a few inches of slow-moving water in it now. The mountain had spent all the water it had. Canyon Creek was almost completely dried up now.

And still no sign of Keith. He was probably half way to the ocean by now.

Grim couldn't help admiring the Yamaha as he approached it, all put back together now, running better than it ever had for its last owner, thanks to Danny. Finishing the Yamaha had been their project during Danny's few days of off time. His wounded shoulder and arm was bandaged and held immobile in a sling, so he'd supervised Grim. There were times when neither thought

Grim could do it, Danny was in an almost constant state of frustration with Grim's apparent mechanical ineptitude.

But they'd finished it, and Danny had been almost as proud as Grim was happy to see it running again.

Grim mounted the bike and stomped on the starter-bar. It was a little stiff still. The Yamaha responded with a throaty grumble, and Grim tore down the trail.

He felt but did not hear the vibration of cars passing overhead as he shot through the tunnel like a bullet through the tube of a gun. As always, he felt a twist of fear as he shot from the other side, splashing up water before reaching the steep bank. He caught a few seconds of air at the lip of the bank and cried out in excitement as he touched down again, throwing a rooster-tail of dust as he raced for home.

*   *   *

Grim was not home, so Michele stood on his walkway for a few moments trying to decide where to look first. She never saw him in town unless he was on his way somewhere else, or happened to be hanging around Clay. She knew they liked to hang out at the salvage yard. There was also Canyon Jack's, it was air-conditioned, and had a game room — a pinball machine, and a few modern video games the kids had finally talked Jack into purchasing. Beyond Jack's, just on the other side of the highway, was the beach.

All three were in the same direction, out of town, so Michele started walking again.

She'd been sweating by the time she'd reached his house, and by the time she was half way to the highway she was wiping it from her face with the back of her arm to keep it out of her eyes.

It seemed full-blown summer had arrived while she was hiding in her room. She guessed it was nearing one hundred degrees by now, and the cloudless sky above offered no hope of relief.

What are you doing out here, she wondered. *Why the sud-*

den fascination with Grim?

She knew that was not quite true though. Grim had always interested her, and scared her a little. He was like a wolf living with a pack of mutts. He was different than the other boys in Clearwater.

It hit her like an electric shock, stopping her in mid-stride along the dust and gravel at the side of the road. The reason she'd avoided him the last few weeks, and the sudden need to see him now. If she hadn't been so screwed up the night that he'd held her in Canyon Jack's, while her mother gave Danny her statement, she probably would have figured it out then.

She thought maybe her mother had—*not as clueless as she seemed*—and that that was the reason she'd made such a point of telling Michele to stay away from him.

Michele groaned and cupped her face in her hands.

It was the big one she'd read about in so many stupid young adult books, or seen acted out in countless movies: her first big crush. And wasn't it just her luck, it was on a boy who would probably never see her as anything more than just another strange little girl. One who happened to have a killer swing.

Go home now, she thought. *Watch lots of Leonardo Decaprio movies and avoid Grim for a few more weeks, and maybe it'll go away.*

Good idea. Great idea. She didn't move though, she was split; half of her wanted to stay away from him until this stupid crush burned out, but the other half wanted to see him, and wanted to make him want to see *her*. She was pretty enough to get a boy's attention.

Not a bad bod, she thought. She filled out her shirt better than most of the girls her age. Her breasts weren't huge, but they were there, the boys in her grade had certainly noticed them.

She pushed out her chest and looked down the small slope of her breasts, then immediately looked away, feeling like the biggest fool in the world.

That was when she noticed the figure standing in the

thick underbrush marking the edge of the woods. Whoever it was, was shaded by the boughs of the taller trees, their features a blur in the green that didn't quite hide them. Then, with a rustle of brush, the watching figure was gone.

"Hey," Michele yelled, now thoroughly embarrassed that she'd been caught checking herself out. "What the hell are you doing?"

There was no reply. Whoever it was, was gone now.

Great, she thought. *Wonderful. Just in case everyone didn't think I was weird enough.*

She'd made up her mind to turn back for home when the low rumble came from around the next bend in the road. Then *He* appeared. Grim, coming toward her on his motorcycle. She felt a flutter behind her ribs and fought the urge to run into the bushes and hide until he passed her. She wouldn't have made it. A few seconds later he was coasting to a stop beside her.

God, he drives fast!

She stared at him, could not seem to turn away, or even blink. She wanted to say something smart, but her brain was on hiatus.

"Hey," he said. "Where are you going?"

"Uh, nowhere." *Oh yeah, that sounded smart.*

Grim smiled. "Haven't seen you around," he said, dismounting the bike. "I thought your mom had you locked up or something."

"Oh, no," she said, then giggled, a nervous, little girl giggle. "Haven't been feeling good." *Great, now he'll think I'm contagious. Guess he won't want to kiss me now.*

"You feeling alright now?" he asked. "You're flushed."

She was blushing again.

Just fine, she thought. *I think I'll go crawl under a rock now.*

She waved a hand in front of her face. "It's just hot is all."

Grim nodded. If he sensed her embarrassment he did not let on. "Climb on," he said, mounting his bike again. "The wind'll cool you off."

"Sure," she climbed on behind him, careful not to brush against him.

"Arms around my waist," he said. "Hang on tight."

She did.

The ride to his house was quick, thrilling. Her heart was hammering when he pulled up next to his porch. She wondered if he could feel it.

"Come on in," he said, mounting the steps to the front door. "Want something to drink?"

"As long as it's not coffee," she said, and smiled when he laughed.

"Lemonade?"

"Yeah, I like lemonade."

She followed him inside.

"I have to make a quick call," he said, and pointed her toward the kitchen.

She walked into the kitchen and sat down at the table.

The call was quick. He joined her in the kitchen a minute later and fished around the cupboard for two glasses. There was a full pitcher in the refrigerator, and when he finished filling their glasses he set it on the table.

"Glad I saw you," he said, handing her a glass that was already slick with beaded moisture.

"Really," she said, then took a sip before she could say anything stupid. The lemonade was sweet, tart, good.

Grim smiled, but it looked forced to Michele. She was about to ask what was wrong when he spoke again.

"Clara's on her way with an old friend of ours."

Rachel? She thought. Couldn't be. She'd only just left. She'd be unpacking today, Michele supposed.

"Who is it?"

Grim told her.

Chapter 10

"She's asking for trouble," Steven Gentry said. "Bringing *that girl* back here." Steven was a logger by trade but unemployed for the summer. He was the kind of man who refused to adapt to the season, an old dog whose tricks had been learned over a lifetime, tattooed into his very soul. He'd rather spend half the year unemployed than look for seasonal work. Danny was convinced the only reason he volunteered to cover the Thursday and Friday day shifts was because he liked the imagined power of being Deputy Steven Gentry. No matter that it didn't pay, or that Danny hadn't issued him a uniform or gun.

Steven had brought his own gun, and Danny wouldn't be surprised if he showed up wearing a Cracker-Jack box badge one morning.

It's temporary, Danny reminded himself, trying not to loose his cool with the man. Soon as the voters make me official, I'll be able to hire a few real deputies. Steven was only here because Danny was hard up at the moment.

Don't get too comfortable, you'll be back at home with your porn and your beer before you know it.

"What the hell is that supposed to mean," Danny asked, hoping he sounded honestly confused rather than pissed.

"Your foster ma," Steven explained, rolling his blood-shot eyes. "I heard she adopted that retard girl who caused the trouble at Jack's place."

"Three points," Danny said, turning to stare at the man who sat with his feet up on Everett's old desk, pushing his chair beyond the limits of its design under the weight of his

reclining bulk. Danny and Everett had had their differ-
ences, but Danny missed him more than ever on his Steven
shifts. Everett had been a damn good deputy, would have
made a good sheriff too.

Steven grinned, raised his eyebrows. "Yes?"

"Point one," Danny said, lifting the index finger of his
right hand. "She is not retarded. She was kidnapped and
drugged."

Steven's expression did not change. He might not have
been listening at all.

"Point two: she didn't cause the trouble at Jack's place.
Wallen did. He was pissed off at the world and drunk that
night, and he lost what little mind he had left."

Danny paused in his argument for a moment, decided
then was as good of a time as any to pick his own personal
bone with Steven. "And speaking of drunk, the next time
you come to work with beer on your breath I'll impound
your car and give you a DWI."

This got Steven's attention. He jerked in his chair,
almost overbalancing, then dropped his booted feet to the
floor and leaned forward, glaring.

"Jesus Christ," Steven said. "And I thought Everett was
the hard-ass."

"Third," Danny interrupted. "Clara did not adopt her,
just took her in."

"But what the hell do we know about her," Steven said,
a little heatedly. "I don't know a god damned thing about
her. You want to change my mind, enlighten me, let me in
on what you know."

Danny shook his head. "It's not my job to change your
mind about her, Steven. You don't need to know any more
about her." Then, almost an afterthought, "she's a person,
not a soap-opera character."

"What I do know don't paint a very good picture,"
Steven countered. He held up an index finger in imitation
of Danny's earlier argument. "One, she was on drugs,
probably someone's sex toy." He held up a raised finger,
"Two, I've known Wallen since before you were a twinkle

in your daddy's balls, and I don't buy the stories. She did something to provoke him, you can count on it." A third finger pointed toward the ceiling. "Third, no one wants her. Her family hasn't come for her." He stretched out his arms and shrugged his beefy shoulders. "I don't see them here, Danny-boy." He looked around the office as if searching for an expected visitor. "Nope, no one here to claim her."

Slowly, Steven's hand closed into a fist, then the index finger appeared again, poking at the air between them. "No one wants her. You tell me why."

Danny rose to his feet, was about to reply when the phone rang.

Steven reached for the phone, but Danny rushed the desk and grabbed it before he could touch it.

"Sit tight for a second," he said to Steven, then lifted the handset to his ear. "Clearwater Sheriff's Department." He stood, silent for a second, then said, "Thanks, Grim. I'll be right over." He hung the phone up and turned back to Steven, who waited with a smug look on his bearded face.

"You're wrong, someone does want her."

Steven's smile faded.

"Her name is Clara Grey, and I'll tell you now that if you have anything smart to say about Clara you can tell me outside."

Steven's smile had vanished, his bravado faded away.

"Clara may not be my mother by blood, but she is my mother, which makes *that girl* my sister." He took a step toward Steven, and was pleased to see the man lean back into his chair, an unconscious attempt to put more space between them. "I don't ever want to hear you talk about my sister like that again."

There was a moment of silence in the office, and Danny knew the argument was over. He clapped Steven on the shoulder, again pleased when the other man flinched at the harmless gesture.

"I've got to run for a bit," Danny said. "Got some personal business."

Steven nodded. "I'll hold down the fort for you." All the bluster was gone from his voice now. His tone was light, respectful, likely an enormous effort on Steven's part.

"I know you will," Danny said, hoping to give the man a scrap of praise to heal his wounded ego. He didn't want any bad blood between them while they still had to work together. "I know you can handle it." He stepped around the front desk, toward the door. "Shouldn't be more than an hour or two. I'll stop by Jack's on the way back and bring you some lunch."

"Sounds good. Thanks."

Danny nodded and pushed the front door open, stepping from the cool office into the wilting heat of midday. He'd fought to keep a straight face with Steven, but once outside broke into a huge smile. His words with Steven had just come back to him, not the argument, but two words in particular.

My sister.

I'll be damned, Danny thought as he walked around to the driver's door of his Jeep. *I have a sister.*

He felt a sudden warmth, and was overcome by an urge to protect the strange girl that had become his sister.

He still did not know much about her, but what he did know was sad and troubling. She'd had a real brother once. He had died two weeks ago, pulled from that pileup outside Orofino as a pulped pile of flesh from the wreckage of that yellow Oldsmobile, along with his runaway girlfriend.

Dick, from the Orofino Police, had searched the luggage and found clothes too small for the dead girl they pulled out of the car. Clothes that would have fit Clara's Angel. Among the other belongings: a family photo of a mother and father from the Baby Boomer generation, a teenage boy (the dead boy from the car), and the girl. Angel.

Under the spare tire, in the trunk, a stash of Rohypnol and Ketamine.

The boy who had kept her drugged, then abandoned her here was not some sex pervert, thank God for that at least, but her real brother.

* * *

"What do you know about her?" Michele asked, then took another sip of her lemonade.

Grim shrugged. "Not a lot." Danny had told Clara and Grim everything he'd learned about Angel, which in truth was not much, but only because they would share a home with her. It was not Grim's right to share what he knew with anyone else, not even his friends, who he would not have trusted the sensitive information with anyway. Not even with Michele, who had saved Angel's life.

Michele waited for an elaboration, and when, after nearly a minute, none came, she said "you're not going to tell me, are you?"

"No," Grim said. "Sorry, it just wouldn't be cool."

He didn't know Michele well enough to know what to expect from her. She'd always been nice, quiet. Not a wallflower, but not some kind of extroverted manic freak who always was in the spotlight, causing problems. The last few weeks though, no one knew what to expect from her. Two fights in as many weeks. No one would have ever believed it before. Now, people were likely to believe anything anyone said about her.

She was different now, still the same Michele, but changing. Grim was afraid she would turn into the delinquent most of Clearwater thought she was. He hadn't seen either of her fights, but he'd heard about the second from Kelly, who had seen it.

He said she'd gone nuts, if Sara Mitchell from the general store hadn't broken it up, she would have kept punching and kicking until there had been nothing left of the other girl.

Grim half-expected her to lash out at him now, for refusing her, but she didn't.

"That's cool," she said with a nod of her head. "She probably wouldn't like people gossiping about her."

"How're you doing?" he ventured. He spun his empty

glass on the table between his thumb and forefinger, watched it smear the ring of moisture it had left on the tabletop.

"I hate this place," she said. Her voice was calm, even, but when he looked up he saw the truth of her words in her eyes.

He wanted to tell her not to let it bother her, to let it slide, but sensed it would be the worst thing he could say. She didn't want a *suck it up* pep talk. She wanted understanding.

And he did understand.

He reached across the table and took her hand. Sometimes where words failed, a simple touch meant everything.

He felt an almost electrical jolt, a quickening of his pulse, when her grip tightened on his hand.

Her hand was small, soft, strong.

The sound of crunching gravel outside startled him, as if waking him from a trance, and he released her hand.

She picked up her half-empty lemonade glass, but she didn't drink, just held it.

"Is that her?"

"Dunno," he said, and walked to the kitchen window, pulling the curtain aside.

It was Danny. He saw Grim through the window and nodded, then turned toward the road again and waved. A second later, Clara pulled in next to him.

Grim saw her clearly; her saint's smile lighting her face as she spoke to Danny through her open window. Next to her, the silhouette of a girl.

Angel was home.

*   *   *

They waited in the foyer at the base of the stairs, watching the doorway. Waiting for it to open. Michele heard voices outside on the porch, Clara and Danny. If Angel spoke, she did not hear.

At last the door opened, a wave of fresh heat from outside rushed in on her. Angel followed it in, stepping over the threshold with help from Danny on one arm and Clara on the other.

Angel moved slowly, head hung from either shyness or exhaustion. A fall of dark hair covered her face. Once inside she tugged her arms from Danny and Clara's grips, then took a few wobbly steps on her own. Clara stayed close at her side, ready to catch her if she fell. Danny stood just inside and shut the door behind them.

About halfway from the door to the staircase, Angel stopped, looked up, and brushed the hair from her eyes with a shaking hand.

She stared at Michele and Grim in turn. Her lips made a little twitch that looked like it wanted to be a smile. She closed her eyes and wiped a sheen of sweat from her face with the back of an arm.

She moves like Ozzy Osbourne on a bad day, Michele thought.

"Is it always this hot here?" Her voice was high, small. It broke into a wheeze on *here*. She spoke as if thinking aloud, at no one in particular, but Grim answered.

"Not always," he said.

Angel turned toward Clara, grabbed at her arm but missed.

Clara bent down next to her, her face close to Angel's. Any concern she may have had was well hidden behind a cheery facade.

"Yes, dear," Clara said, taking Angel's hand in both of hers.

"Kinda thirsty."

Grim heard, and without having to be asked disappeared through the kitchen door. Moments later he was back with another cup of lemonade. A plastic cup, Michele noted. Just in case she dropped it. He stopped a few feet away from Angel, as if afraid to go any closer, and held the cup to her.

Seconds passed before Angel's hands found the cup.

Clara helped her guide it to her mouth. She grimaced at the tartness of the drink, but took another greedy swallow.

Danny watched the exchange from behind, his hand still on the doorknob. His grip on it was tight, Michele saw. His knuckles bone white. His face was pale too, despite the heat. He looked like he might be sick.

Then he noticed Michele noticing him and motioned her to him with a nod of his head.

She went grudgingly. She had an idea she was about to be asked to leave. Instead he bent down and gave her a brief hug, followed by a pat on the back.

"You're a quick healer," he whispered, examining her face. "I can barely see the bruises."

Michele's hand rose to the left side of her face, the side that had taken the worst of Amber's beating. "Still hurts a little."

Danny nodded. "Not surprised. She's got a killer right hook." He shook his head, smiled and said, "I've seen her work before."

Behind them Clara introduced Angel to Grim.

Grim grunted a gruff little "hey."

Michele guessed this was beyond weird for Grim — having to share his home with a new girl. This girl, who was, if it were possible, even more the outsider than Grim.

"Hey," Angel returned, and followed with a yawn.

"How long have you been hanging out with that troublemaker?" Danny nodded toward Grim.

Michele felt a moment of shocked anger at the insult to Grim, then saw Danny was once again smiling.

She blushed and smiled back. "Just today," she said, and felt her gaze drawn back to Grim and saw that he was watching her. So were Clara and Angel.

"Do I know you?" Angel asked.

"Yeah," Michele said. "You know me."

She turned, took a clumsy step toward Michele, and tripped. If Clara and Grim hadn't stepped forward in tandem to catch her, she would have hit the floor.

Probably curled up and went to sleep where she landed.

She looked so damn tired.

"*How* do I know you?"

Standing to Angel's left side, holding her arm to steady her, Clara shook her head and mouthed the words *no, sweetheart.*

"I...uh," she faltered, "we've met before," she said. She couldn't hold Angel's eyes, tired, but very focused. Focused on her. "I don't remember where," she said, looking at her feet. She never was a good liar.

When Michele looked up again, Angel's eyes were still on her, catching her own eyes and looking onto them. "I'll remember," she said, and at last dropped her gaze.

I'll remember.

Michele felt spider legs on her spine and shivered.

"I'm so tired," Angel said, and the pure, low helplessness in her voice, almost a sob, made Michele want to cry. She was swaying on her feet now, would surely have fallen over if Clara and Grim hadn't been there with steadying hands.

"Grim, dear, could you take her to her room?" Clara's cheery facade was cracking. Behind it was not fear or frustration, but a great sadness for the girl that hinted at things Michele could only guess.

All at once Michele did not want to know what had happened to make Angel the way she was. She had an idea that that knowledge would smother the little bit of innocence she had left.

Grim nodded and led Angel away.

Their ascent up the staircase was slow, each step an obstacle, the landing half way up a brief rest on a long upward journey. Finally, Grim and Angel found the second floor, and vanished down the hall.

Clara turned back to Michele and Danny, the smiling mask gone, her grief fully exposed. She looked old, as if the sadness of life had sucked away years from her plump face.

"I'm glad you came," Clara said to Michele. "I know your mother wouldn't approve but I'm glad just the same."

"I didn't know she was coming," Michele admitted. "I

came to see Grim."

Clara gave her a shrewd look, then smiled. The smile looked forced, almost painful.

"There's a lot of goodness in him," Clara said. "Most folks just won't see it. How are you holding up, dear? I know you've had a rough time."

"Okay, I guess."

"You don't look okay. You look like you haven't seen a friendly face in too long."

"They'll get over it," Michele said.

"Yes," Clara nodded. "Eventually. Clay will get some poor girl pregnant or the Pastor's daughter will turn out to be gay and they'll forget all about you."

Behind them, Danny let out a surprised snort of laughter.

"Hush," Clara said, giving Danny a stern look that appeared about as authentic as a three-dollar bill.

"Whenever you need a friendly face you come on over," she said to Michele. "You're always welcome here."

"Thanks," Michele said, and she knew that she would.

"The doctors up at that *prison* say Angel will start to get better soon. She's going to need a friend in this town because I don't think this town is going to be much of a friend to her."

Again, Michele said, "They'll get over it."

But she understood what Clara was getting at.

She understood too well.

Clara shrugged. "Maybe," she said.

*   *   *

Grim hoped Michele would still be here when he went back downstairs. Just a few weeks ago he'd thought of her as *that sweet girl*, and had never thought much about her before then, but now there was the spark. When he'd touched her hand on the table. He'd never felt the spark before, not with any of the girls or women he'd known in Seattle.

It scared him a little, but he liked it.

She's only fifteen, he thought to himself.

Almost sixteen, said the part of him that responded to the spark. *And you're only seventeen, so stop trying to be such a fucking hotshot.*

Angel didn't weigh much, she'd grown very thin while in whatever padded cell they'd condemned her to, but she had little strength left for walking, so she was dead weight. The best she could accomplish was a kind of a one foot at a time scoot.

She'd been silent going up the stairs and most of the way to her room, but as he stopped before the closed door of a long vacant room, one of several on the second floor of the old hotel, she leaned toward him, her lips almost brushing his ear.

"Thanks," she whispered.

"No problem," he said. He nudged the unlatched door open with a foot, it creaked a little on its inward swing, and said, "welcome to your room."

Clara had spent two weeks to fuss over the once drab wood cubicle, and had transformed it into a *Better Home & Garden* fantasy of girldom. The plank walls were freshly stained and hung with tapestries of kittens and flowers and all things cute. The window was framed by lacy pink drapes. A long pastel runner covered much of the floor from the doorway, past a restored vanity—Grim had a hunch it had once been Clara's—to the side of a four-poster bed, hung to match the window.

The four-poster was original to the old hotel, he'd carried it up a piece at a time for her and helped put it together again, but the sheets and thick down comforter were new.

If I was a girl, I'd be jealous.

Grim tried to help her over the threshold of her new room, but she wouldn't move. She only stood there, gaping.

"You like?"

She nodded her head, a weak, jerky movement of the neck. "Yeah, I do."

"Let's get you over to that bed. Let you catch a rest."

Angel nodded again and let him lead her inside.

Once inside she seemed to gain strength, or maybe just momentum. He supposed that bed looked pretty inviting. He swept one of the gauzy curtains aside with one hand and helped her down. She let him pull her sandals off, then tipped over and settled in.

She was asleep before the curtain fell back into place.

Grim set her sandals next to the vanity, and turned to look at her one last time before closing her door.

However bad things had been for her before, they would get better now.

She was with Clara, and Clara was an angel, too.

Smiling, he closed the door.

Chapter 11

It recognized the girl, and so had followed her, trying to remember where from. It could not make the memory come though, only an implacable fear, like an itch on the back it couldn't quite reach. It remembered blood—blood on the stick—but that was all. The girl made it uneasy, so it stayed away, and when she had seen it crouched in the trees, watching her, it ran.

It waited for dark to come out again. In the dark no one would see it unless it wanted them to. It was comfortable in the dark.

It moved through the brush, edging the dry creek with the wild grace of a cat, its eyes always toward the houses on the other side. Where the people lived. It remembered the other side of the creek, like another life, the other side of a strange veil. It didn't want to go back there, but would have to. It was where the food lived.

"Hungry," it said, and twitched at the sound of its own voice, a forgotten thing.

It tested the ground near the edge of the dry creek-bed, not trusting it, then leapt across to the narrow slash of mud and weed, falling to a crouch on the other side. It was in the open now, but a quick search of the horizon confirmed that it was still alone. It sniffed the air but found nothing but its own unwashed stink, the smell of sweat and dried blood.

It crossed a field of crabgrass of thistles, and found a narrow lane between familiar buildings.

Sheriff's Office — Store.

Street-lamps lit blacktop and gravel, houses set in neat rows, and it remembered. It knew where it wanted to go. It knew who it wanted.

*   *   *

Kelly heard tapping on his window and heard his name whispered, like a sigh in the darkness. He lay in bed, not moving, but opened his eyes.

A dream, he thought, but looked anyway.

Saw nothing, closed his eyes again, slipped back into dreams of cars and cunts. Bodies without faces surrounded him; wet skin and tits and open legs, crammed into the front and back seats of his uncle Butch's convertible Mustang — god he loved that car — and spread across the moon-lit hood like offerings on an altar.

All for him.

And then the whisper came again, a voice he knew but didn't believe until he opened his eyes and saw her framed by his dust-caked window, hair in a wild tangle but still hot. Naked, sweat-covered skin glowing in the pale light of a moon that existed outside his dream, in reality.

And though he saw her there, he still didn't believe it until she said his name again and beckoned him, then disappeared into the dark.

Now fully awake, Kelly jumped out of bed and dressed in the clothes he'd worn that day. He moved quietly into the hall beyond his room and took the back door out of his house.

There she was, streaking through his back yard to the street, watching him over her shoulder.

"God damn," he said. Disbelief, shock, lust.

Kelly followed her through Clearwater's quietest hour, through the dim gravel streets to the single-paved road that was Main Street, and into the dark storefronts.

He was too focused ahead to notice Clint, his brother, watching from the open front door, scratching his ass, then following.

When he found her in the shadows on the other side, he was a willing victim.

*　*　*

It was past midnight, and Grim was tired. Life with Clara had softened him, he knew. There was a time not so long ago when the witching hour was when life began, but not now, not here.

He lay on his side, facing the red glow of his digital clock, and sighed as another minute turned over.

He was tired, but sleep wouldn't come tonight.

Grim turned on his other side and faced the wall, turned from the nagging clock toward the dark, and after what seemed hours felt consciousness smooth out into something else, something that might have been a prelude to true sleep. It didn't last long. The sound of creaking door hinges brought him back to a twitching wakefulness.

A warm breeze teased the hair against his neck, on the way to the world outside his open window.

The window would be open in Clara's room. And Angel's too, if Clara had thought about it. Was it the breeze that pushed his door open? Grim turned again, and though his night vision was poor, he could see a little beyond his door. And what he saw gave him a start.

"Clara?" He whispered, afraid the sound of his voice would frighten the watcher in the hallway.

There was no answer. The watcher stood, a thin silhouette, too thin to be Clara's.

"Angel? Is that you?"

"Something's out there," her voice, the shadow voice, said. "And I think it's my fault." A moment later the watcher was gone.

Grim lay there, trying to decide if the watcher had been there at all, or if it was an invention of his exhausted brain. He had decided to get out of bed and walk to Angel's room to see if she was awake, just to be sure, but true sleep finally caught him, spiriting him away to another dark place, one he'd not thought about in a long time.

* * *

It had been years since Clara dreamed of the bees, but when they came the terror of recognition was instant. First the low drone, an insectile wind, rousing her from a pleasant laziness of iced tea at a long gone picnic table in what had once been a well-kept back yard, what she now called the jungle. They seemed to come from the very air around her, dropping from the clouds, springing from blades of grass.

The walnut tree that provided shade for her began to shiver, leaves humming an unnatural tune, and ripening walnuts fell. The shells split open as they struck the worn wood of the table and earth alike, and more bees emerged from the cracked ruins, filling the world with their hungry drone.

Then, as always, they swarmed her.

She screamed, pain and revulsion, as they covered her waving arms, her face, and tangled themselves in her hair. They planted stingers in her, injecting their liquid pain and falling away to die.

"Mommy?"

Angel. Angel was coming.

"Angel, no!" Her voice was muffled abruptly as more bees darted between her open lips and went to work on her tongue. It began to swell almost instantly, pinching off her breath.

"Mommy, where are you?"

And there she was, approaching through a tangle of weeds and knee-high grass. The well-manicured lawn was gone—it was the jungle again, and her Angel was coming through it, toward the danger. Toward the angry, swarming bees.

Clara stood and ran toward her, scooping bees off with pierced, swelling hands. The yellow/black demons fell like rainwater from her hair. Her face, her head, was swelling, the scalp near to splitting. She tried to shout a warning to Angel, but it wouldn't pass her tongue.

Then she saw them, and she stopped, forgetting the poison horde still working at her.

Angel stopped too, staring at the ground, head hung in a posture of shame. "I'm sorry, Mom," she said. "I didn't mean to do it." She was oblivious to the cloud falling from the sky behind her. A cloud that wasn't a cloud. A cloud that sang its approach like a chord strum on Satan's harp. A buzzing, yellow/black cloud.

It was going for Angel, right for her.

Angel raised her head. She was weeping. "I didn't mean to," she said.

And then the buzzing, yellow/black cloud covered her.

Clara awoke with a lurch, her fleshy hands gripping the bed sheets. She could still feel the heat of a hundred stingers, could still taste the pain of her swollen tongue. She felt the scream building in her constricted throat, but it wouldn't pass. Then, as her surroundings came into focus, the dream sensations faded. The phantom buzzing faded, and the cheery chirp of her bedside phone took its place.

She realized it was the ringing of the phone that woke her, and she blessed the fool who would call her at such an ungodly hour.

She picked up the phone.

"Yes," she said, then yawned.

"Where's Grim?" No apologies for waking her, no explanations, just the strange, urgent question.

"Danny? Is that you?"

A sigh, an impatient sound. "Yes, it's me. Listen, Mom, I need you to locate Grim. It's important!"

"Jumpin' Jehosaphat," she said, indignant. "He's in his own bed, sleeping. Where else would he be?"

"I need you to check, Mom. Just go check."

"Oh, good heavens," she said, and slammed the receiver down on her nightstand next to the phone's cradle.

She rose slow, knees protesting the indignity of being

worked at such a foul hour, and went to check Grim.

Clara passed Angel's door on the way. She had closed it before turning in, but now it stood open, a slight breeze wafting through her open window. The open door didn't concern her—flashes of her dream (bees in the trees) surfaced in her barely conscious mind, and suddenly she had to check on Angel.

The girl was asleep, soundly asleep, the rise and fall of her thin chest barely perceptible. She looked healthier though, her color was better and her posture was one of comfort, not collapse. It looked like a natural sleep, not the drug-induced near-coma Clara had witnessed at the hospital.

Angel had kicked her sheets off during the night, and Clara bent to pull them back over her.

Angel was fine. She was getting better.

Memories of the dream blended with memories of a hot summer day in her childhood, the day she'd tried to help her mother, grooming the back yard while her mother cut the grass. Her reward waited in the icebox inside: cool, tart lemonade, her favorite thing on a hot day. Clara had gone to work sweeping dust and cobwebs from the eaves of the back porch, and not knowing the danger, had tried to beat down a bee's nest.

Clara remembered Danny, waiting on the other end of the line, and went to check on Grim. She felt bad for her shortness with him now. He wouldn't have called if it wasn't important.

"You're only human, dear," she said to herself as she walked the dark hall toward Grim's room. "Danny understands."

Grim lay sprawled in a tangle of sheets, snoring lightly. His hand shot up at her—Clara nearly jumped out of her skin—and waved away something from a dream.

Seems she wasn't the only one suffering bad dreams tonight.

Must be the weather, she thought as she returned to her room and the promising comfort of her bed.

"Grim is sleeping," she said.

Danny let out a long breath, a release of building tension. "Thank you," he said at last.

"What in creation is going on?" Clara had done what he had asked. Now he could explain himself.

"Ms. Baker heard a scream," he said. "I didn't think it would come to anything, but she insisted I come." He paused. Clara was about to ask him if he'd fallen asleep when he finally continued. "I found two bodies behind the general store. A couple of teenage boys," he said. "I can't tell who they are." He didn't elaborate on his inability to identify the bodies, for which Clara was thankful. She was sure she didn't want to know.

"Dear God," Clara said, and gave silent thanks that Grim and Angel were asleep, safe in their rooms.

"I'm sorry, Mom. I just had to be sure that..."

"One of them wasn't your brother," Clara finished.

"Yeah."

"I suppose you'll be up for the rest of the night?"

"Uh-huh," Danny said. "State guys are on their way to assist. This is just too much for me," he said, as if an explanation was in order.

"I know, Danny. What time is it?"

"Just past two A.M. I gotta go now," he said. "The state guys will be here soon."

"I'll bring coffee, dear."

"No, Mom!" Then, a little gentler, "I don't want you to see this."

"I don't want to see it either. I'll call you from the sidewalk when I get there." Then she hung up before he could protest again.

Before she rose, she bowed her head, as if in prayer.

"Please, God, don't do this to us again."

Chapter 12

It had been a long time since Grim had dreamt about Green City—that wild hell on the edge of the Seattle Beltway—and the one they called the Rag Man.

*   *   *

It was raining, seemed to Grim it always rained there, the day the Rag Man took him.

People on the street said Green City was the place to go when you wanted to disappear, and they were right. Grim was nine when he went there to hide from the people who would take him back to the group home, and he disappeared.

He was ten when the cops came to clean it out. They caught who they could, chased away who they couldn't catch, then brought bulldozers in to level it. The Rag Man wouldn't be driven out though, and when the cops and their machines came to his den, he killed them as they came.

He killed them until Grim killed him.

But the Rag Man did not die easy.

*   *   *

Wet leaves on his face, yellow and rotting. The stench of Green City, like a dead dog, in his nose, and the damned rain. The rain never stopped falling here, it seemed.

"*Boy!*" The Rag Man searched for him as the surviving cops tracked him through trees and mountains of refuse. "*I'm gonna fix you, boy.*"

He stopped, the meanest man in Green City, only feet from Grim's hiding spot and screamed, a savage whoop of rage. Blood ran from the place in his back where Grim had put his knife, mixing with the rain.

Grim could hear others coming. He hoped they would hurry up.

Then the Rag Man looked down and saw Grim, and his chapped lips split in a black-toothed grin. His face was pale, the teardrop tattoo a sharp blue on parchment skin. His eyes were bright.

"There you are," he said. "My little pin-cushion. I'm going to enjoy this."

*   *   *

Grim opened his eyes on the ceiling of his bedroom, not the gray-green canopy of Green City, but he did not see his ceiling. He saw The Rag Man's face, growing in his vision until it filled everything. A scream built deep in his throat and caught there, stopping his breath.

Slowly, reality faded in.

*   *   *

Michele never really knew her father, only the few things her mother had shared in unguarded moments. All she had were scraps of images, an ugly and incomplete tapestry of memories — beer cans on the floor, cock-roaches on her pillow, the smell of rotting fish guts in the kitchen sink.

But now other things were coming back.

Things that should have stayed forgotten.

*   *   *

Mommy cried, daddy watched TV, and the girl who was too young to remember (except she did remember now) sat alone in her corner, watching the thunderheads gather between them. Waiting for the storm.

It was sports, always sports with daddy. Colorful men in helmets running on the green, chasing each other, hitting each other.

Sometimes daddy hit mommy. More than sometimes. It made Michele mad when he did it. Sometimes she wanted to hit him back, because her mommy never did.

And it started with…"God damn it!" Daddy yelled at the TV, threw the beer can he'd been drinking across the room. "Fucking Seahawks!"

Mommy cried out at the sound of his voice, yelped like a startled dog and started to shake.

Michele knew the storm had started. She saw it reflected in her daddy's narrowed eyes.

"Don't you fucking start in on me. I'll get enough when pay up time comes, don't need any lip from you in my own home."

"I didn't say anything," Mommy said, but that had been too much.

Daddy reached across the couch, almost fell across it, and slapped her.

The sound Mommy made was almost funny, like the sound of a cartoon character hit by a freight train.

Ooofff!

She fell against the arm of the couch, head drooping toward the floor.

Michele looked away, at the carpet before her folded legs. A cockroach stopped in mid-scurry to investigate her, and scuttled away when she swatted at it.

She watched its retreat across the hard landscape of old shag, dirt and crushed cans. It ran in front of her mommy's hanging head and disappeared under the wood-stove a few feet away.

A rack that held the fireplace poker and ash shovel lay on its side.

Michele stood, watched her daddy to make sure he wasn't watching her—tracking her the way he did sometimes—and walked to her mom. She knelt, and spoke into her mommy's ear.

"Hush, Momma. Don't cry. Hush or daddy'll get mad again." Before her mommy could reply, she rose, watching her daddy's face. He didn't see her. He opened another beer and watched the running men, the Seahawks, with a scowl.

It was only a few steps to the tipped fireplace poker. It made a scraping sound as she lifted it from the iron grasp of its holder.

Daddy sat back, head tipped as he sucked his can dry, eyes still on the TV screen. He didn't see Michele walk around behind the couch, behind him.

Both hands grasping the black iron of the poker's handle, she lifted it. It was heavy, but she lifted it over his head...

*   *   *

Michele awoke with a gasp, arms raised above her head, the feel of cold iron fading in her hands. Slowly, her arms dropped into her lap.

The dream wasn't real, just her current guilt intruding on an old nightmare. That last night, as her father worked her mom over one last time before running scared, Michele had only sat, silent and still, not wanting to attract his attention to her. Wishing he would go away and never come back.

Wishing he would die.

*   *   *

Grim heard Clara downstairs in the kitchen, the opening and closing of cabinets, an uncharacteristic curse as she dropped something, maybe the tin coffee pot.

He rose, picked out a thin white T-shirt and a pair of

cut-off shorts, and dressed. By the time he was finished, lacing his shoes and running a quick comb through his unruly morning hair, he smelled coffee percolating.

It was early, the sun only beginning to peek through his open curtains. Clara didn't rise early on her few days off.

He checked Angel's room before going downstairs. She slept as soundly as ever.

"Mornin', lady."

Clara jumped at the sound of his voice and gave him a sour look as he crossed to the kitchen table. "Go back to bed, Eugene. Summer's for sleeping in."

"Not tired," Grim said, then hid a yawn behind his hand. "What's going on?"

"Nothing that concerns you," Clara said, then under her breath, "thank God."

"Danny have another stiff on his hands?" Grim joked.

When Clara didn't answer, he groaned.

He rose, walked to where Clara stood, hunched over the sink, plump shoulders shaking. He put an arm around her. "Not very funny, am I?"

"No," she said. Her voice was strained. She was trying not to cry. "I'm just not in a laughing mood."

Grim saw the frying pan sitting on the stove, heating beneath jets of blue flame, and, on the counter next to the stove, bacon and eggs waiting to be cooked.

"For Danny?"

She nodded.

"Sit down, I'll finish it."

She nodded again and took his abandoned seat at the table. "He's not picky about eggs, but make the bacon crisp."

"Gotcha."

He cooked the bacon first, then the eggs in sizzling grease. When the coffee was finished, he poured two cups and took one to Clara. She didn't comment when he took the seat next to her with his cup and started to drink it.

"What happened?"

"Danny's working early," she said, then rubbed at her

eyes and took a careful drink of her coffee.

Grim stared at her, his eyes fixed on hers until she couldn't ignore him. "What happened?"

Clara sighed. "He found bodies."

"Who is it?" Grim wondered if Keith and Gina had not turned up at last.

"They don't know."

Grim didn't push it any further. He fried the eggs, then packed Danny's breakfast in the last clean Tupperware container. He'd remind Danny to bring the dirties home from his office.

He poured the last of the fresh coffee into a travel mug.

"Finished," he said. "Let's go, I'll carry them."

"No you won't," Clara snapped, and snatched them from his hands. "You're not coming."

"Clara," Grim began, but she cut him off with an impatient wave.

"Don't start with me, young man. I want you to stay in case Angel wakes up."

"She's not going to."

He felt suddenly as if he were being watched. He turned toward the hallway and flinched in surprise.

There she stood, in the new nightclothes Clara had bought for her. She was not the tired and confused girl from the day before. Her eyes were bright, clear, her expression inquisitive.

"Angel," she said, her tone plaintive. "Is that my name?"

Clara smiled, her dark mood suddenly lifted. "No dear, we don't know your name, but you're my new angel, so that's what I'll call you."

The girl stood for a moment, face blank, as if absorbing Clara's words and weighing them before reacting, then she smiled.

"I'll go meet Danny," Grim said softly.

Clara nodded, looking worried, then said, "You go, but please be careful."

*   *   *

Cougar, Danny thought. Had to be.

He stood in the alley, watching the quiet main street, waiting for the State Patrol and the Coroner to arrive, something that was happening too often this summer, hoping they would before the spectators and mourners. Doubting they would. Already too many lighted windows spotted the dusky morning.

Steven had made perhaps a dozen calls, and none he'd spoke with were missing their kids. Many hadn't answered their phones, but he'd expected that. Those he had spoken with knew no details, only that he was looking for two teenage boys. Most jumped to assumptions of delinquency, vandalism, teenage tomfoolery, and he did nothing to discourage that. The truth would be out soon enough, and there would be hell to pay for yet two more bodies on his watch, but he would keep the lid on it for as long as he could. He could only hope they would identify the bodies and clean up the mess before Clearwater fully awoke.

Footsteps in the gravel drew his eyes back to the alley, back to the bodies, and he found one of the town strays, a small, dirty canine of no particular breed, creeping toward the closest body, sniffing at the pool of blood around what was left of…

No, Danny thought, don't think of it as a kid. It's just meat now.

Danny clapped his hands, a firecracker sound in the quiet dawn—nature's chorus seemed to be taking the morning off, mourning the dead in their own way perhaps—and shouted, "scat."

The mutt bolted, sprinted across the trickling water of Canyon Creek and vanished into the trees.

He'd have to keep a sharper lookout. The God-awful carrion smell would bring more scavengers.

And what of the predator?

Danny scanned the dark beyond the trees, felt the weight of unseen eyes upon him, shuddered. He rested the palm of his hand, the one not restricted by his sling, on the butt of his revolver, but found little comfort.

Had to be a cougar. What else? There'd been sightings, and a hunter the previous fall had shot one stalking him. There were bears in the mountains, but they never ventured this far down.

A wolf? Maybe. The Fish and Game had brought the wolves back a few years ago, and they were thriving, spreading, even attacking farm animals farther east.

But not here.

Had to be a cougar.

But he had his doubts. Serious doubts.

"Boss," a silhouette announced itself from the back door of his office down the alley.

"Anything yet, Steven?"

"Nothing yet," Steven said, then turned his head and retched. It was the smell. It seemed to be growing, covering more space by the minute, getting stronger. Danny fought his reflex to let fly as well; pinched his nose and waited for Steven to finish.

"You okay?"

"Not really," Steven said.

He was not the usual self-important prick this morning. Danny supposed it was hard to be macho while puking your guts out. As much as Danny disliked the man, he respected him this morning. He was still here, after all. Puking sick, but doing the job.

"Coy Bradford says he's pretty sure the kids we're looking for were stealing beer out of the cooler on his patio." Steven paused to wipe his lips across the sleeve of his flannel shirt. "I told him if he didn't move the beer inside I'd finish it off for him."

Danny laughed a little, in spite of himself.

Steven nodded. The morning glow was a little brighter; Danny could see Steven's face now, not just the shape of it. "I'll make some more calls." Then he ducked back inside.

Danny turned back toward Main Street.

No State Patrol, no County meat wagon. Just the single bright eye killing what was left of the darkness and the whine of Grim's Yamaha.

Danny figured he could leave the scene long enough to meet Grim at the sidewalk.

"Ready for breakfast, bro?" Grim kicked the stand down and killed the motor. "Bacon, eggs, and coffee." He unzipped the bag hanging from his shoulder, produced a thermos and one of Clara's old tin cups. He didn't wait for an answer, but poured a cup and handed it over.

"Thanks," Danny said. "No food though."

Definitely no bacon, he thought. *I may be off meat for a while.*

He sipped the coffee, and when it didn't come up on him, gulped it. Grim refilled the tin cup when it was empty, then recapped the thermos and zipped the bag.

"Your office open?" Grim asked. "I'll leave it on your desk." He shrugged, "in case you're hungry later."

Danny nodded. "Thanks."

* * *

Grim watched Danny disappear around the corner into the alley and had a morbid urge to follow. Instead he walked the half block to the Sheriff's Office, opened the door, and froze.

"...Incompetent? The man couldn't find his dick with both hands and a flashlight." There was a pause, a commiserate grunt. "Yes, Mr. Commissioner. It's your choice, but you think about it. Six dead bodies—six!—and it wasn't a damn mountain lion this time. I've seen cougar attacks, and this is not a cougar attack."

What the hell?

Grim pushed the door open just far enough to fit his head in, then peeked around. He could see the front of Danny's desk, but the partition—town bulletin board, community services, etc—blocked out the rest, including the speaker. Grim did see his boots. They were work boots, scuffed and dirty. Corked logging boots.

"Yeah, maybe he was a good deputy, but we need a

Sheriff. Mr. Commissioner, there's a predator out there, and we need a Hawk to catch it. Grey is a Dove."

Grim backed his head out of the Sheriff's Office front door, inched it closed, and ran to the side alley where Danny had met him.

"Danny," not too loud, not wanting the man in the office to hear him. He dropped the bag with Danny's breakfast on the sidewalk beside his bike and walked into the alley.

"Danny." A little louder. Still no answer.

Grim could smell the death waiting down that dark gravel lane, just out of sight.

"Danny?"

Grim braced himself and walked down the alley.

Chapter 13

Clara cleared away the dishes from an early breakfast. She was tired, shocked at the news of yet more death in Clearwater. But yet she was pleased to see signs of Angel's recovery.

Angel was much better this morning. She was walking by herself and eating a little which was enough to inspire some hope that she wouldn't continue to wither away.

Clara had done most of the talking between them, asking how she was feeling, how she had slept, how she liked her eggs? Angel was aware and responsive, but otherwise silent.

After breakfast they went to the living room. Clara sat in her rocker with her third cup of coffee. Angel, almost instinctively, found Grim's usual place on the couch. Clara turned the television on to the early AM pre-news infomercials, then turned it off again.

"Angel, dear, would you like anything?"

"No thanks." She sat with her hands folded in her lap, twisting at the fabric of her nightgown. Her eyes flicked to Clara, then back to the hardwood between her slippered feet.

"Dear," Clara said, laying aside the book she'd picked up from the stand beside her rocker. "You don't have to be shy. I can see it in those pretty blue eyes." Clara winked, drawing a smile from Angel. "You want to talk."

Angel nodded, but didn't speak right away. She

released the twist of fabric in her hands and smoothed her gown out over her lap. Clara sipped her coffee, waited.

"Did I do something wrong?" she asked. "Is that why they locked me up?"

Clara could not find her voice at first. Of all the questions she expected, this was not one of them.

Angel must have seen something in Clara's expression, because her own darkened. She found the spot on the floor between her feet again and focused on it.

"No," Clara said. "You didn't do anything wrong." She turned away, wiped at her eyes with the sleeve of her sweater.

Do not let her see you cry, Clara thought. *Keep it together.*

That was one of Grim's sayings — keep it together — that Clara had adopted. Thinking of him now made her feel better. Grim was proof to her that a loving home could bring someone back from the brink of Hell itself.

She faced Angel again. "Honey, look at me, please."

Angel did. There were no tears in her eyes, no shame, just confusion. Confusion and fear.

"Don't ever think it was you."

Angel nodded.

"I don't like that hospital, but you weren't sent there for punishment." *This is where the waters get choppy*, she thought. "Someone left you here, at the diner. You were drugged and abandoned."

"I don't remember," Angel said. I only remember being at the hospital, then coming here." She shook her head, then grimaced and slouched back on the sofa. "Nothing else."

"It's the drugs," Clara said. "The doctors said you should get your memories back, but it might take some time."

Angel smiled, but it was a troubled smile, an expression that didn't sit easy on her tired face.

"It's in here," she said and tapped her temple. "I'll get it back."

"But in the meantime," Clara rose from her rocker and

walked across the living room to where Angel sat, "we'll start making some new memories." She sat next to Angel, took the sickly girl's hands in hers. "Starting today, and as long as you want to stay, this is your home."

Angel raised her head again, a hint of an honest smile lifting the corners of her lips. "I don't have to go back to the hospital then? I can stay here?"

Clara squeezed the girl's cold, clammy hands between her own. "Yes, Angel. As long as you like."

*   *   *

Grim saw the bodies and the blood; he smelled the turning contents of torn bowels, felt the buzz of swarming flies inside his head, but could not equate the lumps of flesh in the gravel as having been human.

"Grim? Is that you?"

He'd heard stories about herds of diseased deer in the mountains to the north, deer that lost their fur and died by the hundreds...

"Hey, Grim. Get away from them."

That made more sense. It was all a big mistake—the mountain lions around Clearwater were real enough, but these were just a pair of diseased, hairless deer, not humans.

"Damn it, Grim, the State Police are on their way. They find you back here and I'll get in trouble."

A hand closed over his shoulder and turned him, forced him to look the other way. It was Danny, looking tired and panicked, who shook him, then started to drag him back toward Main Street.

"Jesus Christ, Grim, what the hell were you thinking?"

Grim blinked, shook the creeping fingers of grogginess away (had he been about to faint?), and allowed Danny to guide him.

"You didn't answer," Grim said. "There's someone in your office."

"I know," Danny said. "Steven Gentry's making some

calls for me."

"Where were you?" Grim leaned against his bike. His eyes wanted to wander back toward the alley, and even though he couldn't have seen the bodies, he forced his eyes back to Danny.

"Parameter search," Danny said. "Grim, you need to get home, the State Police are on the way and you can't be here."

"Here they are," Steven stood on the sidewalk outside their office. He pointed down the road but his eyes were on Grim. "Scat, kid. You don't need to be here now."

Grim opened his mouth to tell Steven to go to hell, but Danny cut him off.

"Deputy Gentry's right," Danny gave Steven a look, none too pleased, but didn't contradict him. "You shouldn't be here."

Grim nodded and climbed on his bike as Danny started down the alley again, but spoke softly. "He was talking to the commissioner, bro. He's trying to get you fired."

Danny stopped and turned toward Grim, eyebrows up, but his expression otherwise neutral.

"That so." His eyes flicked toward Steven, smoking at the curb and waving a hand at the approaching State patrol car. He looked back at Grim, "thanks for the heads up. Better get now."

"Danny?"

"Yes?"

"Let me know who it is when you find out."

Danny started down the alley again. "Sure, Grim."

*   *   *

Danny checked the bodies again, and satisfied that no scavengers had been at them, he turned and waited for the State boys to arrive and make him feel even more like an amateur.

"What's your game, Steven," Danny said, watching from a distance as Steven stepped to the curb to greet the new arrivals. Two sides of beef in State patrol uniforms stepped from the cruiser. They didn't notice Danny standing in the shadows of the alley, and stepped up to meet Steven.

Steven greeted them, shook their hands. "Stiffs're behind the General Store, Officers. Two adolescent males, best as I can tell, but we don't know who yet."

"Better get back to work then, *Deputy* Gentry." Danny covered the distance with a brisk pace, put a finger in Steven's chest. "You and I," he said. "We're going to have us a chat later." He poked his finger a little harder into Steven's meaty chest, forcing him back a step. "We've got to re-establish the pecking order I think."

Steven turned away without a word and walked back to the office.

* * *

Grim passed the single State Patrol Cruiser on his way through town, and a second unmarked car as he slowed for the driveway to his home. Not the station wagon the Coroner drove for pickups. Grim stopped, watched, saw the man driving give him a once over before returning his eyes to the road ahead.

Orofino's Chief of Police Richard Bell if he wasn't mistaken. Probably got a call from the Commissioner.

He did not look happy.

Grim had an idea Danny's reign as Acting Sheriff of Clearwater was about to end.

* * *

The state patrol taped off the scene, took pictures of the bodies, searched for evidence, found nothing.

The bodies were identified tentatively as Kelly Porter, another of Grim's friends, and his brother Clint. They were the only kids unaccounted for, so far. Their father would be here soon to identify them, or try at least, and make it official. In the meantime, Danny covered them with tarps from the back of his Jeep. The town would be out in force soon, and Danny would be damned if he'd let them turn Kelly and Clint into the next sideshow.

Police Chief Bell took charge. He thanked the patrolmen, set Deputy Gentry to watch over the shrouded boys, and requested Danny's company in the office.

"I suppose you have some idea why I'm here."

"Yeah," Danny said. "The Commissioner wasn't up to coming himself, huh?" Danny pulled his wallet from his back pocket, removed his Clearwater County ID card and laid it on his desk. "Overstepping his bounds a little this time, wouldn't you say?" He unbuckled his belt, slipped the holster with his service revolver free, then laid it next to the card.

"Not at all," Bell said. "You were never elected." He picked up Danny's card and slipped it into his breast pocket. "The commissioner is promoting Steven Gentry to full time and naming him acting Sheriff until the elections."

Danny snorted. He'd figured as much.

"You can run in the fall if you want, nothing stopping you." Bell grimaced, "between you and I, if Gentry fucks this up as bad as I think he will, you've got a hell of a good chance."

"And until then?" Danny asked.

"The commissioner wants me to convince you to stay on as deputy," Bell elaborated. "You'd be volunteer until we have a legitimate Sheriff again, of course."

Danny nodded. Again, he'd thought as much.

He unpinned his badge and slapped it onto the table next to his sidearm. "I don't think so."

Chapter 14

Danny spent the next couple of weeks in a happier place, in the mountains miles from his troubles in Clearwater. He called it his *ancestral home* the first summer he brought Grim up for a weekend camping trip. It had been his father's place, and his grandfathers before that.

Ten acres of land, including a small mountain lake with a modest supply of sunfish and catfish, and a one-room cabin, accessible by only one narrow backwoods lane. Besides him, only Clara, Grim, and the propane man came with any regularity, and that was just what Danny needed.

When he was ten, after his mother's abrupt run-out, his father had moved them up there. The cabin was drafty and leaking, the road a washout, no power, wood heat and cooking, no television, no friends. Danny had hated it, and he'd hated his father for taking him there.

He understood now, even if his misgivings persisted, and he was glad he hadn't given in to the childish impulse to sell the place when he'd turned eighteen.

Danny had modernized it over the years, repaired the leaky roof and drafty walls, brought in better furniture for the bottom floor and a new bed for the overhead loft, installed new gas appliances—cooking stove, hot water heater, and a heater to supplement the wood stove. Next would be a propane powered generator, though he didn't know if he'd be able to afford the gas to run it often enough to make it worthwhile.

He'd also set up a two-way radio a few summers ago, like the one in his home on Angel Ridge Grade, just in case Sheriff Davis needed to reach him while he was away. Davis never had, but occasionally Clara would, just to see if he needed supplies or find out when he was coming home.

That morning it was Grim's voice waking him from a late afternoon nap, and he sounded excited.

* * *

It was the second human voice, besides his own, that he'd heard since leaving Clearwater, and it was welcome. The first had been Clara's, a week into his self-imposed exile, just checking up as she always did.

The first burst of static smashed the silence and startled him awake. There was more white noise than usual, a symptom of an approaching summer storm. The second burst came and he recognized Grim's voice. Something about Angel.

Danny rose from the old sprung sofa, stretched, walked to the radio on the small kitchen table and adjusted the tuner.

"That you, Grim?"

"Hey, Danny, thought you might be out fishing." He came through a little better, but the storm would arrive soon.

"Nope." Danny yawned. "You caught me napping. What's up?"

"Got a call from California, about Angel. Someone you called about that picture you found in Angel's things."

"Did they find anything out?" Danny hadn't expected a call back, was a little surprised the investigators had bothered to follow up.

"Don't know," Grim said. "Clara's out and he wouldn't talk to me."

"Shit," even over the phone Grim couldn't escape disrespect, but he handled it well. "You get his name and number?"

"Yep. You coming back to follow up or should Clara call him?"

Danny paused to consider. He didn't want to leave just yet, but it was important, and he knew the law's info maze better than Clara. And beneath that reason, something just as important, maybe more important. He had to leave sometime, like it or not. Danny did not want to deal with other people yet, but if he withdrew any further he might go the way of his father, and that was unacceptable.

"I'll be there tonight, Grim. Let Clara know I'm coming."

"Will do," Grim said, but before signing off added, "if you're going back when you're finished, how about taking me with you?"

Danny laughed. "Sure, Grim. I think I could handle that."

* * *

Michele made dinner, as usual, and when her mom hadn't shown up by seven o'clock, again as usual, she decided to call Grim and Angel over.

Home was becoming a lonely place the last few weeks, her mom spending more of her nights in Lewiston, no friends other than Grim and Angel, and she usually went to their house. Having them over would be a change.

She dialed them, excited at the prospect of not spending the evening alone.

"'Chele," Grim said, sounding pleased. "What's up?"

"Just making dinner," she said, feeling the heat of a blush rise in her cheeks. Damn, why did she always blush when she heard his voice. "Thought you and Angel might come over, watch a movie with me or something."

"Angel's out with Clara," he said. "Should be back pretty soon though."

"Oh, okay." Michele's first impulse was to forget the whole thing, to eat dinner alone, again, and hope there was something good on TV. Maybe even sleep through the night without bad dreams.

But she didn't want to be alone.

Not tonight.

Mom will kill you if she finds out.

She didn't think her mom would. Tonight was looking like another all-nighter. Maybe she would get a call from the office tomorrow morning, maybe not, but she didn't think her mother would make an appearance tonight.

"Do you like pizza, Grim?"

*   *   *

Grim had only just got off the radio with Danny when the phone rang, and by the time he'd hung up his bleak mood had lifted a little for the first time that day. He ran up stairs, changed out of his grungy clothes, ran a comb through his hair.

It felt strange, going to see Michele without Angel, sometimes even Clay (who had finally quit calling Michele "Killer Kirkwood" —at least in her presence) in tow. He knew she liked him, and he was nervous without the buffer his new sister and friend created between him and Michele. Not because he was uncomfortable with the way she felt toward him, but because of the way he felt about her.

True, there was an unresolved tension between them, but it was a good tension. A safe tension.

But it would be good to be alone with her, just for once, to hear only her voice for a while, and for her to hear only his. Maybe to touch her again, to find if they would spark again when his fingers touched her skin.

He scribbled a note to Clara and put it on the kitchen table, knowing she wouldn't approve of his unchaperoned visit, but unwilling to lie to her about it.

The sun was giving Clearwater it's daily fare-thee-well as he stepped outside, walked to his bike, and sped from the driveway, on his way to what might, or might not, be his first date since he made out with Keith's sister in Canyon Jack's game room.

So excited he forgot to obsess on whatever it was Danny's California connection might have found out about his mysterious new sister.

*   *   *

It watched him from the distance between the woods and the road, remembering more. More every day, and hating the memories.

Hating them.

Wanting to snuff them.

Tracking him until he disappeared around the bend to town.

Alone.

It wanted him, wanted him even more than the others because of who he was, because it had known him differently before...

Afraid to go for him though, because the other one was always with him now, and it feared her more than it hated him.

Alone this time.

It went back into the woods, deeper into the trees, and guided by a force part memory, part instinct, part need, to where it knew it might watch him.

To wait until the dark, and hunt again.

*   *   *

The girl was a mystery.

A mystery wrapped in an enigma, shrouded in sadness and locked in a cell of amnesia. Despite what the doctors had said, her memories had not returned with her health. The Rohypnol and Ketamine cocktails that wicked boy had given her seemed to have rubbed all memory preceding State Hospital North away.

Her brother, or so Danny thought, but Clara couldn't believe it. What kind of brother would do something like that to his sister?

It was Clara's job to help Angel find herself again.

To that end, Clara had tried everything she could think of short of taking her to yet more doctors—a youth minister in Lewiston, with some training in child psychology, a used car lot across the Washington border in Clarkston with a similar make, model, and color car as the one her brother had brought her to Clearwater in, every fast food joint and motel she could find on the highway between Clearwater and the Oregon border, any place they might have stopped or stayed along the way. Anything that might jog her memory.

Nothing yet, though she seemed to enjoy the long rides, sitting in the front seat and staring out the windows at the scenery.

Today was a library day. Spent mostly at a computer terminal in the second floor of Lewiston's State College Library. Clara used the library's Internet connection and searched for every California landmark she could think of, none of which meant anything to Angel.

During their last hour before closing, she let Angel wander the isles, just looking at the endless rows of books, and eventually making her way to the Reference shelf, and a row of *Time-Life* hard covers; *Unexplained Mysteries, Curses of The Pharaohs, Ghosts and The Supernatural,* and the likes.

That is where she had her first breakthrough.

"I remember these," she'd said, pointing to a twelve-volume set called *Psychic Phenomenon.* "My dad read these." She extended a shaking hand toward the volumes, ran a finger down a textured spine, closed her eyes. "Number seven," she said. "I remember number seven." She withdrew her hand and turned to Clara. "Does that mean anything?"

"I don't know," Clara said, trying to keep the excitement, and a touch of fear, from her voice. "What do you think?"

Angel shrugged. "Maybe I'm trying too hard." Her hand twitched toward the books again, toward volume seven, but she didn't quite dare touch it. "I can see him in a room full of books, sitting at a desk with his glasses at the end of his nose." She closed her eyes again. "He has short brown hair and a mustache and a scar above his right eye. He's reading number seven." She opened her eyes again; they were bloodshot and tired. "He's afraid of something, but I can't remember what."

"Yes," Clara urged, putting a hand on her shoulder, more to steady herself than comfort Angel. "What else?"

"Nothing," Angel said. "I don't know, maybe I'm just making this up."

Clara didn't think so. She'd just described the man in Danny's photo.

Angel's hand hovered close to the spine of the dreaded volume seven. Clara reached past her and plucked it from the shelf. Angel flinched away from it.

The cover was imitation leather with a yellow front, the diagrammed cross-section of a human head, the brain's hemispheres and vital areas highlighted in different colors and labeled with psychic powers supposed to be associated with them. A laminated tag beneath said: WE DO NOT LOAN REFERENCE TITLES.

"Can we go now?" Angel asked. When Clara looked at her there was fear in her eyes. She was watching the book like it might open up and try to bite them.

Clara slid it back into place.

"Yes, dear, we'd better go. Grim will think we've run away."

* * *

Grim arrived just before dark. Michele heard his bike pull in the empty gravel lot, and met him at the door. She knew there would be faces peeking through drawn curtains and pressed to windows next door, across the street, so she didn't bother to look for them. She didn't care what they thought of Grim, and she didn't care if they told her mother.

Grim kicked the bike's stand down and dismounted with an easy grace, gave her a wave, and walked to the porch. "Hey, 'Chele, what have you got planned for me?"

She laughed, a nervous sound. "Nothing big," she said. "Just pizza and a movie."

Grim climbed the steps and paused at the threshold, waiting for an invite inside. "What's the movie?"

"What do you like?" She pulled him inside by the arm and shut the door.

Grim moved slowly through the foyer, into the living room, taking in his surroundings, familiarizing himself with unfamiliar territory before making himself too comfortable. "Comedies, westerns, and horror," he said. "I'm not picky. I'll watch whatever you want."

"Horror," Michele echoed. "You mean low budget, scare your girlfriend into your arms, slasher films?"

Grim turned, laughed. "Yeah, those are the ones."

I was hoping you would say that, Michele thought.

Chapter 15

Twilight; fire in the sky, shadow trees growing across the pavement, turning into night.

Angel sat with her eyes closed, leaning against the car door as Clara slowed to turn off the highway onto the road to town. Clara thought she was sleeping, then the girl spoke.

"I'm scared."

"You don't need to be, dear. You'll remember in good time. I'll be here to help you." Clara passed Canyon Jack's and sped up. Almost home now.

"No," Angel said. "It's not that." She scanned the darkening world outside her window, hugged herself. "Something bad is going to happen, and I think it's my fault."

Clara's flesh crawled. *Goose walked over my grave*, was the expression that came to her mind. "What on Earth are you..."

She saw the thing in the road out of the corner of her eye. A naked thing, dirty and crouching low.

Clara screamed.

The thing jerked its head, matted hair flying in twists, and bared its bloody teeth at them. It held something small, furry, dead, in its claw-like hands. A rabbit maybe, or a cat.

Clara stomped down on the brakes, but too late.

She slammed into the naked girl, a familiar face on a haggard body. The wild girl flew, arms and legs spinning as she cartwheeled through the air, landed on the gravel shoulder, bounced into the high weeds in the dry creek bed.

Angel screamed, a sound that drilled though Clara's head, made her eyes water, made her ears want to rupture. She felt a warm trickle running from her nose, down over her lips like snot. She wiped her face with the back of her hand and it came away bloody.

"Hush!" Clara tried to ignore the pain in her head and comfort Angel. "You're okay, honey. Just hush."

And finally, Angel did

Clara opened the door and tried to climb out, but Angel grabbed her arm and held it.

"Don't go out there," she said. "Please, it might still be alive."

"Dear God I hope so," Clara said. "That wasn't an animal. I have to see if she's hurt."

"Yes it was," Angel said, her voice no more than an out rush of breath. She looked pale, faint. She leaned in closer to Clara. "I don't want it to hurt you."

Clara was torn between placating Angel and helping the girl she'd knocked into the ditch, not sure which way to go, when the headlights came from behind and washed over them.

*   *   *

Danny heard the shriek first. It burred into his brain, like a parasite feeding on his strength, excreting pain. Then he turned the corner and saw Clara's car parked crooked in the road, its headlights pointing toward the dry creek and into the woods. He pulled in behind her.

Jesus Christ, what was that sound? He rubbed his forehead, but the pain was already receding.

Clara did not come to meet him, so he went to her. Her door was part way open, but Angel clung to her arm, refused to relinquish it.

"Danny," Clara said, her voice quivering at the edge of tears. "I just hit someone. She landed over there." Clara pointed at the ditch. She beckoned him closer, and whispered in his ear. "I think it's Gina Fox. She was naked."

Danny watched as Clara covered her mouth, seemed on the verge of hyperventilating. "Dear Lord, Danny, I think she was eating something off the road."

Danny nodded. "Stay put."

"Danny!" It was Angel. "Be careful."

He nodded. "Yeah, sure. I'll be careful."

Danny walked around the front of Clara's car, keeping his eyes on the light-washed blacktop. The cat looked fresh. Crushed flat, eyes bulging from the sockets like a crank fiend, most of its fur gone, but fresh. It was drawing flies, but not yet rotting. Probably no more than a few hours dead.

Something, or someone, had been feasting on it.

Danny stepped around it, searched the roadside, found blood on the gravel, and followed it.

Aside from the weeds and stones, the bed of the barren creek was empty. But there was more blood, a trail of it spotting the bank to the other side, disappearing into the darkness.

Behind him, Clara's car horn gave a short beep.

Danny jumped, almost tripped headlong down the bank.

"Christ," he whispered.

"Danny?" It was Clara.

Danny walked back to the open car door, Clara hanging half out of it, still anchored inside by Angel.

"She's not down there," he said. "Looks like she ran into the woods."

Clara sighed. "She's alive."

Angel's grip tightened on her arm.

"Yes," Danny said.

A howling sound drifted through the dark, through the woods. From the old Wallen place. A crooning, pathetic sound, a wounded animal sound.

Crying.

"Take my car," Danny said, taking Clara by the arm,

pulling her, then Angel out. "We can't move your car until Steven makes his accident report."

Clara nodded as Danny led her to his car. "Sure."

Angel followed, keeping a close watch on the trees to their left.

"Call Steven, tell him to get his ass out here." He reached under the dash and popped the trunk, then rushed around to the back of the car while Angel and Clara climbed in. A few seconds later, he slammed the trunk closed and appeared at Clara's window, road flares in hand. "You'll have to meet him back here and explain the accident to him."

"Danny, what are you doing?"

"I'm going to look for her," he said.

He half-expected her to try and argue him out of it — *don't you even think about it young man, you'll do no such thing* — but she did not.

"You be careful out there," she said.

"I will," he said, then stepped away and let them go.

He watched their taillights shrink into the distance, then went to work placing the road flares around her car. When they were set, he took a breath to steady himself, crossed the dry creek, and followed the broken trail of blood into the trees.

*   *   *

Knowing how obvious her game must be to Grim, she played it nonetheless. She followed horror movie protocol, cringing when the spooky music score told her to, turning her head at each exaggerated splash of blood, practically jumping into his lap with each small scare.

Grim did his part. He held her when she screamed and let her bury her face into his shoulder through the worst of the gore. But he didn't make a move.

Damn it, Grim, can't you take a hint?

"I'm glad you came over," she said, taking his hand — warm and strong — in hers. "I knew Mom would forget."

Grim turned to her, eyes leaving the screen for probably the first time since the movie had started.

"What did she forget?" When Michele didn't answer, he asked again. "What's wrong, 'Chele? What did she forget?"

Michele smiled at him, a smile that looked at least a little sad, she hoped. "My sixteenth birthday."

Grim gaped. "I'm sorry, 'Chele. I didn't know." He groaned. "God, what a shitty birthday. I didn't even get you a present."

Michele slid an arm around Grim's neck and pulled him toward her. Before he could react, she kissed him.

When it was over she drew away, loving the taste of him, still on her lips. "Feeling a little better now," she said.

Grim sat stunned for a moment, touched his lips, looked at her with wide, surprised eyes. Then grinned. "Glad I could help," he said.

Then he helped himself.

*   *   *

She'd expected to find Grim home, but found the note he'd left instead.

Not pleased, but not surprised. She'd known from the start that Michele had a crush on him, but didn't know how he felt. Kept a pretty tight wrap on his feelings, her Grim did. Hard to know how he felt about anything unless he wanted you to. She knew about Grim and his friend's sister, Gina — oh God I hope I haven't killed her — but not until after the fact.

She'd gone through the same phase with Danny, and knew there came a time when all she could do was give her best council, then hope he'd take it.

Hope he wouldn't get in trouble.

Danny had dated infrequently since the age of sixteen, never staying very long with any one girl, which made her sad, but not getting any of them in trouble. One day he would find a good girl to settle with, and he wouldn't carry any baggage into the relationship.

She crumpled the note and dropped it onto the table, then called The Sheriff's office. The office line rang twice, then routed to Lydia. She was a nice girl, as good a prospect for Danny as anyone else in Clearwater.

She'd have to invite Lydia to dinner sometime, get her and Danny together and see where it goes.

Lydia picked up after the third ring.

"Clearwater County," she said, her ever-personable phone voice singing out over whatever program she was watching in her living room.

"Lydia, dear, it's Clara."

"Oh, hi, Clara. It's good to hear from you." As always sounding pleased to hear from you. Clara didn't know if this was just good phone manners, or if she was always just pleased to hear from her. If it was an act, it was a good one. "How is Danny these days?"

"He's just come back to town tonight," Clara said, then quick, before Lydia could cut in with more time-wasting small talk, "Dear, there's been an accident. I need you to call Steven Gentry."

A short pause, and Lydia's voice came back at her, all business now, not cold, just professional. "Could you let me know what's happened and I'll contact Sheriff Gentry right away."

Clara explained, leaving out the part about how she believed the victim to be the missing Fox girl. "Danny came into town just behind us and couldn't find anyone."

"And you're sure it wasn't an animal?" Lydia asked, concern in her tone rather than doubt.

"I don't think so," Clara said, and then the first tears came, unexpected. "I'm sorry," Clara said.

"It's okay, I'm sure whoever it was is fine. They can't be hurt too bad if they got up and ran away." Wanting to convince, but not sounding convinced.

"I hope so," Clara said. "Dear God, I couldn't live with myself if..." but she couldn't finish the thought aloud.

"I'm going to call the Sheriff now. Will you be all

right?"

"Yes," Clara wiped her eyes. "Tell Steven I'll meet him there." She wouldn't call that windbag *Sheriff*.

She hung up.

Angel watched her from the foyer, worried.

"I'm going to call Grim and Michele back, dear. They can keep you company while I talk to Steven. I won't be long."

Angel nodded.

She walked to Angel, hugged her, and led her toward the stairs. "You go change for bed now. Michele's mom is out of town tonight, so maybe she'll stay over with you."

A ghost of a smile, then Angel turned and ran up the stairs to her room.

Clara returned to the kitchen, to the phone, called Michele's house, praying for the strength not to yell at Grim.

It rang seven times before Michele answered.

"Michele, dear," Clara said, the usual amiability gone from her voice. "Put Eugene on, please."

* * *

It was probably a good thing, Michele thought. She'd lost control and let Grim go farther than anyone ever had, much farther. And she would have let him go farther still, maybe all the way, because losing control had felt so good.

What a birthday present that would have been.

Now, as she sat behind Grim, feeling the vibrations of the Yamaha's engine, it seemed cramps would be all she got for her sweet sixteen. They'd started just after Clara's call, so she'd had enough time to do what she had to do before they left. As long as she lived, she'd never get used to her period.

Yeah, definitely a good thing Clara had called and broke it up.

"Hold on," Grim said as they turned onto Main Street and he gunned it toward his house.

She held him tight, buried her face against his neck, and groaned as they hit a small pothole, her cramps intensifying.

"You alright?"

"Uh-huh," she said. "Stomach hurts a little." Definitely didn't want to talk about her period with Grim. Probably gross him out.

He slowed the bike and the ride smoothed out.

They found Clara waiting outside, standing by Danny's car, shaking her head in dark appraisal.

She crossed her arms as Grim killed the engine. She approached them, tisking.

"I know," Grim said.

"You should know better," Clara said. "Her mom would have killed you if she caught you two alone."

"Mom's not coming home tonight," Michele said. "She's staying in Lewiston tonight, again."

Clara turned to her, frowning.

"Pizza and a movie, Clara." Grim said. "She shouldn't be alone on her birthday."

Clara shook her head again, the *Not An Excuse* expression on her face, but her eyes had softened. "Well," she said to Michele, "you can stay over with Angel tonight, if you want."

"Thanks," Michele said.

"What's wrong?" Grim said.

"A little accident," Clara said. "Nothing you need to worry about, Mister."

Grim nodded, kept his mouth shut. *Mister* meant she was pissed, or stressed, or both. Mister was usually the precursor to a good butt chewing.

"Angel's upstairs, dear. Not feeling well," she said, taking Michele's hand and giving it a squeeze. "Happy birthday."

Then she stepped away from them, clapped her hands together—*Now, Now!* "Inside."

They stood by the porch and watched Clara drive away in Danny's car. Michele's hand found Grim's, as their fingers locked, each feeling the other's pulse.

"She's in trouble," Grim said.

Michele nodded. "I think you're right."

"'Chele, how about a last kiss for a doomed man?"

"What?" *Last kiss?*

"Yeah," Grim said. "Clara's gonna kill me, but I'll be damned if I let her face whatever trouble she's in alone."

Michele half-smiled, relieved, and gave a doomed man his kiss.

Chapter 16

Clara parked on the shoulder well away from the burning road flares, headlights trained on her parked car just in case someone came along. No one did, no townies coming home from an evening out, no strangers who happened to take the wrong exit.

No Sheriff Gentry.

Lazy bastard.

A quarter hour passed and nothing happened.

Then she heard someone approaching from town, and let out a breath of relief. She climbed out into the still night, debating on giving the good Sheriff a piece of her mind, and nearly screamed. Not Steven, but Eugene, determined to get on every last nerve she possessed.

"You turn around and get back home, Eugene, before I take you to the woodshed!"

Grim shook his head. "Tell me what happened. If there's nothing I can do to help, I'll go home. Otherwise, I stay."

She shouted in frustration. "Why can't you just do what I say, Mister?"

Calm, not flinching, not giving an inch. "Because if you're in trouble and I let you face it alone, I'm not worth keeping around." He crossed his arms, leaned against Danny's car. "I'll stand here all night, Clara. You can take me to the woodshed later if you want, but I'm not going anywhere now."

She knew he meant it, and she couldn't stay angry. She was too proud of him to stay angry.

She told him.

"Get back in there and lock the doors," he said. "Don't you dare leave that car. If dumb-shit isn't here in fifteen minutes," Grim said, using his pet name for Sheriff Gentry, "then you go home and wait."

"Eugene, don't..."

"Danny's my brother," he said. "I'm going to help him."

He grabbed the walkie-talkie clipped to his belt. "'Chele, you hear me?"

"Yes, what's going on?"

"Do me a favor and call the number for the Sheriff's Office. Have Lydia light a fire under Steven's fat ass."

"Okay," she said, her voice thin, tinny coming from the talkie's speaker.

"Talk to you soon," he said, and turned it off before clipping it back to his belt.

"You be careful, Mister," Clara said.

Grim winked. "See you in the woodshed."

Then he jumped the dry creek bed and disappeared into the trees.

* * *

"You definitely hit something," Steven said, examining the fractured grill of Clara's little car, then following the spotted trail of blood away from the road.

"Yes," Clara said, unable to help the uncharacteristic sarcasm. "I thought I might have."

Steven turned his tired gaze on her. "I see where your boys get their attitude." He crossed to the edge of the trees, took a step into the wild, jumped as a twig snapped under his feet. He peered into the woods for a time, then turned back and crossed to Clara.

"You should get your eyes checked," he said, patronizing. "I'd bet the bank it was that damn cougar you hit. Go home and pray you nailed the bastard good."

"No," she said, incredulous. "You idiot!"

He climbed back into his Jeep, ignoring her.

Clara reached through the window and seized his arm. "It wasn't an animal."

Steven sighed. "Fine, you crazy old bat, you want me to waste my time looking for a naked girl that we both know is dead and gone, I'll do it." He shrugged her arm away, smoothed out his sleeve. "And when I come back without her, I'm going to book you for making a false statement."

Clara's face reddened. She stepped away, and what she said next would have made Grim cheer. "You are the most worthless turd in Clearwater County. Why our good commissioner," she spat the last word out like something foul, "ever made you Sheriff will always be beyond me."

Steven glowered at her, opened his mouth to speak, but she cut him off.

"Go home, little boy." She waved him off. "The men are out there taking care of it, so just go on home."

Steven pointed a beefy finger out the window at Clara.

"You mind your mouth, bitch. You mind your manners around me."

And then he left her.

*   *   *

"I haven't had a slumber party since Rachel moved." Michele had placed Grim's call fifteen minutes before, then waited for him to get back to her. When he didn't she put the walkie-talkie on Angel's bed and tried very hard not to think about him, out there in the night somewhere.

The nights in Clearwater weren't as safe as they used to be.

Angel sat in a straight-backed chair facing her vanity while Michele stood behind her, combing the knots out of her long hair.

Angel watched her in the mirror. "Who's Rachel?"

"My best friend," Michele said. "Was until she moved anyway. She left before you came to stay." She lifted Angel's hair, ran the brush through from underneath to work out the last few knots, then let it fall. It was long and shiny where it had been a dull, tangled mess the first time she'd seen the girl. "I don't know her new phone number, and she hasn't called."

"I'm sorry," Angel said, and she did sound sorry.

"That's okay," Michele said. "I've got a new best friend now."

"Really, who?"

Michele laughed. "You. Who did you think?" Michele saw Angel's reflection blush.

"Oh. I just thought you hung out with me because of Grim."

"Nope," Michele said. "We're two weird girls in a land full of boring, normal people. We were destined to become friends." She shifted the brush to her left hand and held it loosely as she started to braid Angel's hair.

We bonded when I killed Old Man Wallen.

Michele didn't think Angel remembered that though. At least she'd not mentioned it.

"You do like Grim though," Angel said, then winked at Michele's reflection in the mirror.

"Yeah," Michele said. "I like Grim."

"Does he like you?"

"Yeah, he does." Michele remembered his touch earlier that night. The spark between their touching lips, the strength of his hands when he felt her up.

"Grim's a good brother," Angel said. "Grim and Danny are a lot nicer than my last brother."

Michele flinched away from Angel, dropping the brush.

Angel's half-completed braid unraveled as she turned. "What's wrong?"

"You're remembering," Michele said. "How much do you remember?"

Angel said nothing, and after a moment Michele picked

up the brush, set it on the vanity, and started braiding again.

"A little," Angel said finally. "I remembered a little today, just before I started feeling sick."

As if on cue, Michele doubled over with a wave of fresh cramps.

Angel clutched her stomach too. "Think I ate something bad today."

"It's my time of the month," Michele said, a little embarrassed. "At least I don't have to be sick alone tonight."

"You get sick every month?"

"You know what I mean," Michele said, not wanting to elaborate anymore than necessary.

But Angel only continued to look confused. "No."

"My period."

"Oh," Angel said, then turned away. "I'm sorry. I don't have them."

"Never?"

Angel shook her head.

"How old are you? Do you remember that yet?"

"Thirteen," a pause, "fourteen." She shrugged. "One or the other."

Michele made the last cross in Angel's braid, then tied it off with a pink hair band. "Finished. Want to do mine now?"

"I can try," Angel said. "Don't think I've ever braided before." As she tried to rise another groan escaped her lips. She dropped back into the seat.

Another cramp twisted Michele's guts, and she had a sudden, awful insight. She'd heard that sometimes when girls were close their periods synchronized.

"Angel, I don't think you're sick from anything you ate. I think you're having your first period."

"Oh God, really?" Angel seemed horrified, grossed out. "How do you know?"

"Synchronicity," Michele said. "Do you have..." oh shit, she didn't want to have to be the one to coach Angel through her first period.

"No," Angel said, not needing Michele to elaborate this time.

Another cramp hit Michele. She was sweating. The heat in Angel's room seemed to have risen ten degrees in the last few minutes. She walked to the window, slid it up, letting a breeze only slightly cooler than the inside temperature through the room. Better. She unzipped her overnight bag and dug beneath her clothes for her pads.

Synchronicity was doing Angel a favor tonight, it seemed.

The maker of this unfortunate staple of the woman's curse was good enough to print directions for use, along with a few helpful diagrams. The kind of thing you hid between bags of cereal in the store checkout lane.

"Don't freak out." She held out the box to Angel. "They're easy to use. Just follow the directions."

Please don't ask me to help you, please don't ask me to help you.

Angel took the box, frowned at the diagrams.

Michele's cramps had eased, for now. "Being a girl sucks sometimes," she said.

"Yeah," Angel agreed. She stood, walked toward the door. "This is *so* embarrassing."

Michele sympathized.

"Don't worry, you'll get used to it."

Angel was opening the door to the hallway when the warm breeze carried in a sound that brought her skin to a low crawl. A shriek, something that could have been human or animal, or both.

A pained scream.

An angry scream.

Angel didn't move. She seemed frozen, rooted to the floorboards, her hand clamped, white knuckled, on the doorknob.

She turned, looking not at Michele, but through her, through the open window, through the darkness.

Angel screamed, a hollow sound, a small sound compared to her wide-open mouth, but it went into Michele's head like needles.

Blood stained the front of her nightshirt, spotted the floor between her feet.

Her eyes rolled up in her head and she went limp.

Michele caught her before she hit the floor.

*   *   *

The shriek carried through the still, stagnant air, driving dogs into frenzy, cats into hiding. It owned the night, and everyone that heard it remembered the dead boys behind the general store that morning only a few weeks ago, the missing whom they would likely never see again.

A shriek that could have been animal or human — a cougar on the prowl or a woman in pain.

The two sounded so much alike.

*   *   *

The night was not solid black, it was worse. Black with barely defined gray shapes that rustled and hissed in the warm night breeze. Grim knew they were just trees, almost certainly *all* trees, but that didn't make him any less uncomfortable when they moved around him. Knowing that didn't calm Grim when they reached out with the breeze and touched him.

He'd been immersed in the black/gray for no longer than half an hour, he guessed, though it did seem longer. The sense of dread slowed time for him, and the isolation stretched it.

Alone out here, in the dark, sensing the living danger behind the night's veil of nothing, made him feel very small.

He remembered his nights in Green City. Waiting alone under a veil that snuffed out the stars and moon, knowing they were out there, somewhere, even if he couldn't see them. Waiting for his keeper to come home.

He'd walk for a few minutes, aiming for silence but not achieving it, trying to stay upright but tripping just the same.

Then he'd rest, wait, and listen. After hearing nothing, he would move on with his mind's eye set toward the east. Taking the hard way toward Old Ron Wallen's salvage yard. If he didn't find Danny he'd take the long dirt driveway back to the main road and meet up with Clara again.

He did not doubt that Clara would be there waiting for him. He'd told her to go home if no one showed up, but she didn't take orders from him.

Oh, the trouble he'd be in tomorrow.

"If I had my gun I'd have probably shot you."

Adrenaline surged through his system, dialing his nerves up from frazzled to fried. For a moment he thought his heart had stopped, and that he'd just drop over, dead at age seventeen from a heart attack. Then the beat picked up again, doubled, tripled. He turned to face the voice in the darkness and managed to tangle his feet up.

A hand caught him, one of the gray shapes he'd just passed before he fell.

"Jesus, Danny, you trying to kill me?"

"Nope," he said, his voice all sincerity. "Just thought you needed a good scare. What the hell are you doing out here?"

"Clara told me what happened." When Danny offered no response, "did you find her?"

"No."

"Do you think it was really Gina?"

A pause, then "I don't know."

"If it is, she might be hiding out in Wallen's place." Grim took another step in the darkness in the direction of what he hoped was the old salvage yard, and the Wallen place. "But..."

"Why?" Danny finished for him. "I don't know."

Danny moved past Grim, seemed to know exactly where he was going. "The road's this way. We better get back."

"What about Wallen's place," Grim said. "Shouldn't we at least check it out?"

A sigh. "No. We searched it along with everything else when Gina and Keith went missing. Besides, it's not my job anymore."

"Did you find anything at all?"

"Yeah," Danny said. "Nothing important. Whatever Clara hit is long gone."

Grim followed Danny as best he could through the dark, trusting his brother's apparently superb night vision to lead them out. And sure enough, minutes later he saw a break in the trees, a lighter shade of night where slivers of a moon and the occasional cluster of stars shone through the canopy of evergreens.

Just as Grim's nerves started to settle, he heard a rustling behind him, not the wind this time, he knew that right away. Not the subtle voice of the night through high boughs, but something pushing through the lower limbs. Something running.

And it hit him from behind, taking him to the ground, with the speed of a practiced predator.

Mounting him from behind, claws shredding his shirt to rags, tearing at his back.

"Danny!"

Then hands on the back of his throat, closing, twisting, trying to wring his neck.

Warm, rancid breath against his cheek, making his gorge rise.

"Grim." A whisper.

He heard a grunt of effort above them, saw the vaguest silhouette of a man, arms over his head, wielding something that could have been a sword or a stick.

Grim ducked, closed his eyes as Danny swung.

One swing was all it took. The thing released Grim's neck and bolted back into the darkness, loosing a shriek that made his balls draw up.

Whatever wildlife hadn't been scared away by the struggle, took flight at the sound. Birds exploded from trees with startled cries, squirrels skittered away, small claws scraping wood.

"Come on!" Danny took Grim by the arm and yanked him to his feet, almost dragging him the remaining distance to the dirt road. "Shit, are you okay?"

"Fine," Grim said, but felt his throat for signs of damage. "My back is bleeding. I'll live."

Danny scanned the area.

Grim saw it in his hands, the thing he'd found in the woods. The thing he'd just made that grand slam swing with.

A cane, hand-carved.

The same one Michele had killed Wallen with?

"C'mon," Danny said, and Grim heard real, honest fear in his voice. "Let's go."

They ran, Grim keeping to Danny's side, and didn't stop until they found the blacktop.

"Let me take a look," Danny said when he was capable of speech between gasps of breath. He lifted what remained of Grim's shirt up and inspected his back. "A few cuts," he said at last, lowering the shirt carefully. "Not as bad as I thought."

They turned toward town and walked.

"I don't think we should tell Clara about that," Danny said. "I don't think she could handle it tonight."

Grim agreed.

*   *   *

Twenty minutes later they were home, Grim pulling into the driveway first, Clara and Danny behind him.

Michele was there to meet them before they made it to the door. Her eyes were wide, her face pale.

"I tried to call you on your walkie-talkie," she said to Grim. Then to Clara, "I think Angel's sick."

*   *   *

Clara and Michele flanked Angel's bed, keeping watch while she slept. Clara, sitting in Angel's high-back vanity chair, had drifted. Angel's unconsciousness seemed to have merged into normal sleep.

Michele was still awake.

Grim poked his head in every now and then, but never stayed more than a few minutes. Clara was still clearly upset with him, and he was playing it safe with her for now. Making as small a target as he could.

Finally, Clara gave up her watch. "I'm going to turn in. Maybe you should do the same. Angel will be fine."

"Pretty soon," Michele said, and accepted a brief hug before Clara left her.

Time passed, the dark stayed dark, light from the partially-opened bedroom door providing the only relief from it. She could hear Grim downstairs, but resisted the urge to go see him.

Her father appeared in the doorway, her mother's limp form hanging from his fist. "Think you both need a time out," he said, and stepped through the door, dragging her mother behind.

Michele woke with a jump, eyes wide. The doorway was empty. No father. No time out.

There was movement next to her in the bed.

Angel was watching her with half-open eyes.

"I remember you now," she said.

Then again, a whisper as her eyes closed and she drifted back to sleep. "I remember."

Part 3
BROKEN
ANGEL

Chapter 17

The sting of the iodine kept Grim awake long after Danny retired to his old room and Clara gave up the watch over her sleeping Angel. The cuts weren't deep though, not too much blood. His T-shirt was trash, but he wouldn't need stitches. They'd managed to get by without Clara noticing.

At last he did manage to get some sleep, but it was a short rest. The squeak of bedsprings and stirring of pain in his back as the mattress shifted brought him back from the edge of peace.

"Grim? You awake?"

"'Chele, Clara's gonna kill me if she sees you in here."

Michele giggled, ran her fingers through his hair. "Why would she kill you? I'm the one doing the molesting."

Grim shivered. "Don't say things you don't mean, 'Chele." He reached around, took her hand and laced his fingers through hers.

"Sorry, stud." She said, and cuddled into him, holding him tight.

Grim sucked in a sharp breath, and Michele relaxed her grip.

"What is it?"

"Careful of my back," he said. "I scratched it up looking for Danny in the woods."

She eased her grip, but didn't let go.

"Grim," she said, then yawned. Her breath against his neck gave chills. "I think Angel is getting her memory back."

Carefully, Grim turned onto his side to face her. "What happened to her tonight?"

"I think she's getting her memory back. I guess the shock of it was too much for her."

She didn't elaborate, and Grim did not press her. He drifted again, feeling the heat of Michele's body close to his; feeling her heart beating fast against him. Knowing he was courting trouble, but loving the feeling too much.

"She woke up a little bit ago." Michele said, again bringing him from the brink of sleep. "She looked at me and said 'I remember you now.' Then she went back to sleep."

Grim waited, then said, "Was that all?"

But Michele didn't answer. Her eyes had slipped shut, her grip on him relaxed.

Grim eased himself from her grasp and left her to sleep.

There were half a dozen unoccupied rooms upstairs, but none with beds—one was used for storage and the rest simply stood empty—so Grim went downstairs to the couch, and at last fell into an uninterrupted sleep.

First he dreamed of Michele, of being back in his bed with her, not worrying about Clara, Danny, or even Angel walking in on them. In his dream they were alone.

Then he dreamt of other things. Other times, other places; monsters long gone and a filthy city of green.

*   *   *

Mom?

Clara had lived this day once and remembered it well, even though it was most of a lifetime in her past.

She was seventeen, having just awakened from a nightmare in which she was old, in pain, dying. The bees again, she'd dreamed of them often enough since the day they nearly stung her to death in the back yard.

The sound that had awaken her; a brief scream, and the sound of something heavy falling down stairs. Then silence.

Mom? Are you all right?

She rose from her bed, pulled an old robe around her, and paused on her way out of her room as she caught her reflection in the vanity mirror.

Oh dear, I was beautiful once, wasn't I?

But she didn't stare for long. Something deadly about this day, she remembered. Something bad.

Mom?

Made her way down the hall.

She'd hated this place when they first moved here, but now that it had electricity and running water, it was nice. That great big old house, once a famous old west hotel, and only the two of them. It was like living in a palace.

She stopped at the top of the staircase, stared down at the landing halfway to the main floor, frozen.

Mom!

She lay on her side, back twisted in an unnatural way, neck kinked too sharply to the side. One leg twitched, kicking a slipper from her foot onto the hard wood floor of the landing. Her eyes were open, one staring straight down the length of her long nose, the other turned toward Clara, wide in terminal surprise.

Her dress, a long one piece that made her look much fatter than she really was, rippled, as if stirred by some inner wind.

Hey lady!

The voice was familiar. At first she thought it was Grim, but when he stepped up to the landing from below she recognized him. It looked like Grim, spoke like Grim, even moved like Grim, but it was not. The eyes gave him away.

Small, cold eyes. Eyes full of stupid, cruel curiosity.

She's still moving, Clara. Don't you see her moving? He pushed her mother's body with a foot, rolling her onto her back. There was blood pooled where she had landed. Just a little.   More ran from her nose and the corner of her mouth, streaking her pale, doughy face.

Her leg twitched again, her arm flopped against the floor like a fish. Her dress rippled like a tan, cotton tide.

Then she sighed. A crimson bubble popped from her lips and splattered her cheeks.

Momma, no!

Clara wanted to run down those traitor stairs, to help her momma, if she could, but she couldn't move. She was afraid of the boy who looked like Grim but was not.

He laughed, gave her mom's body another nudge with his foot.

I'm pretty sure she's a goner, lady. He knelt down beside her, hand reaching behind him, into his back pocket. The switchblade came out. *I wonder what's under there, making her move around like that?*

That little bastard, that ungrateful little monster with his switchblade.

Clara thought of the woman he'd cut with that knife, the one in Lewiston who he'd robbed, raped, and cut until she died.

Her first boy, the one who'd broken her heart.

Galen, don't!

But he did.

The blade parted cloth with dreamy ease, and her mother's body seemed to deflate, sinking into itself like a ball with the air let out.

No blood behind the parting veil of tan cotton, no cooling rolls of flesh.

An angry buzzing, an almost electric sound, and the yellow/black cloud…

*   *   *

Michele woke up when Grim left. She wanted to tell him no, to come back, but she drifted again before the words formed.

But in her dream he did come back, stood inside the

open door and watched her, arms crossed, head tilted to the side.

I want you, he said. *I want you so fucking bad.*

Then come and get me, she said, shocked by her boldness. She pulled the sheets off, and was not surprised to feel the stirring of a warm breeze against naked skin.

That was the way of dreams.

How the door closed on its own behind him as he entered.

How a sudden shift of perspective, transported them to her room. Her bed.

He approached, shedding clothes, his eyes locked onto her with a hunger that was a little scary. Exciting.

The sweet madness of dreams.

She watched from between parted knees as he climbed onto the end of her bed, climbed slowly over her, like a prowling tomcat, lingering, exploring her silk topography with his fingers, his tongue.

Knowing it was only a dream, though his touch, and the deep burning it caused inside her, seemed real enough. Not fearing what would come next because it was a dream. Willing to let him do what they both wanted, knowing she would awake afterward, still a virgin.

He slid over her, and she felt his heat trying to push inside her.

And with a sigh, he was gone, and she was alone.

In the dark.

Just another shadow, howling, lonely, in the dark.

* * *

They were all against him, had been from the start, because of his father. Who his father was, what he'd become, and what he'd done. They'd killed his father, and now they were out to get him, too.

Danny sat on the edge of the bed in his mountain cabin loft, hearing the sirens grow louder. Checking the loads in his revolver. He wanted to be ready for them.

Steven Gentry's voice cackled through on his radio downstairs.

You hid in the outhouse like a sissy little girl when they came up here for your poppa.

He laughed, that throaty booming laugh that made the spill of his belly shake over his big Mack Truck belt buckle.

They dragged you out screaming, shit all over ya. Again the laughter.

Danny stood, walked to the edge of the loft, took bead on the two-way, sent it to radio hell.

From the shattered box, twist of wires and shattered circuit boards, blood began to run.

They're gonna sink you this time, Danny-boy.

Not Steven Gentry.

It was his father.

They won't sink me, Danny said, flipping the revolver's chamber open, holding the live round in with his thumb while he dumped the spent shell. He refilled the empty chamber, closed it.

The sirens were closer now. Not here yet, but close. He'd make a good target standing up there. A damn good target.

He took the ladder down, keeping the revolver in his right hand, finger on the trigger.

He kicked the door open, leaned against the jam, waited.

Over the sounds of slowly approaching sirens, the high whine of a motorbike.

Grim popped into view from between the two mammoth Douglas Firs that framed the world beyond his dirt and rock driveway. He held the bike steady with one hand, leveled the other at Danny.

Grim, stop!

Grim's first shot took splinters from the planks on his left, the second from his right.

Behind Grim, his old Jeep appeared.

Clara was behind the wheel. The flashers painted her face red, blue, red again.

They're all against you.

Danny spun, saw a crouched, naked form standing where he had only moments before, and put a bullet in.

She fell, the girl from the woods, but it was Angel who landed. Angel in one of the new nightshirts Clara bought her, a bloom of red spreading from her stomach.

It spread, burned across her chest like fire...

Became the burning light of a new dawn.

*   *   *

The Rag Man was dead.

You're dead, Grim screamed. *You can't come back.*

But he was back. The Rag Man, king of Green City, stalked him down main street Clearwater, the bloody knife that Grim had put in his back clenched in his fist. He wore the same piss and wine-stained pants, the same oversized shirt. Under the fall of oily, unkempt hair was Steven Gentry's face.

Bodies lay in the street behind him. Clara, Danny, Clay among them.

The Rag Man, Steven Gentry, stirring the air between them with the blade of his knife.

You killed me once, boy, but you'll never be rid of me.

Grim, take it.

Angel was there, standing beside him. There, but not there. Transparent, like something in his mind. She held Danny's revolver out to him.

You have to kill him again, Grim. He's going to get me.

Grim reached out to her, his hand passing though her like smoke. He took the gun from her. That, at least, was real enough.

And, as he pulled it from her grasp, she faded like a mirage.

But her voice urged him on, spoke to him from somewhere deep inside. Whispering.

Do it now, Grim.

Grim faced forward again, leveled the revolver, pulled

the trigger.

Lightning shot from the barrel, the smell of electricity and fried flesh, and the boom of thunder shook him awake.

Chapter 18

Grim opened his eyes, the sound of thunder still in his ears. The answering echo chased away the fragmented images of his dream. Another bad one, but he was getting used to them. He'd been having a lot of them lately.

Must be the heat, he thought.

He heard the whistle of percolating coffee in the kitchen, heard footsteps, and rose to investigate. His back seemed to have lines of fire across it, and the bandages felt crusty. He'd have to change them before the girls woke up.

Inside the kitchen, Danny stood, half asleep it seemed, over the percolating coffee.

"Morning, Danny."

Danny turned, startled, and nodded. The morning stubble on his face added years, and the shadows of the long night before darkened the flesh beneath his eyes. "Why'd you sleep on the couch?"

"I let 'Chele use my room."

Danny's eyebrows lifted.

"I was being a gentleman," Grim said. "Don't give me that look."

Danny managed a tired little laugh, an old man's cackle. "Didn't mean to give you the look, bro. I'm impressed; it's hard to be a gentleman when a pretty girl looks at you like Michele does." Danny killed the gas jet underneath the coffee and searched the shelves for cups.

"That obvious?" Grim asked.

"Yep," Danny said. "Tell you the truth, I'm surprised Clara let Michele stay over." He winked at Grim. "Probably thinks you're too afraid of getting into trouble with her to try anything funny."

"She's gonna be pissed about 'Chele sleeping in my room whether I was there or not."

Danny set a cup in front of Grim—his coffee was much stronger than Clara's, just smelling it seemed to start the caffeine buzz—and slapped him on the shoulder, then sat in the opposing chair at the table. "Don't sweat it. I'll cover for you, tell her it was my idea."

"Thanks," Grim said. "I'm already in trouble over not minding her last night."

"Last night," Danny said. "I'm not sure if I believe what I saw out there."

"It wasn't an animal," Grim said. "I know that much."

Danny looked at him, said nothing.

"Was it..." Grim didn't finish. Didn't need to.

Danny shook his head. "I don't know."

"It sounded like her. She whispered in my ear."

"What did she say?"

"My name."

Danny turned his face toward the clock hanging over the kitchen entrance, and Grim followed his gaze. It was early, not quite six in the morning yet.

Grim yawned. "No wonder I'm about to pass out again." He tested his coffee, found it exquisite, and drank.

"Feel like going for a ride?"

"Sure," Grim said, stifling another yawn. "Why not?"

*   *   *

Michele heard the crunch of gravel under tires through the open window and rose in time to see Danny's car driving away from town. She saw the back of Grim's head through the dusty rear windshield, and cursed. She'd hoped to spend some time with him this morning before going home to wait for her mom.

"Why does he always run off?"

She decided to check on Angel.

Angel's bedroom door was open. She was not in her room.

"Angel?" Michele kept her voice down, not wanting to wake Clara if she were still sleeping.

"In here." From down the hall, the room opposite of Clara's.

Michele found the door to the room open. It was one of the unoccupied rooms, unoccupied but not empty. It held perhaps a hundred dusty cardboard boxes, stacked against the walls, on the seats of old chairs, atop and beneath an old folding table.

An old woman's whole life, memories and mementos, packed away, to be forgotten, perhaps.

Angel stood in her nightgown, framed by the morning light streaming through the open curtains of the single window overlooking the front yard.

"Where are they going?" she asked.

"Don't know," Michele said. "I'm glad you're awake. I didn't feel comfortable alone in here."

Angel turned, looking more than just awake. She looked wired, intense. "I know what you mean. Strange places are like that." She closed the curtain and began to sift casually through a nearby box, examining random photos and knickknacks, then placing them back inside. "I've been awake since you left my room last night. Couldn't sleep."

Then, a red-faced apology. "Sorry about last night. That was embarrassing."

Yeah, for both of us, Michele thought.

"It's okay. Don't worry about that. It happens to all of us."

I remember you now...I remember, Michele thought, and shivered.

"Feeling better?" Michele asked.

"Yeah," Angel said. "A lot better. Then, quietly, as if not to be overheard, "I'm remembering things. From before the hospital."

"That's good," Michele said.

"It was kind of scary," Angel said. "I remembered that old guy in the restaurant."

Michele jumped, as if someone had just laid a cold hand on the back on her neck. Her heart fluttered and she felt a little lightheaded. Canyon Jack's was a memory she wished *she* could forget.

"Thanks for saving me," Angel said.

Michele could not find the words to respond, so she faked a smile and nodded.

"I remember other things, too," Angel said. "Not everything though." She frowned.

"What do you remember?"

"I did something bad," Angel said, her voice low, conspiratorial. "I don't remember what, but it was really bad." Tears lined her pretty, wide eyes. "Please don't tell Clara," she said. "I don't want to go back to that hospital."

"I won't," Michele said, and wanting more than anything else, to be out of that creepy room with all its dusty memories, out of that conversation, she said, "Let's get dressed. I want to go to the beach today."

*   *   *

Clara lay in bed, her blanket pulled over her head despite the heat, curtains closed. The thin drapes did not filter out enough of the blasted morning light, so she'd hung her throw blanket over the curtain rod to kill the dawn's glow.

She heard the girls talking in Angel's room, wished for silence, then felt bad for the unkind thought.

It was the damn buzzing in her head. The pain, like a migraine, though she'd not had them since she was a girl herself. The kind of pain that made her wish for unconsciousness.

She closed her eyes, then opened them again when the room began to spin. It was like being drunk, she thought, though again it had been years since she'd taken any kind of alcohol.

"Dear God, please make it stop." She hadn't realized it before, but she was crying.

Giggles from the next room made her want to scream. For a time, her mind seemed to lose focus. Not sleep, but something close enough. The buzzing receded, and with it the pain, and when she was able to move without stirring the wasp's nest of noise and pain in her head, she rose and greeted the day grudgingly.

She caught the girls on the way out the door.

"Hold up," she said, moving down the steps as quickly as her stiff legs and back would allow. "I don't think I want you going out today, Angel."

Michele looked crestfallen.

Angel protested, "I feel better now. Can't I go out with Michele?"

She did look better. More awake than Clara had ever seen her; no tired, sad eyes. On the contrary, they were wide, intense.

"You do look better," Clara said.

"She's been up for a while," Michele cut in. "She's doing good this morning."

Angel nodded and smiled hopefully.

"Well, I'm not letting you girls out without breakfast. You go wait in the kitchen, Angel." She clapped her hands together—*now, now*—and Angel skipped into the kitchen with a wink back at Michele.

Michele didn't need prompting. She met Clara at the bottom of the steps and accepted Clara's standard hello hug.

"How is she coping with..." Clara let the question float.

"Good," Michele said. "It was her first."

"I never thought of that," Clara said. "I should have been prepared."

"She's your first girl," Michele said. "We take some getting used to."

Danny drove them past the spot where they'd followed Gina Fox into the woods and turned off onto the dirt road to Wallen's place. Grim figured they were doing what he suggested they do the night before. Danny was right, it wasn't his job anymore, but Clara told them about her road-side chat with Steven, and they knew he wouldn't do anything until there was more blood. Probably toss the first person who looked at him cross-eyed in jail and call it a closed case.

The place was just as he'd remembered it from the beginning of summer, as he rode beside Danny in the County's Jeep toward Canyon Jack's. The flood of reporters had taken more pictures than Clara could cram into a dozen photo albums, but didn't disturb a single cobweb.

There were more of those now, and a layer of dust one would expect on the site of a place years abandoned.

They pulled up to the front beside an old Charger sitting on blocks. Danny killed the engine, stepped out and walked back to the trunk.

Grim waited a second, feeling a little paranoid, then followed Danny's lead.

Danny opened the trunk and pulled out the cane. The head and shaft was covered with dried blood.

"Where did you find it?"

"In the ditch," Danny said. "When I went looking for her."

"I'm no expert on legal procedure," Grim said, "but shouldn't that be in an evidence locker somewhere?"

Danny turned to Grim, eyebrows raised. "Why?"

"I know Michele wasn't charged with anything, but it was still a weapon."

"Oh," Danny said, understanding dawning on his stubbled face. "This wasn't the cane Michele used on Ron Wallen." He closed the trunk and approached Wallen's porch.

Grim followed. "What?"

Danny pointed toward an old folding canvas chair sitting by the free-swinging screen door. Next to it, a half dozen shafts of wood leaned against the wall, some stripped of the bark, some not, one carved halfway down the shaft from a pine knot handle.

"There will be more inside," Danny said. "The old fart was a carving fool."

And there were more. One leaning against the wall next to a tall hand-worked coat rack, more in a braided wicker basket a few feet from a rocker facing the TV. A few hung from the walls, displayed. These were fancier than the others, one with a wolf's head for a handle, another with the head of a bear.

Grim looked at the one Danny held again. It had a snake's head.

"You knew she'd been here," he said.

Danny nodded. "We don't know if it's Gina or not, Grim, but whoever did it has been here."

That is Kelly's blood, Grim thought. *And Clint's.*

He felt a prickle of dread run up his spine and shivered. The cuts on his back protested, reminded him that he had been next on Gina's list.

"I think I'm going to be sick," Grim said, and almost was. His breakfast of black coffee surged to the top of his throat, and he had to fight it back down.

"Probably shouldn't have brought you with me," Danny said. "Just didn't want to come out alone."

"We going to report this to Steven?"

"Not yet," Danny said. "C'mon."

He led them back outside, off the porch and around the far side of Wallen's shack.

"Where would you hide?" he asked Grim.

Grim shrugged. "The tool shed. Maybe the salvage yard."

The tool shed was behind the shack. It was just as Danny had found it before, following Gina's disappearance, when they'd searched Wallen's property.

They continued on foot toward the salvage yard.

The first thing Grim noticed was the low buzz of swarming insects. It filled the hot air of the industrial graveyard. They heard them, but didn't see them yet.

Next he caught the thick carrion stench.

Danny held a hand up to his nose. "Jesus Christ, something's dead." He looked around. "Where is that noise coming from?"

Grim waved a hand in front of his nose, stirring the rotten air. He searched, spotting a small dark cloud hovering over the old boilers where Bo had nailed him with the spud gun.

"Over there," Grim said, and picked up the pace toward the boilers. "Something is beyond dead."

"Wait," Danny ran to catch up, grabbed Grim by the arm. "You've got my back," he said, then took the lead down the row of old rusted boilers.

Grim stayed close behind, plugging his nose.

Above them, the flies were getting thicker. So was the stench.

Danny tried the rusted latch on one of the boiler's doors. It moved slow, grinding, not wanting to give up its secrets. Powder rust sifted onto his hand. The hinges screamed as Danny pulled the door open.

Grim looked inside.

Nothing.

They tried the next, and found nothing.

They knew the one when they found it. The handle was a deeper red than the others, not rust but dried blood. Danny tried it, and it moved easily.

The hinges gave little protest as he swung the door open.

Danny screamed, slammed it closed. He stumbled away, collapsed to his knees and vomited bile and coffee into the dust.

"What?" Grim followed Danny, crouched beside him.

Danny shook his head, pushed Grim away.

"You okay, bro?"

"Yeah, just give me a minute."

The buzzing around them was louder now as the startled swarm reformed around the top of the boiler, pouring through the steam pipe at the top like black water.

Knowing it was a bad idea, suspecting what he would find, Grim opened the boiler door.

Time and heat had turned what was left of its flesh into a soup. Only the bones that remained were recognizable as something that might have once been human. An arm reached toward the open air, it's blackened hand beckoning to Grim, cracks in the flesh sweating puss. A skull lay on its side, its unhinged jaw grimacing at him.

"Get away from there, Grim." Danny was on his feet again, behind him, tugging at his shirt.

Grim closed his eyes and slammed the boiler door shut.

Chapter 19

Danny dropped Grim off at home and met Clara at the Post Office. "You look like hell," he said, and stepped away from the counter as she took a swat at him.

"Language," she snapped. "You really know how to make a lady feel good, Danny."

"Sorry, Mom. You got a second?"

Clara spread her arms, indicating the deserted Post Office lobby. "I think I can find a minute for you."

"I found one of Ron Wallen's canes by the road last night."

Clara looked up at him, the letters she was sorting forgotten.

"Grim and I went out to Wallen's place today."

"Did you?" Clara paused as someone passed by on the sidewalk. "Did you find her?"

"No." Danny leaned closer to her, whispering, and told Clara what he did find.

*   *   *

Don't tell anyone.

That was what Danny had said, before dropping him off.

No one. You were never there, understand? I'll take care of it. You were never there.

Michele and Angel were gone, Clara at work.

Grim passed the stairs, walked through the pantry to

the back door, stepped onto the back porch, facing the jungle. It was in need of a serious mowing. He reached up, feeling around under the eaves until he found his hidden smokes and a book of matches.

He lit a match with shaking fingers, touched the tip of his smoke to flame, and drew smoke.

Clara would kill him if she knew he'd started again, but if ever anyone had deserved a smoke, it was him. The scent of burning tobacco masked the stink that had followed him home. The smell of his friend, rotting in the belly of the old boiler.

He finished his smoke, stomping the butt out and dropping it in a tin can hidden beneath the porch.

Inside, he picked out clean clothes, took a scalding shower, hoping to burn and scrub the stink off his skin. He bagged the clothes he'd worn to the salvage yard and ran them out to the garbage can.

The girls still hadn't shown up. Probably at Michele's house. He thought about riding over there, then decided against it. Her mother might be coming home today, or might be there already.

He knew Clearwater was going to get busy again real soon, Danny would report what they'd found soon enough, and he wanted a little friendly company.

Clay.

Grim mounted the Yamaha and kicked the starter. Clay's antics got old sometimes, but when he needed a little cheering up, Clay always did the trick.

When the news got around that Danny had found what was left of Keith out at old man Wallen's salvage yard, Clay might need a little cheering up, too.

* * *

Michele's mom had left two messages on the answering machine, the first just after she left with Grim the night before.

Michele, hon. I'm sorry I didn't call earlier. I'm showing a house this evening.

The background noise did not convince Michele; a sea of white noise, made up of equal parts laughter, a rabble of competing conversations, and country music so bad it had to be live.

I'll be home around noon tomorrow and take you out for lunch. Someplace fancy if I make the sale.

"Is that where your mom works?" Angel asked.

Michele hit the erase button, hard, knocking a candle sitting beside it off the end table.

She almost snapped, was a breath away from telling Angel to mind her own fucking business, then realized there was no sarcasm intended in the question. Just curiosity.

"When she's closing a sale she works wherever the sale is." This was technically not a lie, but as far as Michele knew, this had never included bars.

The second message sent spider legs up her neck, teased her heart into a frightened flutter.

Breathing, slow and steady. Snoring in the background, and oldies music, turned low.

Michele was about to punch the delete button again when her mother's voice cut in.

Michele. Where are you, Michele?

She spoke slow, beating a nervous rhythm on the phone with her fingernails.

Michele, what the hell are you doing?

She was drunk. It was not the first time Michele had heard her that way, but it had been a long time, long before she got her license to sell real estate and started her dream job.

Then her mother slammed the phone into its cradle. The message ended with tone of a broken connection.

"You're in trouble," Angel said, her good mood spoiled.

Like hell, Michele thought. *I'm not letting her spoil my whole day.*

"Not until she gets home," she said. "Let's get changed. We're going to the beach."

*   *   *

"Dude," Clay said, poking his head out the cracked front door and squinting at the bright morning. "You're foster ma has ESP or something." He let Grim inside, then handed him his cordless phone.

When Clay's parents had first bought the cordless, Grim had tried to convince Clara to get one too. So much easier being able to talk without being chained to a wall. Clara wouldn't think of it though. She liked the antique phone they used. It was the first phone installed in the old house when she was still a young lady; the kind with coin slots that you could turn into a pay phone.

"Yeah," Grim said.

"Yeah," Clara repeated. "Is that how you answer a phone, young man?"

"Sorry," he said. "Hello, Clara." He smiled at Clay, shook his head. "Is that better?"

Clara had been grumpier than usual since Angel's arrival, and Grim had come to expect the occasional crabbing. Just consider the extra pressure she's under, be cool, and let it slide.

That, and try to make as small of a target as possible when she boils over.

"Not much," she said, but let it go at that. "Are the girls with you?"

"No." Expecting to hear about Michele spending the night in his room, but she didn't bring it up. Michele must have awakened before Clara did, which was strange. Clara was not one to sleep late on her workdays. She didn't like to be rushed in the morning. She rose early so she could meet the rest of the day at her own pace.

"You busted?" Clay asked, always one to enjoy the suffering of his friends.

Grim gave him the bird.

"Did you try Michele's house?"

"Yes. They're not there." She sounded worried, and

Grim didn't have to stretch his imagination far to understand what about. Danny had already been by to talk to her.

"We'll find them," he said.

"Yes," Clay said behind Grim. "We'll put makeup on, play mystery date and talk about boys."

The elbow Grim planted in Clay's stomach didn't stifle the laughter that followed.

"Lord, the smart mouth on that boy." Clara tisked, but Grim thought he detected a smile underneath. Not even Clara was completely immune to the power of Clay. "You tell that boy I'll have a switch handy the next time I see him."

"I'll pass that on," Grim said. "I'll pants him and hold him down for you while you spank him."

Intelligent conversation became impossible after that, as Clay lost his last thread of control and doubled over with laughter. Clara shouted a goodbye and hung up.

"Pull it together, buddy. We need to go look for Michele and Angel."

But it was a few minutes before Clay's laughter died, and Grim didn't rush him. It had been a long time since any of them had laughed like that.

It was good.

*   *   *

Steven was beyond pissed; he was livid, caught in a fit of anger that bordered on rage.

Danny leaned against the town bulletin board, watching Clearwater's new Sheriff from the civilian side of the desk, not wanting to enjoy the humiliated tirade, but enjoying it anyway.

Danny had every intention of going straight to the new Sheriff to report his find, but at the last moment before stepping through the door to the Steven's office, he'd changed his mind and walked a little farther, to the phone booth standing outside Gavin Fox's deserted repair shop. It was a childish impulse, but a strong one.

The commissioner was relieved that the missing boy had been found at last, even found dead was better than staying forever missing. He was not happy that it was a civilian, following up a report Steven had ignored, who had found him, and even less happy that it had been Danny.

Steven was in the same unsettled position Danny had been in not too long ago. Sheriff by default, not election, and until he was voted in, which Danny didn't see happening, the commissioner could remove him just as easily as he'd installed him.

Backstabbing son-of-a-bitch had a little humiliation coming his way, and despite the circumstances, Danny was happy to have been the one to provide it.

An appointment calendar flew toward him, bounced off the wall to his right and fell to the dirt-tracked floor. He hadn't kept up with the office housekeeping. Since Danny's dismissal, all the volunteer deputies had quit, so the place was a mess.

Steven was yelling at him, but Danny had been pretty much blocking it out.

"Sorry, Steven, I didn't catch that."

"I asked you if you were fucking pleased with yourself." He leaned across his desk, Danny's old desk, and poked one of his sausage fingers toward Danny's face. "Going over my head. The commissioner near chewed me a new ass." His large hand was balled up into a fist now. "You won't be happy until I'm fired."

"Not at all," Danny said, perfectly calm, though he wanted more than anything at the moment to break every finger on Steven's fat hand. "It's just that last time we tried to make a report you blew us off."

Steven's face went a deeper shade of red.

"If you're going to hit me," Danny said, "then get on with it."

Steven's mouth dropped open, an idiot's expression. His face lost a shade, returning to its usual shade of ruddy.

"If not," Danny continued, "you can get that fucking

meat-hook out of my face."

Steven backed off, dropped into his seat. Danny heard a protesting groan as Steven leaned back and expected something to snap, spilling the good Sheriff on his back. He resumed glaring at Danny, but the main tirade seemed to have blown out.

"You want me to apologize to you? Is that it?"

"No," Danny leaned forward, pushed the phone across the desk. "I want you to make a call over to the Post Office and apologize to Clara." Danny picked up the handset and thrust it toward Steven.

Steven snatched it out of his hand, looked at it with distaste.

"Once that's out of the way, I'll take you to the scene and let you do your job."

Chapter 20

Michele and Angel stopped for a rest at Clara's house on the way out of town. They agreed some cold lemonade would go down fine. The shade, and what little comfort the old swamp cooler could provide, would be even better.

Grim's bike was gone.

Michele pouted. He came home while she was gone and left again.

"Probably hanging out with Clay," Angel said.

The thermometer in the shade under the front eaves read ninety-five degrees already.

Inside, the door shut behind them, the sweat cooled instantly against her skin. Her T-shirt and shorts stuck to her swimming suit beneath.

"Mind if we hang out for a little bit?" Michele asked.

"Sure," Angel said.

Michele fetched the lemonade and ice while Angel retrieved the glasses.

They sipped at the lemonade, enjoying a break from the heat. Killing time, Michele hoping Grim would show up soon.

"Clara hit something with her car last night," Angel said abruptly. "On the way home. That's why they were gone all evening."

"Really?" Michele asked, shocked. "I wonder why Grim didn't say anything about it?"

Angel shrugged her thin shoulders. "Clara seemed pretty scared. I think it might have been a person."

Couldn't have been, Michele thought.

"You sure?"

"I think so." Then, "I wish we didn't have to walk to the river. She's still out there."

"She? The person Clara hit?"

Angel nodded. "They didn't find her. I think she's mad."

Michele remembered the figure hiding in the bushes watching her the day she'd gone looking for Grim. The feeling of being watched even after whoever it was ran away.

"Who is she?"

"I don't know," Angel said. "She was there when you saved me from that old man. I think she was anyway."

Angel went silent for a long moment. Seemed to brood. Michele was about to ask her what was wrong when she spoke again.

"I like having friends," she said. "I like having a best friend, and brothers who don't hate me." Angel smiled, a smile with more sorrow than joy, Michele thought. "I even like hanging around Clay, and he's weird."

"You act like you've never had friends before," Michele said. "Did your brother really hate you?"

"Yes, he hated me. He was afraid of me, too. He wasn't my real brother, but I still wanted him to like me."

"Were you adopted?" Michele wondered how much Angel had recovered now, and how much of it might be imagination.

"No," she said. "I was found."

"How much do you remember, Angel? You can tell me."

Angel scooted her chair closer to Michele. Her eyes, wide, intense, and unblinking, seemed not to be looking at Michele, but through her.

"Are you sure you want to know?"

"I'm your friend. Of course I want to know."

Angel smiled again, a real smile this time, not the sad attempt of earlier. But it was still not a happy smile. It was hard, manic.

"Thanks."

She leaned across the table and seized Michele's hands with her own.

There was a great snap of energy between them, not the pleasant spark she'd felt with Grim, but much more powerful. Michele tried to pull her hands away but her arms wouldn't respond.

"Thank you," Angel said again, and closed her eyes.

It was like electricity, locking their hands together, coursing from some unseen source, through Angel and into Michele. It was like being electrocuted.

It did not hurt though. It didn't hurt at all.

Like an interrupted thought, Clara's kitchen faded, and they were somewhere else.

* * *

Michele recognizes the study she sits in because Angel recognizes it—her parent's study. Not her *real* parents, she doesn't know who her real parents are. They are just the ones who found her. Her father sits in the chair behind his desk, his normally neat hair standing at odd, greasy angles.

She—Michele/Angel—is tied to the chair opposite him, only half-awake. Barely aware. They've finally found something that works on her. Something to shut her down.

Father is a screenwriter's agent, not a doctor, not a scientist or occultist. He can only guess at what is wrong with her, and he has no idea how to stop it without killing her. She knows that is what he is thinking about now—now that his wife is dead...

...She knows there is something wrong with her, and she tries her hardest to control herself...

...It had been two weeks since she'd slept, but that didn't stop her from dreaming, or having nightmares. Sometimes her nightmares hurt people...

...Her mother—not her real mother, but the mother who found her and took her home—used to be an actress. B Movies, her father said, a few horror movies, a few amazons in space science fiction movies, and one movie that was really good, but had sunk anyway. She didn't act anymore. She was too old for the parts she played and didn't have the range to act new roles, so she was a professional lounge lizard.

She was hosting a pool party the night she died.

Angel (not the name they called her, that was still lost) stood at the third floor window, watching over the audience of the famous and nameless alike. She'd given up even trying to sleep. It just wouldn't happen; she was too full of energy.

Her mother saw her watching from above, and came up to see her. Angel remembers nothing after the moment her mother walks through her bedroom door, but she knows something has happened, because she sleeps for a full day afterwards, and when she awakes, her mother is already dead...

...Her brother never liked her, seemed to sense even before she did, that something was wrong with her. It didn't matter. When her father put the plastic bag over her head, pulling it tight over her face while she struggled, bound to his office chair, her brother came into the room. Drawn by her panic, possessed by her fear, a momentary slave of her will to live...

I didn't mean to make mother die. I couldn't help it.

I'm sorry.

*   *   *

"His girlfriend wouldn't let him kill me, so they kept making me take those drugs to make me sleep and forget and drove me as far away as they could and left me here."

The story had switched from telepathic to oral, Michele could not say when, but she understood, and she believed. She was there, she was Angel, and when she awoke in Clara's kitchen, her eyes burning from dryness, as if she hadn't blinked once during, well, during whatever had just happened.

"Please don't tell anyone," Angel said. "I'm learning to control it, but if you tell people they will take me away."

"I won't," Michele said. That was a promise, as solemn a vow as she would ever make. In that brief time, Angel had shared herself, her lost and found memories, and the link she'd created between them was more than thought, more than mind, more than Synchronicity. They shared empathy, like twins sharing happiness and sorrow, and she could no more betray herself than betray Angel.

"I won't tell anyone," Michele said.

Everything that's happened this summer is because she's here, Michele thought.

"It's all my fault," Angel said, as if picking up on that thought, and for all Michele knew, she probably was. "But I'm doing better."

They were startled from the moment by the high whine of an engine outside and the sound of tires skidding in gravel.

Michele stood, shook the tingling lethargy from her body, and walked to the kitchen window. She pulled the curtain aside and saw Grim and Clay dismounting his bike.

"Grim is going to figure it out sooner or later," Michele said.

"He already has," Angel said. "Everyone knows there's something different about me. As soon as you saw me in the restaurant you knew. You just didn't know what."

There's something wrong with her, Michele remembered herself saying.

"Is that why Ron Wallen tried to kill you?"

"Don't know," Angel said, and shrugged. "But no one tried to stop him, did they?"

"No," Michele said.

"Except for you," Angel smiled. "You saved me."

But did I really, Michele wondered. *Was I a hero, or just another slave of your will?*

The front door banged open and Clay led the way inside with his typical cocky gusto.

"Look, two pretty girls in bathing suits," Clay said. "All

we need now is a wrestling ring and a fire hose."

Grim followed Clay, closed the door, and smiled when he saw Michele.

When Michele saw him, the chill that lingered in the wake of her and Angel's strange sharing faded, replaced with a tense, but comfortable heat.

*   *   *

Clara finished sorting the mail that Robert, Clearwater Post Office's part-timer, brought in from his morning route, and waited for noon to come. There was never much, especially on a Saturday. Most of Clearwater used P.O. boxes, and traffic on Saturday was light.

The only excitement that day was the unexpected call from Steven Gentry, and considering the circumstances she hadn't even been able to enjoy that. Still, she'd have to thank Danny for orchestrating it.

She watched him drive past earlier, Steven following close behind, out of town to Wallen's salvage yard.

Clara didn't even want to think about it.

She was relieved Grim and Clay had found the girls. She'd been able to relax a little more after Grim called.

A quarter till noon, the magic hour, and she swept the floor, then decided to take off a few minutes early.

Danny was waiting for her outside, standing by his car, looking tired, sick. He met her at the sidewalk and gave her a quick hug.

"Hi, Mom. Looks like Grim and the girls are home."

"Yes. He was thoughtful enough to call." She reached up and put an arm around his shoulders, led him toward the shade of the Post Office awning. "So, when does the excitement begin?"

"No excitement," Danny said. Steven wants this kept quiet for now, until the Coroner can identify the remains. It's a good call," Danny rushed to add.

Clara nodded agreement. "What about Gina?"

"We didn't find her."

"She's still out there?"

"I don't know," Danny said. "She's hurt, she might even be dead."

There it was, the last thing Clara wanted to have to consider, the very real possibility she'd avoided. "Oh, dead." She covered her face with her hands. She didn't want anyone to see her cry.

"Clara, don't cry for her."

Those words, coming from one of the kindest humans she'd ever known, startled her momentarily from her worry. "What?"

"I think Gina was the one who killed the boys. She's been hiding at Ron Wallen's."

"No," Clara said. "She couldn't have."

"Mom, she was eating road kill when you hit her. She's been living in the woods, running around naked like a wild animal."

"She lost her brother and her father in one night," she said.

"She attacked Grim last night. She's not who she used to be." A passing pickup truck honked at them. Danny didn't recognize the driver, but waved anyway. When it was gone, he turned back to Clara and whispered. "She's a killer, Mom."

Clara didn't reply. She didn't know what to say.

"Let's go, Mom," Danny said. "I want to check on the kids, and I have to make a call to California."

"About Angel?" Clara had given up hope of Danny's contact in California finding anything out about the photo he'd scanned and emailed, or the old yellow Oldsmobile that had brought Angel into their lives.

"Yeah. He called while you were out but he wouldn't talk to Grim."

"That's why you came back last night then," she said. "Are you going back soon?" She hoped not. She missed having him around. She had hardly seen him since he'd lost his job.

"No. I'm sticking around for a while."

Chapter 21

Michele left early that day to make it home ahead of her mom, and as usual when Michele wasn't around, Angel seemed to deflate. Clara still wouldn't let her out by herself, and they were all careful about where they took her in town. Steven, and some of the old-timers, held a grudge against her, more than Michele even, for old Ron Wallen.

Angel seemed to understand this, almost instinctively, as if she were used to being hated. With Michele, or Clara, she was fine, but without them she seemed to lose all interest in social interaction. She was content, it seemed, to listen to her radio, or read one of the books Michele had brought her, or to just settle back into her own deep thoughts. She did that for hours at a time if left alone. Just sat, as if sleeping with her eyes open, staring at the walls.

Grim and Clay rode to the beach to have a swim. On the way past Wallen's long driveway he kept a watch for the new Sheriff, the Coroner, or anyone else who might be investigating the scene he and Danny had discovered, but saw no one.

After swimming they had target practice with their paint ball guns. It wasn't as much fun without Kelly and Keith. Days like this Grim even missed his old enemies: Alex, Clint, Raif, and Bo. They were assholes, but they played a good game. They kept the days from getting boring, anyway. Their gaming days were over, Grim knew that, and without the war game to vent their mutual animosity, any dealings he had with them would end with the fist.

For Clara's sake, he avoided that, and made a conscious effort to steer clear of Alex, Bo, and Raif. It wasn't hard. They pretty much kept to the south end of town, hanging out around the abandoned lot in front of Gavin's Garage and the old log yard where the locals played baseball, football, and the other games small town kids took part in to stave the boredom. Grim spent most of his time between home, Clay's house, Canyon Jack's pathetic game room, and the beach.

They had the beach to themselves most days in the early summer, when the Clearwater River was still near freezing from the mountain runoff, but as full-fledged summer arrived, the others migrated that way.

Grim and Clay weren't there long when others showed up, dropping down the embankment from the highway above, or through the concrete wash-way underneath the highway, as they had.

Most Grim recognized by face, he tended to forget names once school was over and he didn't have to deal with them daily.

A tall, gangly boy with crew cut red hair, constellations of freckles across his face, shoulders, and back, and a gimpy right leg, shook his fist in the air at Clay, pinkie and forefinger extended in a *hang loose* salute. "Dude. How they hanging?"

"Lean and limp," came a familiar voice from behind. Alex Cain.

Grim turned, saw Alex standing at the water's edge, filling a large rubber raft with a tire pump while Raif shoved beers from a freshly opened case into a cooler. Bo was not there, but he would be. Wherever Alex and Raif were, Bo was sure to be.

Clay raised the bird over his shoulder at them, but otherwise ignored the comment.

"Hey, Freddie," Clay said, meeting the skinny redhead's high five. Grim didn't know the kid well, only that he was one of those rare people who got along well with everyone, despite the gimpy leg, a handicap that would have condemned most kids who suffered it to a kind of social hell. "You here solo or did you drag the troll along?"

"I made her carry the chairs and blankets," Freddie said, and nodded toward the highway above. "If I have to bring her along I might as well put her to use."

Amber, Freddie's half sister, struggled down the embankment, two folding chairs under one arm, two rolled up towels under the other. Grim almost felt sorry for her, watching her almost trip, falling backward on her butt to keep from tipping forward down the embankment. Almost felt sorry for her. Shorter than Freddie but twice as thick, Amber ranked as one of Clearwater's premier bullies. She'd picked a fight with Michele earlier that summer, and if Danny hadn't been nearby to stop it, Michele would have come out of it with more than just a few lumps and bruises.

Clay laughed. "How do you get away with bossing her around like that? You know she could probably kick your ass."

"It's the power of being a big brother," Freddie said. He turned to Grim. "What about your new sister? She ever come out in public or what?"

"She gets out," Grim said.

"Saw her with Kirkwood this morning. About shit my pants," he said. "I heard your foster-mom adopted that girl Wallen tried to snuff, but I was starting to think she was one of those urban legends, or maybe that you guys kept her locked in the basement or something. Then I see her walking through town this morning."

"She's adjusting," Grim said. His tone said, *let it go.*

"Hey," Freddie said, sounding suddenly concerned. "Did you come with Kirkwood?"

"No," Grim said. He felt a pang of loss, wishing she could be here to share the sun and sand with him. Wondering what she looked like in a swim-suit, her hair falling like wet silk down her back as she dried in the sun.

"Word gets around quick enough," Clay said, putting an elbow in Grim's ribs. "Bet the whole town knows you're hot for each other by now."

"Naw," Freddie said. "I live across from her. My mom saw you over there last night, so I figured," he was cut off by Amber's whining voice.

"You gonna help me or what?" She passed him, dropping her burden in the sand, and glared at Grim and Clay as she passed on her way to the water.

Clay turned and whistled at her, drawing scattered laughter from the growing crowd on the beach.

"Tell Kirkwood to watch out," Freddie said. "Amber's looking to catch her alone some time and finish the beating she started."

"Yeah," Grim said. "Thanks for the heads-up. I'll let 'Chele know."

Freddie smiled, shrugged. "Or just make sure she carries a big stick around wherever she goes. I don't think anyone would bitch if she pulled a Killer Kirkwood on Amber." He bent over, scooped up the towels and folding chairs Amber had dropped, then limped off closer to the water. "I sure wouldn't complain."

* * *

It wasn't the revelation Danny had hoped for, but no more than he'd expected. His contact could not positively identify the family in Angel's photo; the best lead was a corpse they'd found in the Mojave Desert who resembled the father. Hard to be certain though. The heat, rot, and scavengers had done a number on the body. The man had been shot point blank in the face, so identification by dental records was out. They were finally able to identify him through a DNA test.

Cecil Bates was a talent agent and low-level player in Hollywood. He had a wife and son, also missing, but no daughter, and no missing nieces or female relatives.

The yellow Oldsmobile belonged to a retired investment banker who lived in New York and wintered in sunny California. The summer home's caretaker had reported it stolen only a few days ago.

The next step would be to try and connect, or rule out any connection, between the Oldsmobile's driver, the boy Danny had assumed was Angel's brother, and the dead man they'd found in the desert.

They would let him know.

Danny thanked the man for his time and hung up.

"What is it?" Clara had hovered close by, waiting patiently for Danny to finish on the phone and fill her in.

"Nothing solid yet," he said. "They think they found the man in that photo, dead, and they're going to DNA test the boy who left Angel at Jack's to see if he's related."

"Well, that's something. Have they found the mother yet?"

Do you really want them to, Danny thought, then felt guilty for it.

"No, but it won't matter if they do or not. They don't have a daughter."

Clara pounded the table, shaking coffee out of her tin mug. She'd been on edge since returning home, tired, frustrated.

"Is that all they can do?" she said.

Danny nodded. "Sorry. They've looked. They can't find her face or fingerprints in any state databases. And without something to compare it to, a DNA test is useless."

"There's got to be something more, damn it," Clara said.

Danny rested his hands on her shoulders and she almost jumped from her chair. The muscles were knotted, tight.

For a time, neither spoke. Danny worked the muscles in her neck and shoulders, trying to massage some of her stress away, and she seemed content to let him.

"Who is she?" Clara said, her temper under control again.

"I don't know, Ma."

Clara surprised Danny again, this time with a laugh.

"Yes, I suppose she is that." She pushed his hands from her neck and rose from the table, turned to face Danny with the same smile she'd always had for him, her *you're a good boy, Danny* smile. "She's my enigma."

* * *

She'd done it again, and this time it was not some little shit-eating dog.

The night she'd killed Mr. Spritzer, that dimwit waitress's dog, was like a waking nightmare. Aware of what she was doing even while she did it; aware of what she meant to do when she caught the little bastard wandering the streets that night, thinking Mr. Spritzer had it coming for all the dumps it had taken in her yard, thinking Darla should know better than to let it wander free to foul her property.

She knew what she meant to do as she carried it, one hand closed over it's throat, tight enough so it could breathe but not bark, and the other hand clamped down over its snapping little mouth so it couldn't bite. She knew what she was looking for when she walked to Robert's house; to the car he used to deliver the mail. The plan had come to her whole, like a present dropped from the sky. Robert's car was unlocked. In the back seat she found half a dozen burlap bags with USPS stenciled on them in bold black letters.

She tied his mouth shut with a length of the drawstring, dropped him inside.

That fucking little dog would never shit in her yard again.

But more important was her special delivery to Clara, and her juvenile delinquent bastard, Grim. For daring to put a hand on her daughter.

But it was like a dream, a dream that you love because it allows you the pleasure of rage—a dream you hate because of the guilt that follows.

She'd been having those dreams since the night at Canyon Jack's, when Wallen had tried to kill that little freak of a girl.

It had been a dream up until the end, the final swing of the mailbag against the light pole, the final crunch of tiny bones.

It was the blood that woke her, the blood, splattered on her arms, face, the blood under her shoes, which made it real.

She'd done it again, and this time it was not some little rat-bastard of a dog. This time it was a man.

Like the best kind of dream it began with her in full control, the man beneath her in bondage. A slave to her whim. He was a willing prisoner, like the rest she went home with, crucified to his bed by silk and nylon, enjoying the pleasure she gave as she rode him, loving the pain she carved into his chest with her fingernails just as much.

An ugly man, and ugly was how she liked them. Ugly men were much more willing, much more open.

Again it was the blood, running in thin streams down his chest, onto his sheets, drying under her fingernails. She licked it from his chest, and it tasted like a dream. A powerful dream. And when she looked at him again, the ugly face of the man she'd picked up at another ugly country bar was gone. The handsome, grinning face of her ex-husband looked up at her.

And when she woke from that power dream, he was dead, pushed past the line of erotic asphyxiation. The ultimate stiffy.

She released the cord around his neck and his last trapped breath gushed out as the atom bomb of orgasms melted her mind and stiffened her body.

She didn't try to hide her crime. When she awoke the next morning she showered, ate, and decided it was time to return to Clearwater.

She had business at home to take care of.

She had left a clear warning for Clara and Grim, and they had ignored it. Worse than that. Thrown it back in her face. Mrs. Ipstien, God love that stupid bitch, had been good enough to check up on her Michele while she was away, and had seen her with Grim.

* * *

Michele heard her mother's car pull into the driveway and braced herself for the trouble she knew she was in. The TV was tuned to some daytime melodrama; white noise. An open book lay on her lap. When her mother's footsteps slammed the porch, she raised it to her face, pretending to read. Hoping that maybe, just maybe, whatever had put her mother in the foul mood that she'd detected on the answering machine, had smoothed itself out. Hoping, for once, that her mother would walk by and ignore her.

Her mother came inside, slamming the door against the invading heat. "Michele, where were you last night?"

Michele had spent hours pondering her comeback to that question, but unable to think of a bulletproof lie, settled on something close to the truth.

She lowered the book and put on an expression she hoped was convincingly pouty. "Angel had a birthday party for me yesterday, since you didn't come home, and I spent the night at her house."

Birthday was the magic word, the silver bullet that seemed to kill her mother's anger, or at least wound it and drive it back.

"Birthday?" Her mother's mouth hung open, her cheeks burned red. "Oh, Jesus, Michele. I'm sorry. I forgot." She dropped her briefcase next to the couch and sat beside Michele, who turned away and raised the book again, pretending to read.

"Michele, honey, I *am* sorry. It's just that work has been crazy. You know that." She grabbed Michele's shoulder. "Baby, look at me."

Dead kittens — Old Yeller — Romeo and Juliet — your mother forgetting your birthday, Michele thought. *Think sad.* She squeezed her eyes shut, willing tears to come, just enough moisture to be convincing. They came, just a few, and she lowered the book, turned to face her mother. It was enough. Whatever anger might have been left was gone.

"I'm sorry," her mother said again, and pulled her into a hug, which Michele accepted greedily. Her mother was not an affectionate woman. Hugs, and words like *I love you*, were not the normal order for her. "I'll make it up to you today. I promise."

"Okay," Michele said. Holding on just a little longer, giving a final, strong squeeze, before letting her mother draw back.

"Let's start with a late lunch," she said. "Your choice. Then I'll take you shopping wherever you want."

Sweet, Michele thought. From being in trouble to being taken out and spoiled with a few well-placed words and well-timed tears. For a moment Michele felt guilty, and a little startled, at how easily she'd manipulated her mother, but it passed quickly.

She did forget my birthday, after all. She owes me this one.

"Thanks, Mom." She closed her book, making a show of folding the edge of the current page down, as if she'd actually been reading, and laid it on the arm of the couch. "Can I change first?"

"That's fine," her mother said. "I need to change too."

Her mother's clothes looked crisp, fresh, as if she'd only just changed into them, but Michele didn't question it. She hurried to her room and stripped out of her sweat-stained T-shirt and shorts, replaced the bathing suit with panties and a bra.

Her mother's voice drifted to her from down the hall.

"Tell me about your new friend. Do I know Angel?"

Michele's relief faded a bit. Grim was going to come into the picture now, and her mother didn't like him.

"She's Clara Grey's new foster daughter," she said. "The girl from Jack's, remember?"

A pause at her mother's end, a long one, then, "how could I forget?"

Michele finished dressing, found her mother waiting outside her door.

"Her name is Angel, huh?"

"Yeah," Michele said, and stepped past her mother

toward the bathroom to take care of her monthly chore before they left. The cramps were still bad this morning, but the flow at least was almost finished.

Her mother followed her and waited outside the bathroom door.

"Tell me about this Angel." Her voice was picking up the tense edge again.

"She's really sweet. All I know is someone abandoned her at Jack's, and that she was drugged. She doesn't remember much from before Clara took her home."

"Hmm," her mother intoned. "When did you two start hanging out?"

"A few weeks ago." She wished her mother would drop it. She didn't want to ruin their day together. "She came over to thank me for saving her," Michele lied.

"Well I don't think I like you being around that Grim very much. I don't trust him."

That Grim? Quit being such a bitch, Michele thought.

She kept the smile in her voice though. "He's always out with his friend, Clay. I hardly ever see Grim around."

This seemed to satisfy her mother. "Okay, you just be careful around him. I don't trust him," she repeated.

Then the sound of feet moving toward the living room, and the potentially dangerous conversation was over.

Michele finished in the bathroom, trying to decide where she wanted to go for lunch. She already knew where she wanted to go afterward. The mall in Lewiston had a Bon and a Fashion Bug. She would pick out something cute to wear for her next date with Grim.

*   *   *

I hardly ever see Grim around.

Lying, sneaking little bitch! She knew damn well Grim had been there just last night.

But if this was the game Michele wanted to play, she would play it, and she would win. If she had to catch them together, that is what she would do. She'd prove to Michele that no sixteen-year-old was going to outsmart her.

And God help them when she did catch them. She was damned if she would let that little son-of-a-bitch dirty up the last pure thing she had in her life.

If he tried, he would pay.

Chapter 22

July arrived, and they met it with the wind in their faces.

The 4th had been subdued, fireworks forbidden out of fear of starting a wildfire. Her time with Grim kept it from being a disappointment.

"Not too fast," Michele yelled, then gasped, hugging him a little tighter as the Yamaha left the pavement, bouncing over the washboard shoulder before dropping into the dry bed of Canyon Creek. They caught air for a few seconds, and she screamed when they hit bottom.

"Slow down," she yelled, and then laughed.

"Fine," Grim said with mock annoyance, and cut their speed in half before bouncing over the concrete lip into the wash way under the highway. Halfway through he goosed the accelerator, and Michele squealed in surprise.

"You're going to get it," she said.

"As long as you're the one who gives it to me," Grim said.

She loosened her stranglehold on him long enough to slap his shoulder.

Grim slowed the Yamaha to granny speed as the river end of the tunnel approached. There were always people at the beach these days, and he didn't want to run down anyone who might be getting ready to use the passage back toward town.

They came out into the sun, horizon to horizon blue sky, and the stares of those already at the beach.

He parked in the bull rock next to the culvert's mouth (Danny always warned him that driving in sand was rough on motorbikes) and helped Michele down.

Clay would already be here, somewhere, and Angel would arrive soon enough with Danny, their unofficial escort.

There'd been no further sign of Gina in or around Clearwater, no more missing kids, no sightings, but Clara would not hear of them leaving town on foot. Especially Angel.

Clara had grown almost obsessive about her, not letting her out of the house unless she, Michele, or both, accompanied her. Grim was not in that trusted circle for some reason. Chalk it up to a nervous foster mom's fear of sibling rivalry, maybe. Grim didn't think that was it, or at least not all of it. For some reason, especially where Angel was concerned, Clara had lost her trust in him.

On one hand that hurt, the new gulf between him and the woman who had saved him. On the other, Clara's attachment to Angel left him with longer reigns. More freedom, and more time to spend with Michele.

And that made up for it.

For everyone else in Clearwater, the tension had eased. Those who had cars drove to the beach, parking in front of Jack's, and crossing the road on foot. There were a few bicycles and motorbikes, but most simply walked to the beach without concern.

As far as Grim knew, no one besides them even knew the remains had been found.

They'd put a lid on that grisly find before anything got out. According to Danny, Steven had parked across the driveway, just out of sight of the main road, blocking it while the Coroner did that day's dirty work. The cane Danny found was in storage, in the downstairs broom closet/evidence room, alongside the cane Michele had used earlier that summer.

"Race you to the water," Michele said, and took off through the sand ahead of Grim.

He gave a half-hearted chase, not wanting to catch up right away, enjoying the view from behind, the way Michele's body looked in the two-piece she'd got for her birthday. She stopped at the edge of the water and waited for him to catch up.

If Michele noticed the way the others moved away from her, staring back over their shoulders with superior looks, whispering into cupped ears, she didn't let on.

If I hear one more person call her Killer Kirkwood I'm going to fucking kill them.

"Looking angry," Michele teased. "You gonna pout because you lost to a girl?" She winked at him. Finally, unwilling to accept the glares in good humor any longer, she turned toward the nearest clustering of girls. Girls she'd played softball with only a few months ago. Girls who'd been her friend before she dared to do what no one else at Canyon Jack's had done that night.

There were many things Grim liked about small town life, but the clannish mentality bordering on xenophobia was not one. Maybe it was better in their minds to spare a mean old drunk bent on violence, because he was *town*, than to save a helpless stranger.

That was probably oversimplification, but that was how it looked to Grim. He supposed he would never be sure. He was not town. He'd always be an outsider, even if he lived a long life in Clearwater and died there, he'd always be that big city runaway Danny Grey had caught eating out of Canyon Jack's trash bin.

"Hey, asshole," Clay called. He stood next to a girl in Michele's class. Dana Brown; her father was a mechanic down-river in Lewiston, her mother an orderly at State Hospital North in Orofino. A friend of the girl Michele had beat up following her beating at Amber's ham hawk fists. Clay took her by the arm and led her toward Grim and Michele. "I scored a couple of tubes. Wanna go floating?"

Grim scanned the water; tubes of all sizes, from garden variety truck tires, to monster tubes salvaged from log yard equipment and patched in a hundred places, Styrofoam coolers dragging behind by lengths of rope, drifted like flotsam. A few nicer rafts mixed with their poor junkyard cousins. Alex Cain and his friends paddled toward the diving rock at the other side of the river in theirs.

"Sounds like fun," Grim said, spotting two of the log yard monsters stacked next to a cooler at the far end of the beach.

"We should wait for Angel," Michele said.

"We didn't invite you," Dana said.

Michele said nothing, just stared at her. Dana glared back. Clay stood, gaping, an *oh shit, didn't see that coming* expression smeared on his face. "Whoa, what's that about, babe?"

Dana didn't answer. She did an about-face and headed back in the direction they'd come. "I'm gonna have a soda. Meet you over there."

"Sorry, Clay," Grim said. "I won't go where 'Chele's not welcome."

Michele took Grim's arm, tugged at it. "I'm not going where I'm not wanted."

"I'm inviting you, Michele. You don't need her permission."

"Is she going to be like that all day?" Grim asked.

"Like what?" Clay said, tilting his chin up and narrowing his eyes.

Do I really have to say it, Grim thought.

A sudden hush fell over the beach, and for a second Grim thought everyone was bracing for a throw-down. Him and Clay. He hoped they were mistaken. The thought of fighting Clay made him sick.

Then, a lone voice in the crowd. "Oh my God. It's her!"

All eyes were facing the trail from the edge of the highway. More voices joined, a chorus of disbelief.

It's her.

You're shittin' me. I heard they locked that girl away up-river.

She's living with Grim. Miss Grey is adopting her.

Faces turned toward Grim, naked speculation, suggesting a barrage of questions to come. That night at Canyon Jack's had been the most exciting and gruesome thing to happen in this small town, and the girl at the center of it seemed to have attained legend status. There had been a lot of speculation, of course, and though it was common knowledge Clara had taken her in, now that they could see her, standing on the roadside with Danny, it was real.

Grim felt Michele's hand tighten around his arm, her fingernails digging into flesh. Grim felt a blush of shame, realizing he had been doing the same thing. Just standing there, staring, useless.

Michele dropped his arm and made her way through the parting crowd, up the trail, glaring back over her shoulder.

Finally, the gawking faces turned away, people picking up the loose ends of abruptly ended conversations. The freak show was over.

"Shit," Clay said, amused. "You guys sure know how to kill a party."

"That your new girlfriend?" Grim asked, nodding toward Dana.

"Wouldn't go that far," Clay said, "but she sure is fun to squeeze." He leered back over his shoulder. "Not bad to look at either."

"Think you can tone her down around 'Chele?"

"I'll talk to her," Clay assured him with an unconvincing grin.

"Buddy," Grim said. "I'm happy you have someone to fondle, if it means you'll keep your hands off me now." He dodged a playful punch Clay launched at his shoulder. "But those two are going to get into it if she mouths off to 'Chele again."

"I know," Clay said, grinning even wider than before. "All we need now is a kiddy pool full of pudding and a vidcam, so we can cherish the moment forever."

"Clay, you really are a shit sometimes." But he was grinning now, too.

"Thanks," Clay said. "I do my solid best."

* * *

Michele met Angel coming down and walked with her so she wouldn't be alone. Everyone's attention seemed to refocus on the business of fun in the sun, but she saw some sneaking quick looks as they descended.

Angel looked more than nervous, not used to crowds Michele assumed. This was her first public appearance in Clearwater since Canyon Jack's.

Had Clara really managed to keep her shut in the whole summer? Yes, Michele realized. Other than a few visits to her house while her mother was at work, and the occasional trip to Lewiston with Clara, Angel had not been out of that old house.

"Danny, you mind if she goes tubing with us?" Michele said.

Danny carried a fishing rod and tackle box, scanned down river for a quiet spot to set up and fish while the kids played.

"You know how to swim, Angel?" he said, turning back to them.

Angel shrugged. "Can't remember."

"I can swim," Michele said.

"Okay," Danny said. "Be careful." He pointed down river. "I'll be around the corner if you need anything."

Faces turned toward Angel as they made their way toward Grim and Clay. "Ignore them," Michele said.

"Hey," came a voice from the crowd. Amusement, cruel glee. A here comes trouble voice. "It's Killer Kirkwood and Freakshow! Did I tell you two you could come to my beach?"

Scattered laughter, and all eyes were on them again.

Angel turned to find the speaker, and Michele tugged on her arm. "Keep walking," she whispered.

But Amber was not going to let them go that easy.

"Hey, bitch, I asked you a question." Amber ran through the crowd and stopped in their path.

Michele searched the shore for Danny, but he was already out of sight, and she was not going to embarrass herself by calling for help. She'd take more lumps before she gave Amber the pleasure of hearing her call for help.

"Would you quit being such a freak," her brother, Freddie, said, and limped toward them through the crowd.

Amber ignored him. "I owe you this," she said, and stepped forward.

"Hey!" Michele heard Grim shout from the other end of the beach, running. Clay was close behind.

Not close enough though.

Amber made a show of cracking her knuckles, put on a fierce grin she'd no doubt practiced in her bedroom mirror.

Michele drew back, relishing the look of surprise that replaced Amber's predatory grin, and put fist to cheek.

Gasps all around, more than a few smiling faces. One "Oh, yeah!" from just behind Michele, and Amber went down ass first in the sand.

Amber shook her head, spit blood into the sand, and looked up at Michele. "You're going to get it now," she said, and stood, keeping a wary eye on Michele.

A circle formed around them, hungry for entertainment. Michele saw Grim trying to push through.

Michele and Amber faced each other, and she knew the beating would be severe this time. That first punch had caught Amber off guard, and now she would pay Michele back for that embarrassment.

Angel stepped between them, drawing Amber's wrath to her.

"You want some too?" Amber said, motioning Angel forward.

"Angel, don't," Michele said.

But she did. She took another step forward.

Amber drew back, threw a fist at her.

Somehow it missed — had she sidestepped, dodged? — and Angel caught her arm.

Amber's rage drained from her face, her red cheeks turned pale. She seemed to shrink where she stood, and Michele realized she was falling to her knees before Angel. Her wide eyes froze on Angel's face.

Then she screamed.

* * *

Danny was working a spinner through a promising eddy when he heard the scream from the beach. He dropped his fishing rod on the stony shore, hoping a monster Rainbow or Cutthroat Trout wouldn't take the bait while he was absent and drag his rigging to Lewiston, and ran for the beach.

Most of the teenagers in Clearwater had assembled at the beach today, and a majority stood in a packed ring around...around what, Danny could not see. He didn't see Angel or Michele in the crowd, but Grim was pushing his way through, trying to get to the center.

"Hey," Danny yelled as he closed in. "Break it up. Now!"

Heads turned to mark him, then turned back to the fight.

"I said move it!" Danny grabbed shirts, arms, and pushed them aside. The rest moved aside to let him in.

The fight, if it had been much of a fight, was over. Michele stood, staring at Angel with open shock. Angel stood, rigid as a board, eyes rolled up to the whites. She had Amber Ipstien by the wrist.

Amber knelt in the sand, a thin line of blood running from the corner of her mouth. She screamed again, tried to pull away.

Angel's grip was firm; the bigger girl could not shake her off.

"Angel," Danny yelled. "Let her go."

Angel reacted to the sound of his voice, turned her head toward him but not seeing him. "He made me do it, Daddy. I didn't want to," she said. "I didn't even like it."

Freddie stood at the inner ring, his face ghost-white except for a burning in his cheeks.

"Shut up," he said, and tried to push himself backward through the crowd. Faces turned toward him, speculative expressions.

"Let go, Angel," Danny repeated. He reached for her shoulder, and stopped. He didn't want to touch her.

Michele seemed to come from her shocked trance. "Angel, let her go." She took Angel by the arm.

Angel's rigid posture relaxed. Her fingers uncurled, releasing Amber's arm. There were angry red stripes, where they had been. Danny thought they would bruise before the day was over.

"Leave Michele alone or I'll tell everyone," Angel said, then turned away from Amber.

"Break it up," Danny yelled.

And they finally did. The show was over, and everyone drifted, a few that Danny recognized as past victims of Amber's were grinning. More than a few giving Angel wary looks, giving her a wide birth as they left the scene.

"What the hell was that about?" Danny approached Amber, knelt down.

"She picked a fight," Michele said.

"She's a bully," Angel said, then yawned. Her previous, almost manic, energy was gone. She looked worn out, used up, ready to sleep.

"What did you do to her?" But Danny didn't wait for a reply. He took Amber by the arm, tried to help her to her feet.

"Don't touch me!" Amber screamed, pushed herself back through the sand to get away, and bumped into Grim.

Grim backed off a few steps, repeated Danny's question. "What'd you do to her?"

"Nothing," Angel said. "She tried to hit me."

"Grim, go get her brother," Danny said.

"He took off," Grim said. "Don't know where he is."

But there was no need. Amber stood, giving Angel a stare full of wonder, terror. "Stay away from me, freak." Then she ran, scrambling up the trail to the highway faster than they had ever seen her move. Danny cringed as she darted across the highway without looking, but there were no cars, and she disappeared from sight.

Others were leaving too, in singles, pairs, and groups.

No doubt the word on Angel would be out soon.

Grim had made his way to Michele, put his arm around her shoulder. "Did you hit her?"

Michele nodded.

"Are you guys okay?"

"Fine," Michele said. "I'm not going to let that bitch ruin my day." She left Grim's side and made her way to Clay and Dana, who stood, waiting at the water's edge.

"Bye, Danny," Angel said, and followed.

Danny shook his head, turned to Grim. "Jesus Christ, you think you guys can keep out of trouble for a while?"

"Whoa," Grim said. "We didn't start anything." He took off after Michele and Angel. "Go fish," he said. "We're cool."

Danny resisted a strong urge to take after Grim, call him on the attitude. Instead he walked back to his fishing spot, knowing he wouldn't be able to relax enough now to enjoy it.

*   *   *

Michele looked back and saw Grim running to catch up.

"What was—" he started, but Michele just shook her head.

She put an arm around Grim's waist.

"That was fucked up," Clay said, catching them half way.

"Were they supposed to let her beat them?" Grim said.

"I didn't say that," Clay said. He looked at Angel. "What the fuck did you do to her anyway?"

"I just messed with her," Angel said. "I don't like bullies."

"C'mon," Michele said. "Let's just forget about it and go floating."

Clay frowned. "Sorry," he said. "Dana threw a fit when you two ganged up on her." He turned to Grim again, who stood with his arms crossed, looking more and more pissed by the second. "She says you can come along, but not them."

"*That* is fucked up," Grim said.

Clay shrugged. "They're her tubes, man. What can I do?"

"You can go," Angel said. "It's fine."

"Sure, go on. I don't care," Michele said. But she did care. She was learning to live with the scorn so many of her former peers showed her this summer, but she didn't think she could take it from Grim. She'd let him go, if he wanted to, but it would break her heart.

Grim shook his head. "Have fun man," he said. "Hope she's worth it."

"Are they?" Clay said, his face reddening to match Grim's. "Are they worth pissing off the last friend you have here?"

"Yes, they are," Grim said without hesitation, and walked away.

Chapter 23

The rest of their day was boring, lonely. After asking Danny if he could drive Angel home, he'd driven Michele back on his bike, not teasing her with his crazy driving, not enjoying riding, as he usually did. At home, Grim sat, brooding on the living room sofa and watching the television. In one of his quiet moods and wouldn't be drawn out yet. Michele understood, and didn't blame him for being upset. Being made to choose between his girlfriend and sister (kind of sister), and his best friend. Michele knew he was pissed at Clay. She hoped he wasn't pissed at her, too.

Danny arrived a few minutes behind them, dropped Angel off, and went back to the river to fish. Angel wasn't in a talking mood either. She sat in Clara's rocker and slept.

Clara was at work and wouldn't come back for a few hours.

Michele decided to go home. "Bye, Grim." She could be bored at home, and wouldn't have to feel guilty, sitting across from Grim.

"Don't go," Grim said. "Please."

She paused, the front door half-open. Already the smothering heat was invading Clara's house. "You're not talking to me, I don't think you even want to be with me right now." Michele realized she was very close to shouting, and made herself calm down. "I'm sorry about Clay," she said, "but I was there, too. How do you think I feel?"

"'Chele, I'm not mad at you," Grim said, walking to the door. He took her hands. "Please don't leave."

"I'll come back when you're in a better mood," she said, but before she could open the door again, Grim turned her around and kissed her.

When it was over Michele smiled, licked her lips. "Okay," she said. "I'll stay."

*   *   *

Grim's mood improved, and so did Michele's.

They talked about nothing for a while. Then Grim asked about Angel again.

"What did she do to Amber? I've never seen that girl back down to anyone." Grim recalled her scream. Not anger, not frustration, not pain, even though Michele had drawn blood.

Full on, ice in the blood, terror.

Michele looked over at Angel, still napping in Clara's rocker. She looked so peaceful.

"We'll talk about it tonight," Michele said. "Not now."

Then she kissed him.

And didn't stop until they heard Clara's car pull up to the house.

Grim pulled away, and Michele noticed a cold absence on her breast, under her shirt where his hand had been. She didn't remember when he'd put it there, and now that it was gone she wished she could relive the moment. No one had ever touched her there like that. If anyone had ever tried she would have decked them.

Except Grim. She liked him going there, wanted him to go back.

"Oh man," Grim said, out of breath. "That was hot."

Yes, it was, Michele agreed.

"I'm sorry, did I interrupt something?" Angel sat up in Clara's rocker, yawned and stretched, smiled at them. "You're getting along again."

"Yes," Michele said, blushed. "We made up."

The front door swung open and Clara stepped inside.

"I heard there was a fight at the beach," Clara stopped

at the threshold to the living room, her eyes falling on Michele, Grim, and Michele again. She did not look happy. "I think it's time for you to go home, Michele," she said. Her eyes were cold, her tone disapproving.

"Okay," Michele said. To Grim she whispered, "call me later. Hang up if Mom answers." She walked over to Angel, bent, gave her a hug. "I'll talk to you later, Angel."

Angel had watched the exchange between Clara and Michele, her face falling into a frown. "Does she have to go?"

"I'm afraid so, dear," Clara said. Then to Michele, "Let's go." *Clap, clap.*

"Later, 'Chele," Grim said.

"Later."

Clara waited for her outside the living room, then followed her to the front door and stopped her on the way out."

"You were always such a nice young lady," Clara said. "But now you're getting into fights all the time, and I know what you and Grim were doing, and in front of my Angel."

This was a speech, Michele realized, not a discourse. Michele knew the difference; her mother was great at speeches. She knew better than to say anything in her defense, so she crossed her arms and waited for it to end.

"As much as I hate to admit it, I know Grim will never amount to anything. It just isn't in him. He'll leave soon and drift wherever the wind blows him, and without a thought for you." Clara took Michele by the arm and led her outside, shutting the door behind them.

"I know I can't control Grim anymore. He'll do what he wants to do, but I will advise you to back off from him if you don't want to get in the kind of trouble that will follow you through the rest of your life."

Michele was stunned. The sweet, generous Clara she knew had taken a walk. She didn't like the new Clara much. She shook Clara's hand off her arm.

"Is that all? Can I go now?"

For a few seconds Clara just stared at her, eyes unblinking, as if considering whether to let her go or take her to the woodshed, as she liked to call it.

"I think you'd better stay away from Angel," Clara said. "You're a bad influence on her."

"But," Michele started, but Clara silenced her with the wave of a hand.

"You're not the good girl I thought you were, and I'm sorry for that. You'd better go now."

* * *

Grim stood at the threshold to the foyer, unable to swallow what he'd just heard. Had Clara's opinion of him changed so drastically since she took him in, or was that how she'd always felt? She heard Michele say goodbye, the door slam, and Clara's footfalls coming his way. He turned to go back to the couch, not wanting Clara to know he'd heard her, not prepared for the confrontation it would cause. He needed to think.

Angel stood behind him.

"I'm sorry," she said, as he pushed past her and took up his usual seat.

As he settled into the worn cushions, Clara appeared. She gave him a look of equal parts fear and disgust, but said nothing. He couldn't stand that look, not from her, so he turned away.

"Clara," Angel said, her tone plaintive, frightened. "What's wrong?"

"Things are changing," she said. It sounded almost random, not an answer to Angel's question, but a statement; disconnected, but not meaningless.

Let it slide, Grim willed himself, but he couldn't let it slide. Her words hurt too much. A burning behind his eyes told him he was about to cry, and he fought it. He couldn't lose control now. He couldn't remember the last time he had cried.

Grim dared to look at Clara. Her eyes had not left him, but her expression had changed. She looked confused and exhausted."I think I need a nap." She wobbled on her feet, latched onto Angel to keep from tipping over. "My head hurts so bad."

She started down the hallway, up the stairs. "Angel dear, will you come with me?"

"Sure," Angel said, and with a last, sad look back at Grim, followed Clara.

"Eugene," Clara shouted from the top of the stairs. "You've been shirking your chores, and I will not tolerate it any longer. I want the Jungle mowed and raked today. Don't bother coming back inside until it's finished."

"Yes, ma'am," Grim said.

Grim waited until he heard her bedroom door close, then went into the hallway. Still trying to wrap his mind around what had just happened. He passed the staircase to the back door, stepped out into the Jungle. He reached up into the back eaves and found his smokes. He'd done well the past few days, but needed one now.

He lit up, dropped the burnt match into his can beneath the stairs, and walked to the utility shed.

Clara acted as if she hated him. What had he done?

He finished his smoke behind the shed, next to the mostly dry bed of Canyon Creek. Only a few shallow, stagnant puddles remained. He tossed his butt into one, then opened the shed door and rolled the lawnmower out.

Clara had paid him less attention since Angel's arrival, but he didn't mind. He'd expected it, he understood that Angel needed Clara more than he did.

He unscrewed the gas cap and checked the fuel level with a dry stalk of timothy grass. Almost full. Should be enough.

The past couple of weeks though, Angel had been much better. Aware, energetic. And as she seemed to improve, Clara seemed to grow more distant. Not just sleeping late on her days off, but excusing herself from his company almost as soon as she came home. Always a headache.

Grim guided the mower to the far edge of the yard, started it, pushed slow through the tallest of the grass bordering the dry creek bed.

The sun was on its decline, but the heat was still monstrous. The kind of heat that killed old folks and people crazy enough to attempt yard work.

He pushed mindlessly, not stopping until he'd reached the halfway point. Sweat ran from his saturated hair, dripped from the end of his nose, and hissed on the mower's hot engine. He released the kill bar and the mower died with a sputter and a pop. The sun was falling behind the western, evergreen horizon, a breeze pushed past him, teasing his skin.

"Fuck it," he said, and walked to the back door, checking Clara's bedroom window to see if he was being watched. He was not. She'd hung a blanket over the window, covering the thin curtain. Probably asleep by now.

He went to the kitchen sink, turned the water on cold, stuck his head under the flow. When the sweat and lethargy was washed away he turned his mouth to the faucet and drank.

He turned the water off and dried his hair with the hand towel.

"What the hell did I do wrong?"

He decided it was time to confront Clara.

He found Angel standing at the top of the stairs, guarding her door.

"You better not go in there, she said. "Clara's sick."

"Why is she mad at me?"

"She doesn't know," Angel said, turning her eyes from Grim's face. "I'm sorry, Grim. I didn't mean to cause trouble, but I did."

"I wish you'd quit saying that," Grim said. "You didn't do anything wrong."

"Not on purpose," she said. "But I did."

Maybe it was the weirdness of the day, or maybe the sad sincerity in Angel's voice. He believed her.

"You better not wake her up now. She's in a real bad mood."

"Okay," Grim said, and left.

*   *   *

Michele opened the door and found Grim waiting, his face somber in twilight color. She poked her head outside and looked around, but saw no witnesses to his presence.

"You were supposed to call," she said. I didn't know if Mom was coming home tonight."

"Sorry," he said. "Do you want me to go?"

"No," she said, grabbed his shirt and pulled him through the door. "I want you to come inside."

Michele was afraid Grim wouldn't come after Clara's words with her, that Clara, in whatever weird state of mind had gripped her, would forbid it.

But here he was, and she had *never* been happier to see another human being.

This is not how a crush feels, she thought. *Crushes fade— only love grows like this.*

There were a hundred things she wanted to tell him that night.

About how she thought her mother was catching on to them.

About her strange vision with Angel, and how she'd gotten her memory back, but was afraid to tell anyone.

About what she thought, or felt, had happened at the beach that day.

About how she was afraid they were moving in a physical direction too fast.

Instead, three words that sounded wonderful and terrible at the same time. Three words that when spoken from the heart, could change a life for the better, or for the worse—she knew the opposite sides of that coin, had lived them through her mother's experience with her absent father.

"I love you," she said, and when he smiled in response, a great weight seemed to lift, the lead in her stomach turned to butterflies.

"I love you, too," Grim said, and his arms closed

around her.

There was no talk of her mother, or Angel, or anything else. There was nothing but the sweetness of them, together. And at the point where she knew she must stop or be changed forever, she did not.

"Is your mom coming home tonight?"

"No," she said. Her mother had not called, so she didn't know for sure, but she didn't care either. Let her mom find out. She could not stop them. She could not keep them apart.

Grim carried her to her room.

They undressed each other, slowly, savoring each moment, exploring new flesh with slow excitement. It was clumsy, but perfect in its own way.

And this time it was real.

He slid over her, and she opened to him, fearing and coveting what would come next. She felt his heat as he pushed slowly, gently inside her. The pain was brief, the pleasure beyond belief.

And with a sigh, they were one, and she felt as though she would never be alone again.

Chapter 24

She cries, and watches the blood mix with water. The colors, pink and red, are like currents of a dream, a daydream of roses in her grandmother's garden, death in a back alley.

That little bitch...

That girl knew about them, her and her brother, their secret was out now. Exposed like a raw nerve in the cold, public air.

"I didn't wanna do it." But she had. And she had liked it, in a deep down place she didn't like to think about, she had liked it, and wanted more.

Every time, he thought it was him, that he was in control, but by the time they were doing it regularly, she was big enough, strong enough, to stop him if she wanted.

But she never did.

And then they were caught, and that moment had been like dying. Every time her mother and father reminded her, with a word, a look, she died again. A little death each time.

Now everyone knew, everyone, and every time they looked at her she would die again in their eyes.

So she cried, and waited, and bled out like an animal before the feast.

Dying one last time so that she would never have to die again.

*   *   *

Clara begged him to stop, begged him on her knees, but he would not.

Grim would not stop.

The little bastard that she'd thought was Galen, her first foster son, the bad seed who had broken her heart, but was not. It was Grim, and Grim was worse, because he had fooled her for so long into thinking he was a good boy.

He knelt down over the broken, twitching body that had been Clara's mother, switchblade in hand.

I wonder what's under there, making her move around like that?

Her mother's body twitched and jittered unnaturally, something under the folds of her housedress. Trying to get out.

How 'bout we find out?

He brought the knife down, slashed across the curtain-like folds of cloth.

No, Clara screamed. She knew what would come out.

The bees.

But it was not the bees.

Hands, dainty, shapely hands, pushed their way out, bare arms, pale flesh sprinkled with freckles, and the perfect, sweet face of her Broken Angel.

She struggled and pushed herself out of the corpse, and Grim watched, a crooked leer twisting his handsome, evil face.

Come to Grim, baby. I've wanted to do this for a long time.

She came out of her mother's shell, naked as if just birthed into this world, and lay panting on the old floorboards.

No, not panting.

Crying.

I'm sorry, she said. *I didn't mean to cause trouble, but I did. It's all my fault.*

Angel!

Clara found strength where there was none before and ran down the staircase. Catching Grim's hand as he reached to unbuckle his belt, she pushed him backward, toward the edge of the landing.

Behind her, Angel screamed.

Pain erupted between Clara's ears, and as she turned to hush Angel — *It's okay, dear, I won't let him touch you!* — the high pitch turned into a drone.

Streaming from Angel's wide-open mouth, a poison cloud of black and yellow.

*   *   *

Though they slept in each other's arms, in his dream, Grim could not find her.

He ran through the nightmare boughs of Green City, and the others followed. The Rag Man chased, and the others followed in their machines. Yellow, crushing machines that wasted everything in their path.

This way, the Rag Man, yelled. *The little bastard is getting away!*

'Chele! Where are you!

One of the machines crashed through the green to his right.

Give it up, Grim. You're never going to find her. It was Clay behind the controls.

Another broke through a wall of young yews to his left, tearing them out by the roots.

You ungrateful, ungodly little son-of-a-bitch! I should have known you'd come to no good. They should have left you out here to die and saved me the heartache! Clara, piloting the second bulldozer, her great gray cloud of hair just visible over the machine's massive blade.

Above him, the whirring blades of a chopper kicked up a wind, drove Green City into a frenzy.

I hate to do this, bro, but you leave us no choice. Danny's voice from above.

And the bullets started to fly.

*   *   *

A scream in the stagnant, heat hammered night. A sound that woke neighbors from uneasy dreams and made their children cry in their sleep. A scream that sent cats into hiding and dogs howling, barking, pulling at their chains.

She'd fallen asleep on the couch watching the Late Show, wondering where Freddie had gone and when he'd come home, but not caring enough to check up on him. Thinking that Amber had been in the bath long enough, the girl was going to prune up like a raisin, but not wanting to check up on her, just in case she was doing something that might embarrass them both.

But it was well past time for them to be home, and in bed, and neither was. If they'd snuck out again she'd tan them both, by God.

She found Amber in the bathtub, laying against the porcelain in eternal sleep. Her eyes open, swollen from crying. Her arms open from wrist to elbow. The blade she'd used, lay on the edge of the tub, stained red in its complicity.

And she screamed, and screamed, and screamed.

*   *   *

Angel stood where she had when Grim left that afternoon. Alone. Clara's troubled moans could be heard from beyond the closed door to her room, but Clara was not with her. Clara was some place else. Some place not so nice.

Angel was not strictly awake, but she did not sleep. She never slept now that the drugs had played out. Her system was clean now. Her mind unfogged. Fully awake, fully aware, but out of her control.

"I'm sorry," she said.

But no one answered.

Part 4
GRIM'S RAGE

Chapter 25

Grim awoke with Michele in his arms, their naked bodies conforming to each other curve for curve. He did not want to let her go, but he had to. It was morning already, and he hadn't meant to stay this long. The barest hint of dawn showed through her curtains. If the neighbors saw him here Michele would be in trouble. It was time to go home.

Home, whatever that meant now.

He dressed quickly, but didn't wake her. She looked so peaceful.

"I love you, babe," he said, and kissed her cheek before leaving her room.

The rest of the house was forbidding without her presence, so he rushed through, cracked the front door open, and froze.

Steven's Jeep was parked across the road at the Ipstien's, an ambulance parked idle nearby.

In the driveway, Evelyn Kirkwood's car.

"She killed herself last night," Michele's mother said. "I'm surprised you didn't hear Mrs. Ipstien when she found Amber."

Grim turned, dread slowing his reflexes, and faced Michele's mother.

"I was hoping Sheriff Gentry would leave before you woke up." She held up a blade, long, serrated, wicked-looking in her clenched fist. "I was going to cut it off while you slept," she said.

Grim believed her.

His mouth had gone dry, his throat frozen. He swallowed hard, licked his lips. "Mrs. Kirkwood," he said, but she cut him off with a wave of the knife.

"Don't you dare speak to me, you little motherfucker. If the Sheriff wasn't out there you'd already be dead." She turned her hateful, narrowed eyes toward the hallway, Michele's room. "As for my little tart, she won't see the light of day for a very long time. She'll wish she was an orphan," she turned back to Grim, pointed at him with the blade of her knife, "like you, by the time I let her out."

"Please, Mrs. Kirk—"

"Get out," she said. "You're never to see Michele again, and if you try, I *will* kill you."

*   *   *

Grim drove home, crept upstairs. He passed Angel's open door, saw her standing at her window. Her bed looked untouched since Clara had last made it.

"Good morning, Grim," she said without turning.

He didn't feel like talking. He went to his room, stripped down to his shorts, and went to bed.

He dreamed of the Rag Man, and all the people here who had once been his friends and family.

*   *   *

"Angel, where are you?" It was Clara's voice, shocked, frightened.

Grim rolled onto his back, opened his eyes. Michele stood in front of his bed, hands crossed at her belly. She was like a vision at the center of a kaleidoscope, the one clear image in a room of foggy shapes and twirling colors.

He sat up. "'Chele?"

"Grim?" A question. "Where am I? I can't see."

Grim reached out to her, took her hands in his. "It's okay," he said. "You're with me."

She'd been staring at nothing, but turned at the sound of his voice. Her eyes were rolled up, only a sliver of their pretty blue showing.

"No I'm not," she said, and let out a sob. "I'm lost, Grim. I'm lost and I can't see."

The room around her cleared, and Grim felt a shock of panic when he saw Angel's face, not Michele's, looking back at him.

"Let go of her!" Clara entered his room behind Angel and pulled her away. "Don't you ever touch her again!"

Then they were gone, and Grim was alone, confused, exhausted.

He put a pillow over his face to block out the sun, and cried into it until he slept again.

* * *

Steven never was much with the ladies. He'd always been able to satisfy the ones he'd had, but the prime ones had never given him much of a look. He knew he wasn't much to look at. A little on the heavy side. Lookers like Evelyn didn't go for his type of man.

Which was why he was surprised when she'd appeared outside her front door, while he stood next to his Jeep. She was dressed in her night clothes but not looking like she'd slept. She looked like she'd primped and made up all morning. Making herself look extra hot for someone.

"Sheriff," she yelled.

Steven blushed. She'd caught him looking.

"Pardon," he said, and turned to make as dignified of an exit from the scene as he could.

"No, come here," she said.

He turned, poked a finger at his chest, making sure he was the one she wanted.

She smiled. Nodded. Beckoned again.

* * *

Michele lay on her bed, too tired to continue her struggle. The nylon ropes securing her to the bedposts gave too little slack, and the knots only tightened when she struggled. She listened to her mother and that pig, Steven Gentry, in the next room, horrified, disgusted.

Unable to push a scream past the gag in her mouth, she gave up, and felt the silent tears of shame and fear soak into the dark cloth that stole her sight.

*   *   *

"You're telling me Eugene Grim was here last night?" Steven was thrilled to hear this, though he tried not to let it show. The girl next door was an obvious suicide, but even if he could conjure up a reasonable suspicion that Clara's little bastard was involved…

"Yes," Evelyn said. "He took advantage of my Michele while I was away at work." She leaned back in her seat across from him, uncrossed her legs, made a show of stretching. "I am very unhappy about it, I'm sure you can understand."

Steven hoped he could keep the conversation going just a while longer. If he had to stand up now to leave, he was likely to offend her mightily.

"Yes, ma'am, I can understand that."

"Michele's quite upset, too," she said. "Seems once he'd done what he wanted, she was no longer quite as interesting to him. She was crying when I found her."

Steven was silent for a moment, tuned for the sound of weeping, but he didn't hear it. "If I might ask, where is your daughter now?"

"Somewhere where Grim can't bother her," she said without elaboration.

"I'd like to question her, if I could. It would be helpful to know when he was here and when he left."

"I'm sure that won't be necessary," Evelyn said. "I bet

you could get that information from Mr. Grim."

"I'll bring him in for questioning. You can count on that," Steven said. Was it his imagination, or was her nightdress riding a little higher than a few minutes ago. He could see her knees now, and the shadows of thigh beyond. Was she coming on to him?

"The mornings are getting so hot," she said, as if speaking to herself. She fanned at her throat with one hand, tugged at the folds of her blouse with the other, pulling loose, inviting in the air.

Her breasts were large, firm, barely contained by the pink frill of her bra.

"Of course, knowing Eugene Grim, he won't want to cooperate. He might even fight you." She smiled. "It would be good riddance if you were to shoot him while defending yourself. No one would blame you." Another tug at her blouse. He could see the darkness of a nipple though the thin pink of her bra. "A lot of folks here would be grateful to be rid of him."

Steven gulped, forced his eyes back to hers. "Ma'am, I'm beginning to get the notion a few might even encourage it."

"Is that the notion you're getting, Sheriff?" She pulled the rope of her nightdress loose with a thumb, let it slide off her shoulders. "I can't fool you can I, Sheriff?"

*   *   *

Grim slept away most of the day, and awoke, feeling sick, to pounding on the front door.

He peeked through his curtain, hoping to see Michele.

Steven's Jeep sat in the driveway, where Clara's had been the night before. Grim let the curtain close and lay back down.

The pounding continued for a time, then stopped, and Grim heard Steven's Jeep pull out.

He dressed, checked Angel's room. Empty. Clara's was empty too. That was fine. He wasn't sure if he was up to seeing Clara's face now.

He called Michele's house, ready to hang up if her mother answered. No one did. He hung up after a dozen or more rings.

He should finish mowing the Jungle before Clara came home. Maybe she'd be in a better mood if she saw he'd done as she asked.

He took a shower, mourning as the hot water washed Michele's scent away. Dressed, called Michele's house again. Nothing.

There was enough gas in the mower's tank to finish, and he did, drenched in sweat and needing another shower by the time he was done. He put the mower back in the shed, fetched the rake and a fistful of lawn bags, and began raking the grass shavings into piles.

"Grim? You back here?" Clay, coming around the side of the house.

Grim ignored him and kept raking.

"Grim," walking up behind him now.

"What do you want?"

"Did you hear about Amber?"

"Yes, so?" He topped off his second pile and moved on to start another.

"Sheriff Gentry has an idea you had something to do with it," Clay said. "Because of the fight at the beach. I told him you were with me, but he's looking for you. He was headed toward the beach last time I saw him."

"Thanks," Grim said, and continued raking.

"You going to turn around and talk to me or what?" Clay asked, unusually somber, frighteningly serious.

Grim dropped the rake and turned. "I have nothing to say to you right now."

Clay nodded. "Didn't figure you would, but I have something to tell you."

"Go on then. I have to finish this before Clara comes home."

"I just wanted to say I'm sorry if I hurt Michele's feelings. I know you like her."

"Clay, Michele couldn't give a shit what you think of her."

"I know," Clay said, not sounding the slightest bit offended. "She's cool that way." Clay kicked at the mower-carved remains of a pinecone, perhaps blown from the top of one of the trees on the wild side of Canyon Creek.

"Grab a bag, would you?" Grim asked.

Clay did, held it open on the ground while Grim raked grass shavings from his first pile into it.

"Where's your *new sister*?" He spoke the words like a bad joke, something funny, but rotten at the same time.

"With Clara. I don't know."

"There's something wrong with that girl," Clay said. "I never liked her, there's something just not right about her. She's—" he seemed to struggle with what he wanted to say, and settled on, "strange."

"I know," Grim said. He'd known all along there was something different about her. Since that first night at Canyon Jack's. He thought the others had sensed it too, old man Wallen most of all perhaps, and that an instinctive fear of her *strangeness* had stayed with them from helping her when Wallen attacked.

Maybe. He didn't know.

He did know that Clay was right. He also knew it made no difference. She was his sister, even if Clara was not his mom anymore. She was a loner, like him, but even loners needed family.

"Everyone is talking about her," Clay said.

Of course they are, Grim thought. *How could they not?* She was the new outsider.

"They think she made Amber kill herself."

Grim threw down the rake. "What do *you* think?"

Clay dropped the bag, stood. "I think I don't want to be around her anymore, even if it means not hanging around you."

"Get the fuck out of my face," Grim said, and Clay did.

Get out.

You're never to see Michele again, Evelyn Kirkwood had

said.

"Fuck it."   Grim left the rake where it lay, the grass unraked. He had to talk to Michele. He had to prove to himself that Evelyn Kirkwood was wrong. She would not keep them apart.

He loved Michele, and no one would keep them apart.

He called again.

No answer.

Chapter 26

When Lydia called Danny and told him about the Ipstien girl, his first thought was for Angel. The town kids had all seen what Angel had done to Amber, and they'd be talking about it now; shock to grief, grief to anger. Anger for the outsider. They'd be out for blood.

He called his mom's house, and Grim answered on the first ring.

"Michele?" His voice sounded almost panicked.

"Sorry, bro, just me."

Grim was silent on the other end.

Not in a talking mood, Danny thought.

"Is Mom there?"

"No, she took Angel somewhere this morning."

"Did you hear about Amber Ipstien?"

"Yeah," Grim said. "Everyone thinks it's Angel's fault."

"I know," Danny said. And he had to bite his lips against the next thought that popped into his head.

I think they might be right.

"Clay stopped by. He says Steven Gentry thinks I had something to do with it."

"What?" Danny's stomach did a sick flip.

"Steven stopped by this morning but I didn't answer the door."

"That's crazy," Danny said. "Why would he think that?"

"Because I was at Michele's last night. Her mom caught

us together, probably told him I was there."

Shit. This was not good.

"Get up here, Grim. Come straight over and stay here until I talk some sense into Steven."

"Sure," Grim said. A pause, then, "Danny, can you do something for me while you're in town?"

"Depends," Danny said. "I'll have my hands full talking to Steven."

"Drive by Michele's house. Just to see if they're home. Could you do that?"

"Sure," Danny said. "You're worried about her?"

"Her mother's crazy," Grim said. "She threatened to kill me."

Danny chuckled at that, despite himself.

"That's not crazy, Grim. That's her being a protective mother. You'd do well to stay away from Michele for a while."

"I can't," Grim said. "Just check, will you?" "I'll check," Danny said. "You get up here now. Don't go anywhere else." Danny considered for a moment and added, "bring a change of clothes in case you need to hide out for the night. Just in case."

"He'll know to look for me there."

Shit. "Yeah," Danny said. "He will." He considered for a moment. "Okay, if it comes to that you head up to my place in the hills. He doesn't know about that."

"You used to be the Sheriff," Grim said. "You sure you want to harbor a fugitive?"

"Did you do anything I should worry about?"

"No." Emphatic, definitive. Danny knew he was telling the truth.

"Then yes, I am."

"Danny?"

"Yes?" Growing impatient now. Too many bad things cooking. He needed to get moving.

"There's something wrong with Clara. She's been acting strange for a while, but I thought once she got used to having Angel around she'd calm down."

Danny closed his eyes and sighed. He'd noticed it too, and chalked it up to stress. But she wasn't improving. If anything, her temperament was getting worse.

"I'd noticed," Danny said. "I'll talk to her later, Grim. I've got too many other things to deal with now."

"I think she's going to kick me out," Grim said.

"Then you can stay with me," Danny said. "I've got to go now. I'll be in touch."

*   *   *

Danny suggested he stay off the main road and take his bike up the trail behind Clara's house, through the woods, that led up to Angel Ridge Road. Grim agreed, but that path was slow, and by the time he reached Danny's house on the hill, Danny was already gone.

There was a note beside the two-way on his nightstand. *Turn the two-way on and keep your ears open. Channel 18. I'll keep you posted.*

Grim turned the radio on, tuned to 18 and adjusted the squelch until it cleared.

Pulled a chair from the kitchen table, and waited.

The phone sitting next to the radio beckoned.

Reluctantly, knowing it was a bad idea but needing to hear from Michele, just to know she was alright, he picked the receiver up and dialed her number.

No answer.

Grim counted the rings, thirty, then hung up.

*   *   *

Clara searched her house, a once safe, now hostile place, for Grim. She held Angel's hand, ready to place herself between her Angel and Grim if he were to appear. He was not home.

"Come on dear, hurry." Clara dragged her by the arm to her room, closed the door from the inside, and emptied the contents of a paper bag onto her bed. A bolt lock, screwdriver, a box of wood screws, and a small canister of Dog Away. She'd bought it because it was the closest thing to pepper spray she could find. She figured it would work just as well on a teenage boy as it would a vicious dog.

"Sit tight, dear. I'll be finished in a few minutes."

"What are you doing?"

"Just a little extra security, dear. One can never be too safe." Angel seemed not to remember what had happened in Grim's room that morning, and that was good. It was the kind of thing that could scar a young girl.

Clara installed the bolt lock, tested it, and was satisfied it would hold an intruder at bay long enough for her to intervene.

"Take this." Clara handed the Dog Away to Angel. "Careful. Don't point it at your eyes."

Angel turned it over in her hands, looked at it with skepticism. "Why do I need this?"

"I want you to keep it with you. If…someone tries to hurt you, spray them in the eyes and run."

Angel looked shocked. "Who wants to hurt me?"

Clara couldn't face her, hated to see her troubled. "Honey, I'm afraid Grim might try to come back and hurt you."

"No," Angel said, her shock giving way to confusion. "Grim's my brother. He's my friend."

Before she could stop herself Clara seized Angel by the shoulders and gave her a shake. "You get those ideas out of your head, baby. Grim is bad."

"Let go," Angel said. "You're hurting me."

"Not until you promise me you'll stay away from that wicked boy." Clara brought her face down to Angel's, could see her own wild-eyed reflection in Angel's eyes. "He's got the same demon in him that Galen had. He is not my son anymore!"

"Let go," Angel cried out, and grabbed Clara's arm.

The headache that had plagued her the past weeks, had been circling all day, kept at bay by ibuprofen and prayer, dropped on her like a predator. It hit her with a white, blinding force, pounding her to her knees. Her hands left Angel's shoulders and clenched her temples, pushing back against a pain that threatened to burst her skull.

She prayed silently for relief or death, whichever was quicker.

Prayed until the agony faded and the blinding white behind her eyes dulled. When she opened them again, Angel was staring down at her, confusion given way to anger.

"Why are you doing this?"

"Because I love you," Clara said, finding her feet. "I'm doing what I have to do for you."

"Grim didn't do anything wrong," Angel said.

"Lord," Clara said, casting eyes toward the ceiling. "Please open this child's eyes and let her see the danger. Protect her from the demon lust, and give me the strength of your resolve."

Clara dropped her gaze, cast a reproachful look at Angel. "Please don't make this harder for me than it has to be. I loved him too once, before I knew the monster he would be."

She left Angel standing, alone. There was more work to do downstairs.

Uninterrupted, she changed the front lock and added a dead bolt in less time than it would have taken to get one of her boys on the task to do it. She heard footsteps at the top of the stairs, Angel coming, and rushed to the back door and went to work. She was not finished yet. She had to make this home safe for her girl.

She would kill, she would die, before she saw Angel hurt again.

"Clara?"

Clara saw her coming and shut the door. "Angel, you go back to your room now. It isn't safe for you to be down here."

"Don't do this. Please don't make Grim leave."

It broke Clara's heart to hear her pleading for the boy who would have hurt her this morning. If Clara hadn't found them in time…

Give me strength.

"Go, now!"

Clara saw the doorknob turn, and grasped it before Angel could open the door. After a few moments, of twisting, the pressure from the other side of the door was gone. She waited for a few moments, cracked the door open, and found an empty hallway within.

She removed the old doorknob, tossed it to the grass.

"Clara."

Clara turned to the sound of the voice and found Angel standing in the back yard at the far corner of the house. Out in the open where anyone could see her. Where anyone could *take* her.

"Angel," she said, straining to keep a reasonable tone of voice. "Baby, I told you it isn't safe for you out here."

"You can't kick him out," Angel said, defiant, determined. "He didn't do anything bad. You're wrong about him."

"I am not wrong about him," she said. "He's bad."

The buzzing had started in her head again, the precursor for more pain. But she would not give in to it now.

"Come here this instant, Angel!"

"No," she screamed. "Not until you change your mind!"

"He's evil!"

The buzzing grew louder inside her head, so loud that it threatened to split her brain's frail bone cage. A small swarm of bees seemed to congregate before her, as if drawn to the kindred sound between her temples. She backed away from them, swatted at the air and shooed them.

The day was suddenly darker.

Angel stalked forward, arms crossed, all the sweetness and innocence gone from her face; frightening in her anger.

"Take it back!"

"I will not!"

The first bee darted in from its small swarm and stung the side of her neck.

She screamed, swatted. It fell away.

The others followed in its wake.

"Clara!" The anger seemed to have drained away from Angel's face, replaced by a dawning fear. "I'm sorry." Angel ran toward her. "I didn't mean to do it!"

Flashes of a memory, the memory of an old, dreaded dream.

The bees seemed to be coming from everywhere now. From the trees on the other side of the creek, from the old walnut tree behind her, from the eaves of her old monster of a house, springing from the air itself, as if plucked from a nightmare. Swarming her.

"Angel, no! Go back!" Her voice was stolen abruptly as more bees darted between her open lips and went to work on her tongue. It began to swell almost instantly, pinching off her breath.

"I'm sorry!"

Her Angel was running toward her, toward the danger.

Clara swatted them, killed them by the scores, scraped them from her arms, face, hair with pierced, swelling hands. The yellow/black demons fell like rainwater from the sky and replaced their dead. Her face and her head were swelling, the scalp about to split. She tried to shout a warning to Angel, but it wouldn't pass her tongue.

Then she saw them, and she stopped, the poison horde still working at her, forgotten.

Angel had stopped too, fallen to her knees in the freshly-cut grass, and vomited. "I'm sorry, Clara," she said again. "I didn't mean to do it." She was oblivious to the cloud falling from the sky behind her. A cloud that blotted out the sun over her home. A cloud that wasn't a cloud. A cloud that sang its approach like a chord strum on Satan's harp. A buzzing, yellow/black cloud.

It was going for Angel, right for her.

Then it was on her, blurring her form in its mass.

And passed her.

They fell on Clara like a plague from God, drove her to the ground. Injecting their poison into a million holes, raping her with pain.

And after a torture she was sure would have driven Jesus himself to unrepeatable despair, oblivion took her.

Sweet, black oblivion.

Chapter 27

Good God damn!

Steven watched, his right hand lay forgotten on the butt of his revolver, as the swarm of bees that had descended on Clara Grey thinned, faded, vanished.

What was left of her looked almost human.

He saw Angel lying in the grass a few feet away, remarkably alive. Fainted, but upon closer inspection, completely unmarked by the killer swarm that had seemed to congregate around her before killing the old woman.

He'd come again hoping to find Grim, with an eye on gaining more of Evelyn's favors. But it wasn't Grim that had caused Amber Ipstien to slash her wrists that morning. He'd heard through the grapevine that this girl had fought with Amber, and had done something to her, what exactly, no one could say for sure.

It was this girl, Clara Grey's Angel, who had conjured that swarm of bees with her anger and set them upon her foolish foster mother. All the craziness in Clearwater had started with her, from the very night she'd arrived at Canyon Jack's place.

Steven put a boot against her arm and gave it a nudge. She didn't wake. Didn't even stir. He looked closer to see if she was still alive. There was some motion in her chest, light breathing. She was down, but not out. For how long, he didn't know.

He left her there, and returned to Clara's back yard a minute later with his Jeep, parking it a few feet away. He opened the back door, cleared off the seat.

I don't want to touch her, he thought. The thought made him feel cold, knotted his stomach. But he'd have to.

He put cuffs on her, closing them as far as they would over her small wrists, then slipped on the old leather work gloves he kept for messy work before lifting her from the grass. She was lighter even than she looked. He lay her on the back seat and shut the door without bothering to buckle her in, then reversed out of Clara's back yard and back onto the main road.

He drove slow, not wanting to stir her too much, afraid she might wake. People waved, and he waved back.

The alley behind his office was empty. Good.

He opened the back door, double-checked that no one was coming from either direction, then carried her to the downstairs cell.

* * *

Danny reached the bottom of Angel Ridge Road and parked at the edge of the road, undecided as to where Steven might be. He was usually in his office, or eating lunch at Jack's, nursing an endless cup of coffee on the side. He didn't go out on patrol as a matter of routine, but today would be different. He would have actual work today that didn't involve holding his office chair down.

He turned left, taking the road out of town toward Jack's. The parking lot was mostly empty, only a few kids visiting the beach today. Most were probably in shock about Amber, who was never a popular girl as far as he knew, but had achieved a notoriety akin to celebrity in Clearwater.

Evelyn Kirkwood's car was among them, and a quick look through Jack's front window placed her at the counter. Sitting alone.

He thought of Grim, worried sick over Michele, and resisted the urge to use the two-way in his car. First thing first.

He parked next to her car.

* * *

She turned at the sound of the door chime ringing behind her, and had to suppress a moment of panic. Steven hadn't caught Grim yet, she was sure. Steve would have found her to brag by now if he had.

But Danny was not the sheriff anymore. She didn't have to acknowledge him if she chose not to. She was in control, not he.

"Morning," Danny said.

Except for a grunt and a wave from Darla, who was wiping down tables in the wake of breakfast, no one replied. Danny's name was mud these days, as it should be. Clara, Danny, Grim, and Angel, all of them were finished in Clearwater. It was only a matter of time.

Grim would be first.

She smiled, and turned in her stool.

"Mr. Grey," she said, and gave a little nod.

"Where's Michele?"

"That's really none of your business, is it?" she replied, and turned back to her late breakfast.

Danny shrugged. "Just curious," he said. "Angel was asking about having her over today."

Liar, she thought. *I suppose you want your turn with her now, don't you?*

"Have you seen Sheriff Gentry around?"

A shake of her head, then back to breakfast.

"He was here a while ago looking for your brother," Darla said. "Grim in trouble?"

"Not that I'm aware of," Danny said. "Thanks, Darla."

He left, and she turned as the door chime rang again, watched him walk to his car.

"Something wrong?" Darla asked, startling her from dark thoughts. "You look mad enough to eat nails." Darla walked around the counter, grabbed the coffee pot, and refilled her coffee.

"Not at all," she said. *Everything is peaches and cream,*

you dumb bitch.

She watched Danny drive away, and decided once Grim was dealt with, she'd have to talk with Sheriff Gentry about Danny Grey. The thought of fucking that pig again killed her appetite, but she'd do what she had to do.

Anything to keep her baby safe from the men in this town who would hurt her. That was a mother's love.

* * *

Grim waited by the two-way radio, resisting the urge to call Michele's house again. If anyone was home, they were not answering.

Danny's voice broke through the silence. Grim was hungry for whatever news he might have.

"You there, brother?"

"Yes," Grim said. "You check on Michele yet?"

"Haven't had a chance to check their house, but her mom is at Jack's at the moment." A moment of static cut them off, then Grim heard "...not with her."

"What?"

A pause. "Michele's not with her, so if you're thinking of doing it, now is a good time to go check. Just keep an eye out for Steven Gentry. I'll keep looking for him."

"Okay," Grim said. "Thanks."

And he was on his way. Not a smart thing to do, he knew that. But sometimes the smart thing, the safe thing, was also the wrong thing. The cowardly thing.

I shouldn't have left her, Grim thought. *Fuck it all, I shouldn't have left her there.*

* * *

Danny put down the radio mic and kicked up his speed. He wanted to be in town, hopefully keeping Steven busy when Grim went to Michele's house. Best-case scenario, he finds out what's in Steven's head, diffuses the whole thing. More likely, he just ties Steven up long enough for Grim to look for, maybe find, Michele.

It wasn't perfect, or even very smart, but suddenly Danny was very worried about Michele, more so even than Grim. Grim was tough, he could take care of himself if he needed to, had done it for years on rougher streets than these.

Something about Evelyn today, something in her stance, her attitude, a crazy shine in her eyes. He'd never liked the woman. A lot of people here thought she was a snob, and he was inclined to agree, but this morning she was worse. Hostile.

Sure, she'd just caught Grim with her daughter, and that would bound to cause some hostility, so maybe he was overreacting.

Maybe not. These days the folks in Clearwater were likely to do anything, it seemed.

He saw the tire tracks running through the grass beside Clara's house, and slowed. They started in the driveway, went through the sparse patch of mostly dead lawn in front, around the side, and disappeared behind the house.

Clara had parked her car in the usual spot, not even close to where the tracks started.

Maybe Steven had already been here.

Danny pulled in, parked beside Clara's car, and followed the tire ruts to the back yard.

"Jesus Christ." Danny ran to where Clara lay, not knowing what to expect. Heart attack, heatstroke.

Gunshot.

What he found looked like a stripped, bloated carcass in a Sunday dress. Swollen to grotesque proportions, her features obliterated by the stings of what might have been a million bees.

He stumbled; fell to the grass beside her. "Mom!"

She'd always been afraid of them, stung badly as a child and never quite forgot the fear and pain they inspired. Danny had always done his best to keep them away from her house, and had passed the job to Grim when he'd arrived.

"Mom!" He took her by the shoulders and shook her, knowing she would not awaken from her poison sleep, but unable to help himself. "Wake up, Mom!"

Grim was a slacker where the yard work was concerned, but he'd never let the bees nests get out of hand. He checked for them himself, and when Clara or Danny found one, it would be gone within minutes of them informing him.

Danny scanned the eaves of the house, the shed, the old walnut tree. Nothing.

"Mom," he slipped an arm under her back and lifted her. She was dead weight, uncooperative. He heard something rip in her back, something that sounded like rotting canvas stretched beyond its endurance. Blood and pus poured from the hidden wound, soaking through her dress.

Clearly, irretrievably, dead.

The grief hit him like a blow from a sledgehammer, knocking him to his back, sobbing. And just as quickly, grief was replaced by fear.

Where was Angel?

*   *   *

Steven sat in a chair facing the cell, and after a time, dozed. The girl's lethargy seemed to be catching. Contagious, like the madness that had spread since the night she'd come to Clearwater. In his dream, he was in the cell, curled against the corner on the small bunk, shaking with fear.

And she sat outside, watching him with cool, inhuman eyes.

He awoke with a jump, as if someone had goosed him.

Goose over my grave, he thought, and shivered, despite the stagnant heat of the basement.

She stood at the bars of the cell. Watching him. Her face was ashen, slack, the eyes barely open.

"Is Clara okay?"

"Not really," Steven said, loving the hurt look in her

droopy dog eyes. "She's dead."

"Oh," Angel said, and cast her eyes to the floor, shedding silent tears.

Not surprised though, Steven thought.

"You did it, didn't you?" He said. "You set those bees on her."

"I didn't mean to," she said.

"But you did it. You killed her." He stood, walked to the cell, laced his fingers over the bars. "I'm gonna have to do something about you."

Angel turned her face up to his. The droopy dog eyes were gone. They were wide, her glare intense.

"You don't have the guts she said."

Steven considered drawing his gun, shoving it in her face, giving her a little reminder of where she stood with him, but he knew if he did that, he might just pull the trigger.

He was ready to kill Grim, eager for it, but not this girl. Not until he got a better bead on how the wind blew through Clearwater.

Not yet in other words.

Until then…

He'd read the report on her. Rohypnol and Ketamine, Roofies, are what her real brother had used on her, and he thought he understood why now.

He had a prescription for pain pills over a year ago after hurting himself in the woods, had filled it, but never felt the need to take them. It was nothing he couldn't handle with a couple of aspirin. He didn't like being drugged. It was like losing a little bit of your mind.

The pills were still in his medicine cabinet.

That should do the trick.

"Don't you go anywhere now," he said, and thumped the bars with his knuckles. "I'll be back."

Chapter 28

Grim found the Kirkwood driveway empty, the door locked. Across the road at the Ipstien's house, cars overflowed the driveway and into the street. Condolence calls. The windows facing him were blank, the curtains closed against the world.

No one on the streets. If he was quick, no one would notice him.

He stepped back to the porch rail, and charged forward, putting a shoulder into the door. It popped open on his first hit, and he stepped inside, closing it behind him.

"'Chele?"

No answer. The kitchen and living room were wide open and empty.

"'Chele, are you here? Answer me."

No one in the hallway, or in her mom's room at the far end of it. The door was open; he could see her bed, messed up beyond what even a violent sleep would do.

Michele's door was locked. The kind of old fashion lock you saw in these old trailers, designed for no more than keeping rug rats out. Through a narrow hole in the center of the knob, all that was required to turn the tumbler was a wooden match or nail.

Grim pried at the molding by her door, loosening half a dozen paneling nails, and pulled one free, let himself in, expecting to find Michele, upset with him, her mother, the world, maybe scared, maybe regretful, maybe sleeping, but there.

"Oh my God."

She was not there, but she had been. The blood on her pillow was still fresh, still tacky. Nylon chords hung from the four corners, tied to the bedposts at one end. The clothes he'd stripped from her lay on the floor where they'd tossed them the night before, next to her shoes.

Panic squeezed his insides.

"'Chele!"

No answer.

*   *   *

Danny found the Sheriff's Office locked. He ran around the building, past the deserted main street — it was unusually quiet, even for Clearwater, as if the town sensed an approaching storm and were shut inside against it — and around to the back alley.

The back door was locked too, so Danny reached up above the door jam and searched with his fingers until they closed around cold metal.

Davis had always kept an extra key there in case of an emergency, a little detail Danny had not bothered to share with Steven or the commissioner when he'd turned in his own keys.

He let himself in, grateful he'd forgotten to mention it.

"Steven, are you here?"

Nothing from Steven, but from somewhere below, like the voice of a premature burial victim, he heard Angel's voice.

Steven had been there, in his mom's backyard, had brought Angel in for some reason and put her in the cell.

Danny had a sudden, strange impulse to leave her there. Just walk away and forget about her. He squashed it quickly. That was his sister, through Clara's love, if not through blood. No matter what was wrong with her, she was family.

"I'm coming, Angel!"

He took the narrow stairs three at a time and hit the basement running.

He found Angel sitting on the bunk, and was shocked with the change in her face, her eyes. She looked little better than the girl they'd brought back from the State Hospital North at the beginning of summer. Exhausted.

"Clara's dead," she said.

"I know," Danny said. "I'm sorry, Angel."

"It's my fault," she said, and the certainty in her voice stopped him in mid stride. "I didn't mean to, but I did it. I'm sorry, Danny," and she began to cry. A warping of her pretty face, silent tears.

"It's not your fault," he said. "You couldn't have stopped it." But again, he wondered. There was something about her, something not right. Everyone had sensed it from the very start, except maybe Clara, who was too in love with the girl to see.

Bringing her back had been a mistake, and that had been his doing. But he couldn't abandon her now.

Danny's only warning was the familiar, low chuckle.

The gunshot was like an explosion in the small basement, and then Angel's scream drowned it out, the impact like a blow to the back from a jackhammer. It picked him up and dropped him unkindly against the wall past Angel's cell.

"Damn, but that felt nice," Steven said.

Danny didn't have the strength to turn and face him, only shuddered, spilling blood down his back, onto the concrete floor. No exit wound, he noted grimly. The slug hadn't passed clean through, but had probably fragmented and ripped him up from asshole to throat.

"You cocky son-of-a-bitch," Steven said. "I've wanted to do that for a long time."

I bet you have, was Danny's last coherent thought before the darkness took him.

*   *   *

Grim hit Main Street bound for Canyon Jack's, if Mrs. Kirkwood was still there he'd make her tell him where she was, and god help the bitch if she'd hurt Michele. He would kill her.

The gunshot was clear, but muted, like a firecracker.

Grim stopped, searched, saw Danny's car parked in front of the Sheriff's Office.

Grim gunned it and was there in seconds, parked on the sidewalk next to the front door. It was locked.

Nothing but locked doors and unanswered calls this morning.

He saw movement inside, the door to the basement opened, and Steven's fat gut led the way from behind it.

Grim ducked to the side before the rest of him emerged.

The back door, he thought, and ran to the corner of the building, and around it.

"Grim!" Steven's voice from the front.

He'd left his bike out in plain sight. Nothing he could do about it now.

He ran down the alley, found the back door open, found Steven waiting inside, a satisfied smile stretched across his bearded face. He hadn't given chase around the front as Grim had hoped.

Steven went for his revolver, and Grim charged.

Hitting Steven was like hitting a wall made of concrete and blubber, but the big man stumbled backward, the gun falling from his hand as he struck a chair in the foyer and tumbled backward over it. The floor shook under their combined weight, and Grim heard a crack as Steven's soft head hit hard floor.

Stunned, but not out of the fight, Steven struck out and thumped the side of Grim's head.

That fist was not soft, it was like a boot upside the head, and when the stars cleared, Grim was on his back, groaning.

The gun lay on the floor between them, inert, but full of deadly potential.

They both reached for it, their hands scrambling over each others for a grip. Steven's found the muzzle, Grim's the butt. He found the trigger, squeezed.

Steven's scream of pain rivaled the thunder of his gun.

Grim rolled away, barely holding onto the gun. The recoil had nearly torn his hand off. He stood, fighting the dizziness and the throbbing pain Steven had inflicted on his head, and raised the gun, steadying it with his other hand.

Steven lay on the floor, clutching and unclenching the air with his good hand. His eyes were squeezed shut, his mouth open in a prolonged wail. His other hand lay at a sick angle on the floor, nearly separated where the bullet had torn through. The fingers still twitched.

Grim stepped up, crouched down, and shoved the barrel of the gun into his wailing mouth.

Steven's eyes opened, tears of pain making clean tracks down his grubby face.

"Shut the fuck up or I'll shut you up," Grim said.

Steven complied.

"Where's Danny?"

Steven lifted his good hand, extended an epileptic finger, pointed toward the open basement door.

"Get up."

He did, and Grim shoved the gun in his back, smiling as Steven stifled another scream, an ammonia smelling flood of piss wetted his pants.

"Go on," Grim urged, pushing forward with the gun. "Fat, sissy pieces of shit first."

Steven led the way down.

*   *   *

Grim saw Danny crumpled, face against the wall, blood everywhere, Angel laying face down on the small cell's bunk. He felt murder in his soul.

"You cock-sucker!" Standing on the bottom steps, just above Steven, he brought the gun down butt first against the top on his head.

Steven went to his knees with a howl of fresh pain, then tipped over sideways.

Grim bent, the gun pointed at his head, finger resting

on the trigger and ready to fire, and pulled the key ring from his belt.

He didn't go to Danny. There was nothing he could do for Danny now, it was all played out, and he didn't think he could stand to look into his brother's dead eyes.

Grim had seen death before. He didn't want to see it in the eyes of his brother, a man his opposite in so many ways, but still his hero.

He tried half a dozen keys from Steven's oversize ring before he found the right one.

"Angel, it's Grim. Are you okay?"

She turned over, sat up. Danny's dried blood stained the pale skin of her face, streaked her hair. She ran to him and almost knocked him over with her hug.

"I'm so sorry, Grim. I thought I could stop it, but I can't. I didn't mean to do it."

He shushed her, returned the hug, keeping an eye on Steven. "It's fine, Angel. You're fine. It's not your fault."

"It is," she said. "Clara's dead, and Danny," she went silent, and Grim stroked her hair.

Nonsense, she was half crazy from shock. None of it was her fault.

Or was it?

"C'mon, lets get out of here."

Angel released him, went to Danny, knelt next to him, the pooled blood staining her dress.

She gave his still form a hug, a kiss on the cheek. "I'm sorry."

Then she left him.

She paused beside the closet door, eyes wide, as if someone inside had spoken her name.

"Angel, we have to go."

She ignored him and walked to the closet. She opened the door, and Grim cringed in dire expectation. No one jumped out and said boo. Nothing emerged, slouching toward them to gobble them up. But there was something nonetheless that gave him a jump.

Two blood stained canes. The one Danny had found

that night in the woods near Wallen's place, and the other one. Michele's cane. The one she'd killed Old Man Wallen with. The cane she'd used to save Angel's life. Angel seemed to recognize it. She picked it up, held it to her chest with crossed arms.

"You remember, don't you?"

She nodded. "Yes."

Yes, Michele thought she had. But she'd not told him, or Clara as far as he knew. She'd hoarded the memories of her life before Clearwater, as if sharing them would damn her.

"Go upstairs and wait for me," Grim said. He was watching Steven. The large man's breathing was rougher. He was beginning to stir. Grim pointed the gun at him. "Get up there, sis. I'll be right behind you."

"Don't do it," Angel said, and touched his wrist.

His hand seemed to lower on its own accord, the finger slipping from the trigger.

Then she stepped between them, and before he could stop her, she bent down and grabbed Steven's thick shoulder.

The man awoke at once, eyes bloodshot, bulging from their sockets. His scream dwarfed the one upstairs, as if the pain of his demolished hand was a sliver compared to this spear that Angel delivered.

Angel squeezed down on him, her tiny fingers pushing divots into his fat, her fingernails in search of blood.

Her face was cramped in effort that bordered on pain.

Steven's scream rang out, his tongue blowing in its wind like the tail of a kite. Tendons bulged in his neck, veins popped, turning his skin a mottled brown. The color of blood on dirt.

Grim dropped the gun, pressed his palms to his ears, and gave echo to Steven's scream.

Steven's face had gone a bright red, and like a cheesy horror movie visual, one of his eyes popped from the socket, lay against his cheek.

Blood from his ripped throat sprayed from his mouth

like rain.

Then Angel released him, and he fell over again.

Grim did not have to wonder. He knew Steven Gentry was dead.

Angel turned to him, a look of savage satisfaction, almost joy, twisting her sweet face. Then her eyes rolled up, the cane fell from her white-knuckle grip, and she collapsed.

Chapter 29

Grim carried Angel up the stairs, she was feather light, as if what she'd done to Steven had sapped more than her energy, but her physical mass. Steven's gun belt hung low on his hips. It was home made and fit bad. Small loops were worked into the front to carry extra cartridges. There were enough for two reloads after he spent the four left in the cylinder of the gun.

Grim knew if he'd heard the first shot from the street, then others would have heard the shot that had taken Steven's hand almost clean off. He carried Angel to the back door and laid her in the back seat of Steven's Jeep. He was climbing into the driver's seat when inspiration struck.

A propane tank sat next to the building's brick wall, and he followed its copper fuel line to the wall, where it coupled with iron pipe running into the base of the wall. The building's furnace was propane.

He ran back inside, saw the first cluster of townies headed across the street, and ducked into the hallway next to the basement stairs. Through the hallway, a bathroom, closet, and small storage room. In the storage room, boxes and boxes of files pre-dating their computer system, and the furnace.

The propane line ran an inch from the wall, then up a foot before a black iron elbow connected it to the furnace.

I'll have to be quick, Grim thought. *Damn quick.*

He lifted a foot, sole out, and kicked the pipe. It bent, but held. Another kick and it bent in further. A stress crack appeared, barley visible, at the fitting near the base of the wall. A third, and fourth kick, and he heard the hiss of propane escaping into the air.

The fifth kick did it. The pipe snapped at the threads connecting it to the wall fitting, and the hiss became a wind of propane vapor.

Grim pushed his way into the bathroom. A window above the toilet let sunlight in through a parted curtain. Grim pulled the curtain aside, found a single privacy window reinforced with wire mesh.

Damn, he'd been afraid of that.

But it was his only way out. He didn't want anyone to see him escape, maybe give chase.

He stripped his shirt off, wrapped it around his fist, and punched the window. The window erupted with a spider web of cracks, but thanks to the wire mesh, held. His fist erupted with a similar broken glass spider web of pain. It too held. He punched again and glass fell in rough beads, exposing wire. What was left caved outward. He shoved with his shirt-wrapped hand, and it popped from the frame. The hole it left was just large enough for him to slip through.

His back alley landing was rough, but he shook it off and rose to his feet within seconds, adrenaline powering his muscles, deadening the pain. He checked his pockets, found his book of matches, lit one and set flame to the curtains inside.

No one in the alley, just him and Angel. Good.

He lifted her from the back seat and ran as fast as her weight would allow. Steven's Jeep sat abandoned, waiting for the flame. He couldn't be seen driving away in it. He wanted everyone to think he'd died in the explosion.

For now anyway.

He'd be back soon enough.

He crossed the bone-dry bed of Canyon Creek, and into the field beyond, toward the cover of the woods.

A phantom voice in his head scolded, *a lot of people are going to get hurt, Eugene.* Clara's voice. *People will die.* Not the shrieking hag she'd been that morning, but the old Clara. Reasonable but firm, loving, but disappointed.

They can go to hell, Grim thought.

Expecting that great, white-hot rush of air to pick him up, roast him alive as it tossed him, Grim pounded the dust harder, panic fueling his steps. At last he found the woods, and it felt safer than being out in the open, but he slowed only a little. He didn't go deeper into the woods, but toward home.

A safe place for Angel until he could return for her. And if Clara really was dead, as Angel seemed to think, a place of rest for him too. But not a long rest. No, not long at all. Danny was dead, but he had rescued Angel. He had to find Michele now. Somewhere, Michele waited, maybe in trouble, as Danny's last panicked transmission led him to think.

And if she were beyond his help, he would avenge her.

*   *   *

The deep, numb blackness receded, and he still felt Angel's kiss on his cheek, lingering. He didn't know *how* he knew it was Angel, but he did.

I'm sorry.

He'd been dead, somehow he was also sure of this.

As a fucking doornail, he thought. How could he not be? His insides were hamburger, and he was pretty sure Steven's slug had severed his spine.

Danny tried to stand, and proved his theory. He fell over onto his shoulder, grunted in new pain.

Wasn't as bad as he'd have expected, really. Like someone had given him a sledgehammer kick to the balls, driven them halfway up his throat.

His arms worked though, so he used them and pulled himself toward Angel's cell.

"Angel, are you there?"

No reply, and when Danny boosted himself up he saw the cell door hanging open.

He pulled himself across the cold floor, hand over hand

towards the stairs.

Help.

Steven, very dead, very large, loomed ahead, once more a pain in the ass.

Danny tried not to look too closely as he pulled himself over the top of the man's mountainous gut.

All sorts of dead. One thing to be happy about today.

He found the stairs, dug his fingers into the seam of the bottom step's rough planks, and pulled himself upward. It felt like an eternity before he reached top, but he knew it was probably no more than a quarter hour. Bars of light fell through the front office windows at roughly the same angle as when he'd come in. But now there were shadow men darting in, out, between them.

"Help me!" Danny tried to scream, but was dismayed by the weakness of his voice. He crawled around the open basement door, another obstacle, blocking valuable space in the narrow passage between the front office and the back door. He saw the shocked faces of those outside, hands cupped over eyes, faces all but pressed to glass.

Then he smelled the gas.

And smoke.

He turned his head, stretching his neck at a painful angle, and saw the black, serpentine cloud, creeping along the ceiling from the bathroom.

"Go," he screamed at the people outside. But they didn't.

He mastered his impulse to crawl for the open back door, knowing even if he escaped the office, he'd never get far enough away before it exploded. Instead he pulled himself toward the locked front door. All the time screaming.

"Get out of here. Run!"

The outside faces marked his progress with horror, shock. Someone tried the front door, but it only rattled in its frame.

He was close enough to touch glass now. Someone whose face he recognized but name he could not remember crouched down. "Hang tight, Danny. I'll go for help."

"Get away," Danny screamed, and at last comprehension dawned on the faces outside. "Gas!"

And the face he recognized but had no name for looked up, saw the smoke, mouthed the words *Oh my God.*

*   *   *

The first blast shook the ground, and Grim fell to his knees on the needle-blanketed forest floor rather than fall over on his face. No screams. Not yet anyway. Those who'd been close enough to see him duck back into the office were dead and in hell before the devil saw them coming.

He was about to rise again when the second, unexpected explosion threw him forward onto his face. The second blast sounded like the end of the world, the sky getting ready to fall. He remained prone, guarding his sleeping Angel, just in case.

Yes, the propane tank. That had been the second explosion. One hundred gallons of compressed liquid propane would make a pretty impressive boom, he thought.

He scooped Angel into his arms again and ran.

Within minutes home was in view.

He found Clara in the back yard, felt a stab of sorrow. She'd been so kind to him, like a mother, almost until the end. She'd lived like a saint, and died horribly.

Angel groaned, stirred in his arms.

Grim carried her inside, upstairs, his legs burning to be free of her weight, little as it was. He laid her down on her bed, then collapsed next to her.

He wanted to sleep; he was beyond exhausted.

He gave himself a few minutes, then rose, sat on the edge of Angel's bed, and reloaded the gun.

*   *   *

It watched from the trees, still hurt, but still angry. And very, very hungry.

Grim had carried the monster girl inside, then come out alone.

The girl was sick, weak.

Gina waited until Grim was out of sight, then made her way toward the old house.

Chapter 30

Clearwater was burning, and he didn't mind. It was nice, actually. Like a giant bonfire on a cold beach.

The day's titanic heat was ebbing, making his stroll much less tedious than it would have been. Cars approached and passed on their way back to town. Had the explosions been heard all the way out to Jack's? Probably.

He ducked behind the high, dead grass bordering the dry, dead creek and waited for them to pass. At last, Mrs. Kirkwood's car came around the last bend before the highway.

This time he did not hide. Grim stood tall and stepped into the road, arms out. *C'mon, bitch, I dare you.*

She did speed up, her car's engine whining as she kamikazed toward him.

He was quicker. He pulled his gun, aimed, fired.

She veered to the side at the last second, but too late. The front passenger side tire blew out and her car jerked back toward him, then skidded to a sideways halt, blocking both lanes only feet from him. He advanced, gun pointed at her head. In his hand, he held Michele's cane. Like a talisman, though how it could bring good luck he did not know. He carried it because she had once, and it made him feel closer to her.

Evelyn gripped the wheel, watched his approach with a sick mixture of hatred and fear.

"Where is she?"

"Go ahead and shoot me," she said. "I'll never tell you."

He pressed the muzzle against her cheek, slipped his index finger through the trigger guard. "I'm not bluffing," Grim said.

She offered no reply. Just sat, rigid, staring through the windshield at the darkening evergreen horizon. The blood seemed drained from her fingers, they looked like bleached, skin-covered bones gripping the wheel.

"Three," he said, and her breath quickened.

"Two," she said nothing, but her eyes darted back to the road, as if expecting the cavalry to come swooping in at the last moment to save her ass.

"Sheriff Gentry is dead," Grim said, and that got her attention. She whipped her head around and faced his, the barrel of his gun now centered on her forehead. "You can consider me the new law in town, if that helps."

"You little bastard."

"One," he said, then yelled, "bang," and tapped the barrel of the gun against her forehead.

She shrieked and closed her eyes, as if being blind to her death would halt it.

But death did not come for her. When she opened her eyes again, Grim was still there.

"One more try," he said. "Tell me where she is."

Evelyn lunged forward, and Grim almost shot her before he realized what she was doing. She pushed the trunk release button beneath the dashboard.

Behind them, an ominous creak as the trunk lid lifted.

"Give me your keys," he said.

And she did.

He pocketed them. "The only reason you're not dead is because 'Chele still loves you."

Evelyn covered her face, wept.

He found Michele inside the trunk, still naked, but wrapped in a sweat drenched bed sheet. Gagged, bound.

"'Chele?"

She was still.

He dropped the cane, dropped the gun. Untied the strap at the back of her head and freed her mouth of the gag.

She was not breathing.

Grim bent and picked up the gun. Evelyn didn't see him draw, didn't see death approaching in his eyes.

But it took her anyway, a sad trophy compared to the girl he loved, whom death had already taken.

The revolver's boom echoed through Clearwater.

Evelyn fell forward against her gore-splattered dashboard.

Her death didn't sate Grim's rage.

* * *

He carried Michele back to Clara's old house, knowing there was nothing he could do for her now, but unwilling to let her go. He found Clara's car waiting in the driveway, and lay Michele in the back seat.

He had to get Angel out of town before it was too late.

"I thought you were dead." A voice from the road.

Grim turned to face it and found Alex, Bo, and a few men from town he didn't know, watching him. One of the men, standing next to Bo, like a redneck familiar in bib-overalls, held a shotgun at his side.

"This is where she lives, Dad," Bo said. "She's the one who caused all this."

The man nodded, stared at Grim. "Don't care one way or t'other about you, kid." He chambered a shell with the pump action on the shotgun, "but the devil girl is coming with us."

A voice in Grim's head told him to stand aside, let them take Angel. They were right. Angel, whatever she was, had been the cause of it all.

Grim shouted that voice away, drew his gun.

The man's eyes bulged, and he wrenched the shotgun upward to take his shot.

Grim was quicker. His slug punched a hole through the man's chest, and he stumbled once before tipping over on his back.

"Dad!" Bo lunged for the shotgun, but didn't make it. Grim put a slug in his back.

He fired another shot at Alex, who dove to the gravel, putting Clara's car between them.

Still screaming, he took a bead on the other man who'd come with them, fired, but missed. The man turned and ran back toward town, and Grim tracked him. Fired again and clipped him. Fired once more and put him down.

Saw Alex leave his cover, crawling for the shotgun lying between Bo and his dad.

Took careful aim, smiling as he did so, and squeezed the trigger.

The hammer fell on a dead chamber.

Grim sprinted, racing Alex for the shotgun. Alex beat him, but not able to aim in time, met Grim's charge with a wilting blow to the gut with the shotgun's stalk.

Grim doubled over and fell, rolling across the gravel.

He struggled to find his breath again, knowing it would be his last.

But the expected blast did not come.

He rolled onto his back, clutching his stomach, and found Alex standing over him, cradling the shotgun, but not aiming. Waiting.

"I'm glad it gets to be me," Alex said, and lifted the shotgun to his shoulder as a shadow fell over him.

Clay came at Alex from behind. His fist found the back of Alex's head and put him to his knees, groaning. A second blow spread him out in the gravel between them, and a kick to the head made sure he stayed down.

"Clay?"

Clay bent and picked up the shotgun.

"I should go up there and take care of her myself," Clay said. But he made no move toward the house. He kept the distance between them, shotgun ready.

"Get her out of here," Clay said. "Just take her away,

and don't ever come back."

He dropped the shotgun, turned his back on Grim, and walked way.

*   *   *

Running out of time.

Grim found Clara's car keys on the kitchen table and pocketed them. He reloaded the revolver while he climbed the stairs, rushed down the hallway toward Angel's room, paused when he found the door open.

He found Gina inside, pulling herself, hand over hand, wearing nothing but a season's worth of filth and her own dried blood, across the floor toward Angel's bed. She pushed with one leg. The other dragged behind, twisted and useless.

"You-you-you," more a panting rasp than words. She grabbed hold of the bed's frame and pulled herself up.

"Gina."

She turned and hissed at him, an animal sound, and dropped back to the floor, wriggled toward him. A twisted thing; a creature of madness and pain.

A shot to the head put Gina out of her misery.

Grim reloaded the empty chamber before carrying Angel downstairs to Clara's waiting car.

Still sleeping her unnatural sleep.

Chapter 31

He passed no other cars on his way out of town. Evelyn Kirkwood's car still blocked the road.

He pushed her into the passenger's seat and drove it around Clara's, blocking the road again from the other side. Before getting out, he pulled the keys from the ignition and threw them as hard as he could across the dry bed of Canyon Creek.

Grim removed his shirt, wiped the sweat from his face, and unscrewed the gas cap.

Michele's mother faced him, slumped against the passenger side door. Watched him with her one remaining eye and no face.

He ripped a long strip from his shirt and fed it into the gas tank, then used the matches in his pocket to light it.

That ought to slow them down, Grim thought as he climbed into Clara's car and left Clearwater behind.

* * *

Grim met a State Patrol cruiser on the highway. It flew down the road, lights flashing, siren chirping an advance warning, and Grim slowed, pulled to the side of the road like a good boy. It passed him without slowing. Seconds behind it, a small fleet of ambulances and fire engines from

Orofino.

Word had finally got out.

They'd come looking for him soon.

* * *

Traffic was light on the highway as he passed Orofino, and once he turned off onto the mountain road to Danny's cabin, it was nonexistent.

For three miles the single lane road was gravel, slow, dusty, but passable. The trail to Danny's cabin was something else. Not so much a road as a stripe of bare, stony earth through the trees. Clara's car was not made for this kind of driving, but Grim made it to Danny's cabin.

Angel stirred as Grim carried her over his shoulder, into the deserted cabin, up the ladder to the loft. Her sleep looked more natural as he laid her on Danny's bed. She would wake again soon, her strange life force building once again toward critical mass, and the deadly cycle would begin again.

He returned for Michele, and when he saw her on the back seat, wrapped in the bed sheet they'd made love on, a fresh wave of grief drove him to his knees.

Grim howled his rage at the emptiness. Shrieked curses at the unfairness.

Somewhere in the trees above, an eagle answered his cry, then exploded into the sky.

Grim carried Michele, as he had Angel, over his shoulder, up into the loft. She was limp, cold. Soon she would stiffen and begin to smell. He would bury her then, he supposed, if *they* didn't come for him first.

But not yet.

In the loft above him, Angel cried out in her sleep.

Grim saw Danny's two-way radio sitting on a table, turned it on, and tuned it to the frequency the law used.

After a few minutes of almost incoherent babble, Grim heard his name.

Yes, they were coming for him.

He pulled a chair up to the cabin's open door and sat, gun in his lap, and waited.

* * *

Green City was dead, ripped from the ground and plowed away, but still the Rag Man came for him.

Grim was ready this time.

"Come and get me you sick fuck!"

The Rag Man said, "Drop the gun, kid. Now! Don't make me shoot you!"

"Fuck you," Grim shouted.

He stood his ground, even as he fired, and missed, and the Rag Man fired bullets from his eyes.

Grim stood until he died.

* * *

Angel awoke to the sound of frantic footfalls on floorboards below. Michele lay next to her, wrapped in a sheet. Very quiet, very still.

"I'm sorry," Angel said, but had no more juice to weep.

She held Michele, even when the men from below, big men with guns and dark blue uniforms, found their way up to her.

"Oh no," one of them said, and in a second was at her side.

"Are they alive?" A voice from below.

"One dead, one alive." Then, to Angel. "Let go of her, there's nothing you can do for her. She's gone."

But Angel would not let go. Would not let go. Even as the big man tugged at her, would not let go.

"Gonna need some help here," he said, and others joined him on the loft, at her bedside.

Another voice, a new one. "You have to let her go, darling." A kind voice, soft and strong. A good man, Angel thought. He touched her shoulder, then drew away, as if shocked.

Would he go home tonight, eat dinner, tuck his children into bed, and murder his wife in her sleep?

Would he have nightmares and slowly lose his mind.

Angel held Michele tight, would not let go.

"Hold on," someone else said. "This one is breathing. She's alive!"

Michele stiffened in her arms, gasped, and Angel felt it, the slow but regular rise and fall of her chest. The pounding of a living heart.

Michele lived again.

Only then did Angel release her, and amid the new commotion, let herself drift once more toward darkness. The strange force that drove her not fully replenished, but once again spent.

It was so much easier to destroy things. She remembered that now. Fixing things took much more out of her.

Grim was gone now too, she'd heard his departing soul's cry in her last moments of sleep. He was beyond her powers, his body too damaged to hold his spirit.

There were no more memories. No revelations. Only guilt, and the knowledge that as long as she continued, those around her would be cursed.

Forever a mystery, even to herself, but not the miracle that Clara had thought she was.

A broken angel.

Brian Knight, author of *Dragonfly*, *Feral*, *Broken Angel*, *Hacks*, and others, lives in Washington State. You can visit him online at www.Brian-Knight.com.

Printed in the United States
'BV00003B/49-93/A

9 781929 653898